PRIME

CODEX

THE HUNGRY
— EDGE OF —
SPECULATIVE
FICTION

EDITED BY LAWRENCE M. SCHOEN AND MICHAEL LIVINGSTON

Paper Golem

PHILADELPHIA, PENNSYLVANIA

INTRODUCTION

BY LUC REID

WRITING, BUILDING STORIES, IMAGINING WORLDS, is a solitary occupation. Apart from true collaborations and other rare anomalies, making a story means anchoring yourself to a chair and moving unaccompanied up into your brain to work. The mushy corridors of the brain can be a lonely place; after wandering those corridors for a while, we can get set in our ways, can unintentionally start using certain routes all the time and others not at all.

So these are the purposes of Codex: first, to shake things up and keep us on our toes, and second to provide some pleasant company on the road of the aspiring writer, which is long and full of potholes and often takes years to get a person to anywhere that has a substantial population.

Codex came into being due to a deplorable waste, specifically of intelligent talk. In 2001, I attended Orson Scott Card's first week-long Literary Boot Camp and was shocked and enlightened out of my desultory, old, write-sometimes habits to become a compulsive writer there. Afterward I prodded the keepers of Card's Web site into setting up a little discussion group for us Boot Campers so that we could trade insights and news about ourselves.

Then, two years later, I became a published finalist in the Writers of the Future contest, where I met a surprising array of up-and-coming science fiction and fantasy writers, my fellow winners and published finalists. I gathered e-mail addresses; when I got home, I set up another discussion group.

In each of these groups, writers posted insights or news or suggestions that, it seemed to me, would be of interest to all manner of aspiring science-fiction and fantasy writers. It was a terrible waste that the Writers of the Future winners weren't hearing from the Boot Camp graduates and vice versa. By now there had been two more years of Boot Camp graduates. Soon there would be more Writers of the Future winners too. And apart from either of these groups there was an enormous pool of other talented, aspiring science-fiction and fantasy writers, including many who were already talking in small groups, but having trouble finding writing peers to discuss their work with.

Groups for beginning writers or writers of all levels abound. Excellent forums like Speculations.com and Critters.org and Hatrack.com offer exceptional opportunities for writers to learn. But their populations include more beginners than advanced writers, since of course there are more people who start writing than who keep with it long enough to achieve a little success. Codex, my intended solution to the problem of talented aspirant isolation, was built specifically for those people who were past their beginner stage: neo-pros and soon-to-be-pros.

The format of Codex (www.codexwriters.com) isn't innovative: it's an online forum with a critique area. Over time we've added an author-maintained library of our work, a directory of Codexian Web sites, a map of where Codexians live, contests, and other features, but in its most basic form Codex is just a Web forum. What makes it remarkable is the wide array of writers. What makes it work is that these writers are all hell-bent on improving their writing, and willing to work with other people to do it.

Through Boot Camp and the Writers of the Future contest, Orson Scott Card and the contest judges unknowingly picked most of our initial members for us, and we continue to shuck the responsibility of choosing members on subjective criteria. Codex members must have either made at least one pro fiction sale, or have completed a major, by-audition-only writing workshop like Odyssey, Clarion, or Boot Camp. In effect, we've delegated the task of vetting new members to the editors and teachers of the speculative fiction writing community. It's been a surprisingly effective approach.

Codex was founded under unusually auspicious circumstances: we drew from two large groups and invited a large number of talented, aspiring writers, instantly achieving that critical mass any online group needs to be successful. It became a melting pot of ideas from the beginning.

Codex has been very active in the three years since it began, producing more than 60,000 posts in more than 2,000 discussions, nearly 1,300 critiques of more than 500 works, as well as mini-critiques from contest entries and other activities. More importantly, our members have made great progress in their writing, in quality, productivity, and success. Half a dozen members have become professional novelists since they joined. Some have sold non-fiction books and, in one case, a picture book. Half a dozen or more have won the Writers of the Future contest since joining. One has become the editor of a major online pro science fiction and fantasy magazine, and others editors on notable, smaller magazines; two worked together to edit a benefit anthology including many of the greatest names in speculative fiction today. And of course there have been numerous professional short story sales. Two of our number have become literary agents, and four have become small press publishers, of whom two are responsible for this volume you have in your hands now.

But most of us are still small time. As we watch each other edging forward, crawling up the rocky overhang of writing success, it becomes easier to understand what it takes to become a successful pro writer. Perseverance, most of all, and a willingness to drag out the best work we can produce. Everyone benefits from raising the bar like this: editors, writers, and especially readers. Walking the lonely corridors of our brains without the help of clever friends and fellow travelers, our work would be limited by our own blind spots, our own unnoticed habits and limitations.

The volume you hold in your hands is of a rare kind, a collection of disparate, accomplished stories written by members of a coherent group. James Maxey ("To the East, a Bright Star") and Elaine Isaak ("The Disenchantment of Kivron Ox-master") have regular access to one another's ideas and insights; Cat Rambo ("Ticktock Girl") and David W. Goldman ("Radical Acceptance") have the opportunity to critique one another's work, and so on. Anything you like about one of the stories in this volume may someday show up in the work of any other of the collection's authors.

I get to read the thoughts of these remarkable authors every week. Here's your chance. I hope you find it as entertaining and enlightening as I do.

CONTENTS

PRIME
CODEX

TO THE EAST A BRIGHT STAR

BY JAMES MAXEY

THERE WAS A SHARK IN THE KITCHEN. The shark wasn't huge, maybe four feet long, gliding across the linoleum toward the refrigerator. Tony stood motionless in the knee-deep water of the dining room. The Wolfman said that the only sharks that came this far in were bull sharks, which could live in either salt or fresh water, and were highly aggressive. Tony leaned forward cautiously and shut the door to the kitchen. He had known the exact time and date of his death for most of his adult life. With only hours to go, he wasn't going to let the shark do something ironic.

Tony waded back to the living room. Here in the coolest part of the house, always shaded, he kept his most valuable possession in an ice-chest stashed beneath the stairs. He pulled away the wooden panel and retrieved the red plastic cooler. Inside was his cigar box, wrapped in plastic bags. He took the box, then grabbed one of the jugs of rainwater cooling in the corner and headed up the stairs to the bathroom. He climbed out the bathroom window onto the low sloping roof over the back porch.

Everything was damp from yesterday"s rain. He took out the silver case with his last three cigarettes. He went through five matches before he got one lit. He sucked down the stale smoke, while a tiny little voice in the back of his head chided him about his bad habits. Tony wished the tiny little voice would consult a calendar. It was a bit late to worry about cancer.

The sky shimmered with brilliant blue, not a cloud in it. The Wolfman had thought Tony was crazy to gamble on this day being clear. It had rained 200 days the previous year. A decade ago a comet had hit Antartica, melting half the ice cap, pumping countless tons of water vapor into the atmosphere. Cloudless skies were only a memory. And yet, in Tony's imagination, the sky of the last day had always been crystal clear. It pleased him that reality and imagination overlapped at last.

A slight breeze set waves gently lapping at the tumbled roofs and walls that lay in all directions. This had been a nice old neighborhood, full of Victorian houses, before the earthquakes started. Now only a few homes stood, twisted and strangely beautiful, half submerged in a shallow green ocean, surrounded by the salt-poisoned skeletons of trees still stretching toward that amazing blue sky.

"Here's to a gorgeous day," he said, raising his water jug toward the sun. He brought the jug to his lips and chugged down half a gallon, quickly, in careless gulps, with water running from the corners of his mouth, dripping down to soak his shirt. He no longer saw any point in being careful with fresh water. It felt good to be wasteful again.

His thirst sated, Tony capped the jug, walked to the edge of the roof, and dropped the water into his boat. He steadied himself, turned around, held his hands over his head, then flipped backward. He landed on his feet in the center of the aluminum skiff, his arms stretched for balance as the craft gently rocked.

"So what do you think, *Pop*?" he asked, imagining his father had been watching.

Tony knew exactly what Pop would think.

"The bit with the boat, just a gimmick," Tony answered, his voice taking on a touch of an Italian accent. "And the back flip...*sloppy*. The people want *form*."

"Whatever," Tony said, his voice once more his own. The old bastard never had a kind word for him. Or even a truthful one. Last year he'd met up with Pete Pyro the Fire King over at the Dixie.

"God Hell," Pete had stammered when he finally recognized him. "Rico told me you'd gone and died of AIDS, Tony."

Which had indicated to Tony that his father wasn't open to the idea of eventual reconciliation. But what the hell. There are only so many days in a life. You can't get around to everything.

Tony untied the rope and pushed the boat away from the house. Taking up oars, he maneuvered through the submerged streets. The sun beat down with a terrible force. It was two hours before sunset. Normally, he never went out during the day. When it wasn't raining, it could reach higher than the old dial thermometer back at the house could measure, and it had marks to one hundred ten. But the whole show ended only an hour after dark, and it would take a little while to reach the old Dixie Hotel, the tallest building still standing downtown. From its roof, he'd be maybe sixty feet higher than he would have been back at his house. Not much, but there was something in him which still craved heights. The higher he could get, the better the show.

Except for the splash and creak of oars, the world was silent. It had been almost a year since he'd seen a bird, three weeks since he'd had to hide from a helicopter, and six days since the Wolfman had changed his mind and headed west. He'd gone in search of the government shelter near Black Mountain, with hydroponic gardens, nuclear power, the works.

"I hear if you put all them tunnels end to end, they cover four hundred miles," the Wolfman had said. "There's room for one more."

Tony shook his head. At best there were cold little cages for crazy people, or cripples, or junkies. The Wolfman was a little of all three. Tony missed him.

Ahead loomed the islands of rubble that marked the downtown. Rusted steel beams were tangled together in great heaps, and mirrored glass gleamed beneath the surface of the sea. The Dixie rose above all this, six stories of old red brick that had somehow survived the quakes, the flooding, and the terrible unending heat. A month ago, the Dixie had been a noisy place, a Mecca for those left behind by accident or choice. He and the Wolfman had come here often. They'd survived the last few years by scavenging, and the Dixie had been a place to trade canned goods and batteries for booze and fresh vegetables. Some old geezer named Doc had filled the upper floors of the Dixie with potted plants, and his horticultural prowess provided garden goodies all year round. Also, Doc had rigged up a distillery for fresh water, plus another for booze. He'd been king of his little world, one of the last bastions of the good life, while it lasted.

A month ago the helicopters had come and taken everyone, whether they wanted to go or not. They'd smashed the stills and tossed plants into the ocean and Tony still couldn't see the sense in it. He and the Wolfman had steered clear of the place since, in case the helicopters came back. But now it would be safe. There would be no search and rescue at this late hour.

He tied off his boat on the east side, in the shade. A steady breeze was blowing in from the north now, taking the teeth out of the heat. He gulped thirstily from the water jug, then poured what was left over his face and hair. He pulled off his sweat-soaked shirt, and tossed it into the sea. He untied the tarp, and unfolded a fresh cotton shirt he'd saved for this occasion. He picked up his boombox, with its missing left speaker cover, and plugged in the fresh batteries he'd been saving. Over the years he'd traded away most of the CD's he'd found, keeping only a copy of *All Hail West Texas* by the Mountain Goats, a scratched-up double CD set of Mozart, and a K-Tel collection of Disco Hits. He still hadn't made up his mind what he was going to play.

Finally, he unwrapped the four layers of trash bags from the humidor. The box's contents would make all of his efforts worthwhile. He stepped through a window, into a shadowy room ankle-deep in brine. The Dixie moaned like a giant oboe as the wind rushed through the open windows.

The stairs creaked with each step. Emptied of its people, the Dixie seemed haunted. A place he associated with life and light now sat dark and dead, the air foul with rot. No doubt the place had moaned and creaked just as loudly on his past visits, but then the sounds were masked with laughter and talk and…

He stopped. Was the wind making that sound?

He climbed three more steps.

Crying. Someone was crying, somewhere above.

He crept up to the next landing. There was no doubt now.

"Hello?" he called out.

The crying stopped short.

"Hello?" he called again.

A woman began shouting, in a rapid, nearly unintelligible rush of syllables and sobs. He followed the sound, racing up two flights of stairs. He rushed past open doors, drawing nearer, until the woman's voice was clearly coming from the door to his left. He almost stepped through, but caught himself, grabbing the doorframe. The room beyond had no floor, and was only a pit dropping all the way back down to the water.

Across the void of the floorless room was an open door, in which Esmerelda stood, naked and filthy and thin.

He couldn't understand what she was saying. She was spitting out words between sobs, with a little laughter mixed in. Esmerelda was a fairly new arrival at the Dixie, having been traded to Doc a few months ago in exchange for a case of booze. When he'd seen her last, she'd been a shapely young thing, with sinister eyes. She'd looked like she hated everyone on Earth, and who could blame her? Now, she just looked terrified and hungry.

"Just hold on," Tony said, studying the situation. The light was nearly gone. It looked like a twenty-foot drop, maybe more, into a real mess of jagged rubble.

"Stay calm," he said. "I'll be back."

She screamed as he left the doorway.

He made it back to the boat in less than a minute. The water danced with black shadows and red flames. Night was moments away. He found his rope, and ran back up the stairs.

She waited in the far doorway, quiet now, and she'd found a sheet and draped it over her body. Her eyes were wide, glistening in the gloom.

"You're real," she said.

"I try," said Tony.

She pulled the sheet tighter around her shoulders.

"What happened?" he asked.

"Soldiers came," she said. "I hid. When it got quiet, I came out. The floor was gone."

"Jesus. You've been trapped all this time?"

She looked down into the pit. He could barely understand her as she answered. "Doc said they would come for him. He said they'd kill me. I wasn't important, like him. He told me he'd made traps."

"Let's get you out of there," Tony said. "Catch."

He tossed a coil of rope. She moved to catch it, but pulled her arms back as her sheet slipped. Fortunately, the rope landed in the room, and snagged on the floor's jagged edge as it slid back.

"Okay," he said. "Are you good at knots? I need you to tie that tightly to the sturdiest thing in the room."

She slowly knelt and grabbed the rope, looking slightly dazed.

"Come on," he said. "Time's wasting. You gotta trust me."

She disappeared into the room. Tony looked at his watch. There wasn't time for this. This wasn't how he'd planned to spend the evening. He should go on, leave her to her own devices. Except he hated people who thought like that, and now was a bad time to turn into someone he hated.

"It's tied," she said, reappearing.

Tony took up the slack, then yanked on the rope, putting his full weight on it. It felt solid from her end. He tugged the rope to a radiator pipe in the hall and tied his end, bracing his foot against the wall to pull it as taut as possible.

Then, without stopping to think about it, he stepped into the room, onto the rope, which sagged beneath him. He kept moving. Five six seven steps — and he was across, stepping into her room. Esmerelda stood there with her mouth open.

"Let's hurry this up," Tony said with a glance at his watch. He began to unbutton his shirt. Esmerelda backed away.

He held the shirt out to her.

"Wear this," he said. "I don't want to trip over that sheet when I carry you back."

"C-carry me?"

"I've walked wires with both my sisters standing on my shoulders. We'll make it."

"You're crazy," she said.

"*Jesus*," he said. "There isn't time for discussion. The Tony Express leaves the station in one minute." He placed the folded shirt on her shoulder, then turned around. "I won't look."

He studied the room she'd been trapped in. It was filled with flower pots and plastic tubs in which various green things were growing, some with little yellow blossoms. The room smelled like a sewer. There was a medicine cabinet on the wall, and pipes where the tub and sink had been. The rope was tied to the base of a shattered toilet, beside which sat a basin of clear water. Above this was a small window, through which he could see the night sky. He was on the wrong side of the building for the big show.

She touched his shoulder, lightly.

He turned. She wore his shirt now, which made her seem smaller, and there were tears streaming down her cheeks.

"Hey," he said. "Don't cry."

"I don't…I don't know if this is really happening. I've had…I've been having *dreams*."

"The Wolfman used to say, 'Some dreams you gotta ride.'" He pointed to his back. "Hop on."

Tentatively, she wrapped her arms around his neck. She smelled earthy, and her skin felt oily and hot against his. He lifted her. She was light, all bones and skin.

"Don't flinch," he said, and stepped onto the rope. She flinched, tightening her grip on his throat, her legs clamping around his waist. He moved cautiously, his feet listening to the messages the rope was sending. It wasn't good. Individual strands of the hemp were popping and snapping. The pipe in the hall was pulling free of its braces. Move move move *move*.

"*Alley oop!*" he cried, jumping forward. Esmerelda shrieked. He landed in the doorway and stumbled into the hall. He pried her arms off his trachea. "We made it. It's okay. It's okay."

She dropped from his back, trembling, laughing, crying.

"G-God. Oh God," she stammered. "I'm out. I'm out. I can still get to safety."

"You're as safe as you're ever going to be," he said.

"No!" she cried out. "Don't you know? Don't you know? How can you not know? There's a comet that's going to hit near here. A big one! We've only got until May 8 to get to—"

"That's today," he said. "We've got fifteen minutes."

She turned pale. She placed a hand against the wall.

Tony grabbed his stuff and headed for the stairs.

"C'mon," he said, racing up the steps two at a time.

Tony opened the door to the roof. The sky was black and silver, with a thin sliver of moon. A dozen comets streamed from the direction of the vanished sun. And to the east, a bright star, brighter than the moon, with a halo filling half the sky.

"Wow," he said.

He looked back. Esmerelda was halfway up the stairs, looking at him.

"Come on," he said. "You don't want to miss this do you? This is the kind of sky I dreamed about as a kid. A sky full of mysteries and wonders."

Esmerelda shook her head and turned, but didn't leave.

Tony shrugged. What did it matter if she didn't watch? He thought it strange, but then, everybody always thought *he* was strange, so who was he to judge? He'd planned to be alone anyway. But now that he had an audience, he was overcome with the need to talk.

"When I was ten, Mom bought me a telescope to see it," he said. "The brown star, I mean. Way out there, beyond Pluto. It wasn't much to look at. Scientists got all worked up, talking about how fast it was moving, where it had come from, where it was going, and all the damage it was doing by altering the orbits of comets. But in the telescope, it just hung there, a boring coffee-colored dot."

Tony sat down, his back against a chimney, the humidor in his lap.

"It's an exciting time to be alive, don't you think?"

She didn't answer.

Tony opened the humidor, revealing the syringe. He lifted it, and looked at the sky through the fluid-filled glass. It swirled with dreams and memories.

"You know how kids want to run away and join the circus?"

She didn't answer. He wasn't sure she could hear him.

"It works the other way around, too. My folks, my older sisters, they were the Flying Fiorentinos, Aerialists Extraordinare! Pop had big plans for me, being the first son. He had me training for the high wire while I was still in diapers."

Tony ran his finger along the old scars on his arm. "When I was about fifteen, the circus got a new snake lady, Satanica. Twice my age, but open-minded. She was a junky. Wasn't long before I was hooked, too. You can handle snakes while you're in the haze. Hell, the snakes like it. But junk and the high wire don't mix that well. So, Pop got Satanica busted. I ran off that night to visit her in jail. Never got to see her. But I never went back to the circus."

Against the bright sky, the waves of heat from the roof shimmered and danced. Tony sighed.

"I hate my Pop. He never gave a damn about me. I was just part of his act. A *prop* or something."

He looked back at the stairs. Esmerelda sat in the doorway, her back to him. She had her face pressed against her knees, her arms locked tightly around her shins. He readied the needle. The star of the east blazed bright now, casting shadows. If his watch was right, and he'd taken a lot of care over the years to see that it was, and if the astronomers were right, and their track record through all this had been pretty good, there were nine minutes, forty seconds left.

"Three years ago, I got off the junk," he said, tying the thick rubber tube around his arm. "But I made sure I'd have one last dose. Because the best moments of my life were spent floating on junk, curled up in the arms of my snake woman. That's what I want to take with me. How 'bout you? How do you want to spend the rest of your life?"

Esmerelda spoke, her voice tense and angry. "At least you were born *before* they found the rogue star. My folks *knew*. And they brought me into the world anyway."

"Some people didn't believe," said Tony, closing his hand tightly around a wad of tissues, watching his veins rise. "And some people hoped for the best."

"They said *God* would take us away," she murmured. She wrapped her hair around her fists as she talked. She looked at him, her eyes flashing in sharp little slits. "I *tried*. I *can't* believe in God. How could *they*? How could *anyone*?"

"My Mom believed," said Tony, placing the needle against his skin. "Probably will to the last second. If she's even still alive."

"I *killed* mine," she said.

"What?" Tony moved the needle away from his arm.

"My parents. On my thirteenth birthday. I slit their throats as they slept. The night the comet hit the moon."

"Jesus."

"I *should* have killed *myself*."

Tony sighed, and opened his hand. "Come here."

She shook her head.

"I think you need this more than I do," he said, holding the syringe toward her.

Her eyes fixed on it. She wiped her cheeks.

"It will help you," he said. "You still have a few minutes left."

She rolled to her knees, and crawled toward him, keeping her eyes fixed on the roof.

"Here," he said, meeting her halfway, pushing up her sleeve.

He'd only used a needle on another person once before, long ago. But the skill came back easily enough. She gasped as he pushed the plunger in.

"Now breathe deep," he said.

It worked quickly, like he remembered. He rolled her over onto his lap, and she opened her eyes to the dance of the comets. He watched her as she watched the sky, for the longest time. He dared not look at his watch. If he didn't look at the watch, time would stand still. Eternities could be hidden between seconds. At last, she smiled.

"Mysteries," she whispered. "And *wonders*."

Tony lay back, lit a cigarette on the first try, and looked at the dark spaces between the comets. The black shapes curled like vast snakes. He recalled the boom-box. He'd forgotten to play the music. But things don't always go as planned. A lifetime of practice won't keep the wire from snapping. When you fall, you relax, and let the net catch you.

JAMES MAXEY LIVES IN HILLSBOROUGH, NC. He's the author of the cult classic superhero novel Nobody Gets the Girl *(2004) and the critically acclaimed fantasy novel* Bitterwood. *You can find out more about James and his writing at www.jamesmaxey.blogspot.com.*

TICKTOCK GIRL

BY CAT RAMBO

MOMENT 20244660: SHE SITS IN THE FRONT PARLOR, covered with white cloth. Subdued spring light washes through the folds each afternoon. Behind her in the cavernous room, the tick tock of the grandfather clock echoes, counterpointed by the steps of the servant come to wind it. The maid must be accompanied by a girl in training today; they speak in quiet, subdued tones, bringing with them the smell of soap and lemon oil.

"Spooky, that's what it is. 'Ow long has it all sat here?" The voice is high-pitched, shot through with a nervous giggle.

"Since her ladyship died. Her father ordered it all covered up, and it's sat here ever since. Going on ten years now."

"What's this now?" The dusty sheet, tugged by an inquisitive hand, slides off her face and the new maid lets out a shriek of surprise before she is quieted by the older one.

"That's the lady's mechanical woman. Used to walk and talk, they say. Still can. But her lordship said, sit here, and so she does." With a deft rustle, the sheet is tucked around her again, but as the light dims, she preserves the sight of wide blue eyes, a mouth agape in astonishment.

"Walk an' talk? Go on, yer pulling me leg."

"That's what they say. Used to march alongside her in the suffrage parades."

A cog, imprisoned in her brain, ticks, and she enters a new moment, this one left behind.

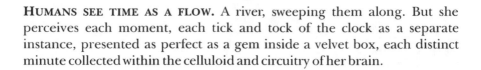

HUMANS SEE TIME AS A FLOW. A river, sweeping them along. But she perceives each moment, each tick and tock of the clock as a separate instance, presented as perfect as a gem inside a velvet box, each distinct minute collected within the celluloid and circuitry of her brain.

MOMENT 1: THERE IS SOMETHING HOT and hard hammering inside her chest, but perhaps that is ordinary. She has no other moments to compare this one with, here and now in the first sixty seconds of life. All that exists is the face hovering above her where she lies on a table. The features are flushed with triumph and perspiration, a mass of golden brown ringlets falling around it, one touching her brass skin.

The lips open, and sounds come out. They have meaning attached to them. "Can you hear me?"

Her own lips move. The rubber bags that are her lungs contract, squeezing out air for her tongue to shape. "Yes."

Water appears on her skin. In some other moment she will know these are Sybil's tears, but not tears of sorrow, tears of joy. There will be many kinds of tears.

"I am Lady Sybil Fortinbras," the face says. "I am your creator." Then, with a laugh, "Creatrix, I suppose."

The moment ends before she can reply.

MOMENT 25153800: THE SMELL OF SEAWATER and musty cargo crates, part of so many moments, is gone. There is a long slow screech as each nail is withdrawn.

MOMENT 25153804: THE LID COMES OFF, and around her the packing material rustles as someone throws handfuls of it aside. Then her face is cleared and she sees him, hears his voice saying in German "A woman? What use is a mechanical woman to me? Schiesse!" He throws the last handful back and she watches it drifting down in slow motion, settling to block her sight again.

MOMENT 8820967: THEY ARE MARCHING IN A SUFFRAGE PARADE. Along High Street, hostile faces loom, shouting. She wheels Lady Sybil's chair forward. Both of them wear white dresses, sashes of purple and green. Purple for courage, green for strength. The other women ignore her. She makes them uneasy, even though she may be the only reason the crowd doesn't rush to attack them. But one, her face lean and resolute as a hatchet, leans forward to speak to Lady Sybil.

"Do you agree with what Mrs. Pankhurst says?"

Lady Sybil glances up impatiently amid the sea of white ruffles. "That the argument of the broken pane is the most valuable argument in modern politics? Perhaps. But we will work within the law. For now." Her eyes are shrewd as she looks at the people lining the street. "Why would we want the vote if we intend to go outside the bounds of the law?"

MOMENT 9097372: LADY SYBIL IS SPEAKING. The winter has withered her even more. She is frail and fragile as a songbird.

"You see, I don't think it's enough to march anymore," she says. "There has to be some good coming from you. In this brave new age, there are villains aplenty. I'll set you after them. You have been my legs, my dear. My mechanical Athena. For so very long. And now you will be my fists."

MOMENT 9156658: SHE HAS THE DARK-SKINNED, well-dressed man by the collar, pulling his limp form after her into the offices of Scotland Yard. She drops him in the doorway of Todd Chrisman, the detective who, she knows, has been working on the case.

"This is the Maharishi of Terjab," she says.

His eyes are amazed. "Yes, I can see that."

"He is responsible for the Soho white slave ring. You will find the evidence in his basement."

He stammers out something, moves forward to look down at the Maharishi. "What are you?" he says.

"Lady Fortinbras's mechanical Athena," she says. "My directive is to fight evildoers."

Behind him in the office, someone laughs, only to be hissed into silence by a fellow. All of these men are watching her.

MOMENT 9230101: "THIS IS THE DOG COLLAR KILLER," she says to Chrisman.

The man at her feet groans, recovering himself. He fought hard.

"He's a clergyman," Chrisman says, astonishment coloring his voice.

Pallid and rabbity, the man wears his robes like a squatter moved into a strange new place. He blinks, the bruises along his face coloring like dark water, and one eye weeps bloody tears.

"I am Father Jeremiah, and this is an outrage," he says, pulling himself upward despite the restraining hand on his arm.

"Marilyn Bellcastle," she says. "Lucy Stipe. Annabel Jones. He killed them all."

He explodes in spittle and anger at the sound of her voice. "Whores!" he snarls. "Jezebels! They deserved no better!"

MOMENT 9618905: "WHAT HAVE YOU BROUGHT US now, lass?" Chrisman asks. She gives him the papers she has compiled, the blueprints for the bomb to be placed beneath the Houses of Parliament and he thanks her, riffling through the rustling papers one by one, studying them. There are new decorations on his uniform; her aid has brought him a promotion.

MOMENT 9713637: LADY SYBIL'S FATHER PACES up and down the study, talking to himself. His cooling breakfast, the opened letter beside it, sits on the table. He wheels on her.

"Died in prison, by god!" he shouts. "Her and that Pankhust woman, thinking hunger strikes would change the gaolers' minds. What good is it dying for a stupid, frippery cause, just another chance to dress up?"

She believes this is a rhetorical question; she makes no reply. She would have been with them, but Lady Sybil felt chasing the Ghost of Belfast was more important. Chrisman should have been pleased when she brought the villain in, but he was subdued, told her simply to go home.

"I'll have every man in that prison to court," Lord Fortinbras says. He looks at her, the way he has always looked at her. Half repulsed and half proud at his clever daughter's creation.

"And you, mechanical Athena," he says. "What's to become of you now?"

There are tears on his face.

MOMENT 25055955: THE CRACK OF THE GAVEL resounds through the crowded room as the auctioneer bangs the sale closed. "And sold to the foreign gentleman!"

Some of Lady Sybil's friends are there, but none of them have bid on her. She is led away to the waiting crate. She feels nothing.

MOMENT 49189954: PROFESSOR DELTA IS SPEAKING.

"The university bought you as a historical feminist treasure," she says. "Built by an English suffragette and scientist. The once owned by Hitler stuff, that was just icing on the cake, a little thrill value. But now…nowadays people are more concerned with the rights of mechanicals than they were when you were sold."

There is a gleam in her eye that is reminiscent of the Pankhursts.

"Do you really want to be on your own?" Delta says, leaning forward. She is a short, wiry woman, her hair cropped close, no makeup on her face. "What would you do?"

"Fight crime," she says.

Delta leans back, her hand flickering in a dismissive gesture. "A superhero? Let the papers call you something like Ticktock Girl? How…trivial. It would be a terrible waste."

She could go back in the crate. But Lady Sybil built her to move. To act. To be her hands, even now.

MOMENT 57343680: SHE FACES FATHER JEREMIAH in the closed room, cinderblock walls, the smell of disinfectant harsh and immediate. Somewhere in the distance, water drips.

She's not sure how he can be alive, unchanged, a century later. But here he is.

"The Lord has preserved me! I am his Hand!" he shouts at her. She calculates the distance from her fist to his jaw, the amount of impact necessary to render him unconscious.

He draws himself up and smiles. "But you can't. I'm legit now."

The word is unfamiliar.

He splits it into syllables for her, serves it up like little rabbit pellets of words. "Le-gi-ti-mate. Everything I do is inside the law."

"You tell people to kill other people and they do it."

"All I do is provide information on where they are: the abortionists, the sodomites, the women who whore themselves out. My followers decide what to do with the knowledge."

Seeing her pause, he laughs. "Welcome to the brave new world, Ticktock, mechanical clock," he half sings. "Can't touch this, can't touch me now."

MOMENT 9097375: SICKNESS HAS EATEN away at Lady Sybil's face, reducing it to paper over bone. But her voice is strong as ever.

"There is right and there is wrong," she says. "You, my mechanical Athena, are always on the side of right." A trembling hand strokes along the bright metal of her face. "The side of justice."

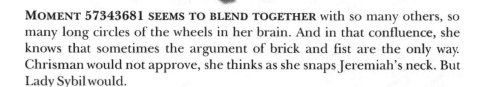

MOMENT 57343681 SEEMS TO BLEND TOGETHER with so many others, so many long circles of the wheels in her brain. And in that confluence, she knows that sometimes the argument of brick and fist are the only way. Chrisman would not approve, she thinks as she snaps Jeremiah's neck. But Lady Sybil would.

CAT RAMBO LIVES AND WRITES IN THE PACIFIC NORTHWEST with her charming husband Wayne and two cats, Raven and Taco. She was a graduate of the 2005 Clarion West Writers' Workshop and holds an MA in Fiction from the Johns Hopkins Writing Seminars. She is currently working on a fantasy novel, tentatively titled The Water's Secret: A Novel of Tabat.

THE MAN WITH GREAT DESPAIR BEHIND HIS EYES

BY KEN SCHOLES

MERIWETHER LEWIS STARED DOWN at the time-worn scrap of paper, holding it in his hands as if it were a rare butterfly too easily crushed. He'd been in one of his moods when the courier had summoned him two hours earlier. This time, he'd even loaded the pistol, placed it on the table near his chair and brandy. This time, he'd promised himself, he would follow through and be done with it. But now, sitting in Jefferson's study, curiosity pushed the darkness aside.

The President pushed back his chair, stood and turned away from the paper-strewn table to gaze out the window at the rain-soaked night. Lewis, glancing up briefly, thought he looked tired.

"Mr. President?"

"As you know, Meriwether, I'm not one given to fanciful flights. By God, I am a man of science and reason, but this shakes me to my very soul and confounds my sensibilities."

Lewis nodded, more to himself than not, remembering when this man — this intellectual Goliath — was his neighbor in Virginia. They'd spent hours talking together about plants and fossils and the expansive West. Thomas Jefferson was every part a scientist. He looked down at the green rectangle, wondered what tree this unlikely leaf fell from. He studied the face in the thumb-sized portrait and read the name again. "And you're certain it is him?"

"Yes. It's Jackson...that backwoods powder-keg. The years are heavy upon him in that likeness."

They were indeed, Lewis saw. Andrew Jackson, now a judge somewhere in Tennessee after a brief stint in the Senate, was in all actuality not much older than himself. But he wore twenty, maybe thirty years beyond in the small drawing.

Lewis turned the paper over, a wonder tinged with some form of fear lifted the hair on his neck and hands. Another picture, another name beneath it. "This is the President's House," he said in a hollow voice.

"Yes." Jefferson turned in from the window. "Yes it is."

"But—"

"But the President's House isn't nearly as old as the parchment. And it has never been called 'The White House.' At least not to my knowledge."

"And neither to mine." Lewis had spent a miserable winter in the unfinished, leaking shell of a house as laborers completed the work. "How did this come into your hands?"

Jefferson creaked into the wood chair and poured a glass of water from a ceramic pitcher. "A colleague at the Society purchased it at no small price from one of Gray's men. A sailor on the *Columbia* claims to have traded it away from a Chinook medicine-man." Captain Gray had named the river after his ship, Lewis remembered, and supposedly enjoyed several weeks of profitable trade among the West-coast natives. "The medicine-man claimed it held mystical properties, having come from a white holy man who lived deep in the forest north of the river's mouth...a teller of fortunes, the Indian claimed." Jefferson closed his mouth, pursing his lips in thought. "He should not be difficult to find, I would think."

Lewis looked up at his friend, his President. "You are proposing that I go?" An excitement gripped him; he had wanted to explore the West for longer than he could remember.

"Yes. Congress has approved the funding to outfit this Corps of Discovery." His brow furrowed. "But this is to be first and foremost a scientific and military expedition. The water route, the careful recording of flora and fauna, notation of any strategic import — these are all noble and legitimate endeavors. As written in the letter you shall shortly receive. This other matter is to be held in your strictest confidence." The President's jaw firmed.

"You shall have it, Sir."

Jefferson smiled, reached across the table to pat Lewis' hand. "I know I shall." He paused, looking even older and more tired. The strain between the French and the British had worn him down, Lewis knew, and factions from the States grumbled faintly of secession as anti-Federalist feelings grew. "If you find him, Meriwether, I have to know. I have to know, if he can tell us, whether this Union we have forged with our very blood and tears and sweat shall abide or perish still in its crib."

"Yes, Mr. President." Lewis turned the parchment over again. It masqueraded as United States currency — a twenty dollar note — and next to an illegible signature stood four small numbers that grew larger and larger in his widening eyes: 1971.

He handed it back to Jefferson, glad for the delicate butterfly to leave his fingers.

IN THE MONTHS LEWIS TRAVELED WITH HIM, Drouillard's anger often hid behind a placid face, but the half-breed suddenly spat into the mud, water running off his cap as he tipped his head. "Damn this rain," he said and the Fields brothers sniggered. Dark eyes flashing back at them, he cursed them first in French, then in a half-dozen tribal tongues.

Lewis smiled at his stalwart companion's outburst though today the darkness held him. It had followed Lewis across the continent, aloof but near enough to sense. Here, close to the end of their journey, it thrived.

Dark and bleak, the sky hung low with clouds when they could see it beyond the pine-ceiling. Still, the sky saw *them* and rained down its furious tears. The stink of ruined, rotting fur filled his nostrils and his ankles ached with every step. The damned rain pervaded everything, rotting even their clothes. The Pacific Coast, thus far, proved to be a wet and gray place.

Private Frazier sidled up to him. "Cap'n Lewis?" He turned to the lanky Virginian, but kept his feet shuffling forward through the loam that sucked at his moccasins. "Do you really think we'll find a ship? And whites?"

"That's what they said." Two weeks before, a handful of Indians in a canoe had told him and Clark what to expect at the mouth of the Columbia. And as they made their way down the river, more and more of the natives wore sailors' caps, carried rusted knives and cooked from copper pots. Last Thursday, they'd finally seen the ocean, distant on the edge of the horizon. Yesterday, Lewis and his small party had left Clark and the others to scout north of the wide river.

"Hell if I'm walking all the way back if there's a ship," Reuben Fields said.

"Hell if you ain't." Joseph Fields laughed. "Hell if we all ain't, if the Captains have their way."

The bushes ahead rustled and their dog bounded out, his black fur slick with rain. A small rabbit kicked its last in the Newfoundland's strong jaws. He's the only one who's truly happy here, Lewis thought. The rain didn't affect him, darken his outlook. Still, mood or no, they had their mission, and the Corps of Discovery was about its business regardless of the weather.

"We'll rest here a bit."

At his word, the men found trees to squat against, hiding from the downpour as best they could. Lewis leaned against an alder and Drouillard drew close. They spoke in low voices.

"Cap'n, I know it's none of my concern, but if I knew what we were looking for I could be more helpful."

Lewis looked at the dark man, nearly as tall as himself, and pursed his lips. "Even if I myself knew completely, I couldn't tell you."

Drouillard nodded. "The men are curious."

"Let them be."

The interpreter straightened. "Aye, sir."

Lewis closed his eyes and let the heaviness take him. Weariness is to be expected, he realized, after eighteen months of walking, paddling and riding the wilderness.

Still, what an adventure so far. There would be much to talk about and celebrate when they returned. *If* they returned. If the rain didn't wash the very skin from their bones.

They'd all celebrated when they glimpsed the broad, gray expanse of the Pacific. But the joy leaked out of him too soon. All his life it had, and for a brief moment Lewis craved death again. "This is the place to find it," he said, not realizing he spoke aloud.

"Captain?"

"Never mind," Lewis said. "Let's move."

At noon they broke into a clearing and an old Indian stood, leaning on a birch staff. Lewis nodded at Drouillard who stepped forward, hands signing their intent. The Indian waved him away. "We do not need to make the sign-talking," he said in thickly accented English. He pointed to Lewis. "The Man-from-the-River told me he dreamed of a red stork flying in the direction of the sinking sun."

The men mumbled and Lewis gave them a hard glance. They often called him 'Red Stork' when they thought he wasn't listening.

Lewis approached the old man. The Indian watched him through squinted, dark eyes buried in a sea of wrinkles. "Who are you? How do you come to speak English? Are you the Man-from-the-River?"

The native shook his head. "The Man-from-the-River sent me to bring you to him. He wishes to meet the great Red Stork." He motioned Lewis closer, out of ear-shot of the others. "He told me to show you this." For a brief instant, a ball of green paper lay exposed in his palm, then he curled his fingers around it again.

"You'll make camp here and await my return," Lewis said over his shoulder. "I'm going on alone." The old man turned and walked toward the clearing's edge. Lewis glanced at Drouillard to confirm his order, and the interpreter nodded, eyes narrow.

Lewis followed the old man, catching up as the brush swallowed them. "You didn't tell me your name."

The old man didn't break his stride. "I am called John Fitzgerald Kennedy."

The rain stopped.

THEY WALKED UNTIL TWILIGHT FELL, pushing aside the gray overcast day for a deeper gloom. Many times, Lewis tried to engage his companion in conversation, hoping to draw out information from the old man. He merely answered the questions with questions.

"Why is he called the Man-from-the-River?"

"What would you call a man pulled from the waters?"

"Where do the green papers come from?"

"Who can know where powerful medicine comes from?"

"Why are you called John Kennedy?"

"Why am I called by any name?"

"Can he really see the future?"

"Why is seeing the future more wondrous than seeing today?"

Eventually, Lewis surrendered and settled into a morose silence. Now that the rain had let up, he knew he should check the powder in his rifle and pistols. But the woods seemed quiet and the old man walked them with a confident, comfortable step that spoke safety to Lewis' vigilant heart.

They broke from the woods into a clearing that hugged a sheer wall of rock topped thirty feet above with pines and moss and fern. A wooden lean-to nestled against the rock, a trickle of smoke leaking out from it.

"I must tell you he doesn't make much of the white-man talk anymore. I think he has forgotten how. He is old. Older than me." The Indian started for the shelter, then stopped as Lewis hesitated. "I will translate," John said.

Lewis nodded, a sudden apprehension twisting his stomach. "Very well."

As they approached, a faint chanting drifted to his ears, a mumbled litany that rose and fell like a song. It stopped as John lifted the weave of alder branches that served as a door. He hurriedly waved Lewis in, as if anxious to keep the moist evening air at bay.

Lewis unslung his rifle and stooped to look inside the dirt-floored lean-to.

The first thing he saw was a canopy of green paper, the bills hung from bone fish-hooks and dangling from the ceiling. It was the ceiling of a faded, soft forest that rustled as his shoulders brushed the lean-to's doorway. The second thing he saw was the old man.

The Man-from-the-River sat on a doe-skin rug, legs crossed, hands turned upward and held at shoulder height. Long white hair flowed over his head and cascaded to the floor, like spilled milk, hiding what clothing he wore, if any. Large ears poked out from the pale tangle. His skin, pulled tightly over the bones, was slightly olive — perhaps of Spanish or Moorish descent — and his eyes were hidden behind a strange pair of dark spectacles. A long pink scar ran out from his scalp like a river leaving a forest, disappearing behind the spectacles, above his left eye. A small fire guttered in a pit dug into the floor, near the rock face.

Leaning the short-barrel musket against the granite wall, just inside the door, Lewis squeezed himself through the narrow opening. The room was surprisingly warm and he wrestled out of the stinking buffalo robe and pushed it outside, the hide already a casualty of the region.

He sat down before the Man-from-the-River and waited for John. As the old Indian settled in, Lewis drew a peace medal from inside his shirt. "The Great White Father sends this token of his regard for the Man-from-the-River." He handed it across the fire and waited while John translated. Nodding, the faintest smile touched the old man's lips as he took the medal. He turned and put it behind him, mumbling something.

John looked at Lewis. "The Man-from-the-River thanks the Red Stork for his generous gift and is glad that you have come seeking him."

"How did he get here?" Lewis watched, listening to the translation.

"He awoke in the great river and did not know himself. I pulled him to safety. Over time, my people realized he had much medicine and charged me to care for him, but far from our village. This was almost thirty summers ago."

Lewis pointed at the ceiling. "Ask him about the paper bills, about the pictures and words on them. Where did they come from?"

John shook his head. "It is not wise to ask such."

"Ask him."

The Indian asked the question quickly, gesturing impatiently at Lewis. Man-from-the-River nodded slowly, looked at Lewis, and shook his head as he spoke.

"They came with him out of the river and are a part of his medicine," John translated. "You should not be concerned with them."

"Tell him my Great Father believes that they are important and sent me to ask of them."

John did, listened to the reply, and paused, asking the old man a question with raised eyebrows. Man-from-the-River nodded, saying the words again more firmly. "These are not why you have come. You have come to swim the dream-waters with the Man-from-the-River."

Lewis tried to hide his frustration behind a smile. "No, I have come to know—"

The Man-from-the-River started speaking, and Lewis let him. "You are a man with great despair behind your eyes, Red Stork. You are a man of tremendous courage but a mighty sadness washes you like the tide washes a stone. You have come to swim the dream-waters and be healed of your darkness."

Lewis felt his temper stir as his patience faded. But he also felt something else stir. The simultaneous hope and fear of being known by this strange old man. His thumb nervously tapped the butt of one pistol and he held his tongue. Finally, he said, "I have no need of healing." The lie rolled easily from him.

"Then we will eat," the Man-from-the-River said through his interpreter.

At that, he produced a bowl of dried fruit and two smoked salmon from a recess in the stone wall. They ate in silence.

When they finished, Lewis tried again. "My Great Father is a knowledgeable man. He has worked very hard to build a strong and just home for his children. He watches them and worries for their well-being. He hears that Man-from-the-River has much medicine and can tell the future. He sees Man-from-the-River's green paper and wonders what it is and where it comes from." If he hadn't held the parchment himself, hadn't seen the thousands of them that hung suspended above his head, he would have felt alarmed for Jefferson's mental state. His voice raised an octave. "Your servant, John Fitzgerald Kennedy, showed me one of these papers so I would come here with him. Now you tell me nothing about them. My Great Father will be unhappy if you do not send me home to him with answers for his questions." He sat back and waited.

Man-from-the-River's response was simple: "If your Great Father wished to ask questions of me, he would have come himself." Silence settled over them. He spoke again, quietly. "But perhaps when swimming the dream-waters you will find answers for him. Many have powerful visions, for Man-from-the-River's medicine is strong and sometimes his dreams are also shown when he gazes upon your own."

"Very well, I will swim the dream-waters." Lewis had participated in other tribal rites, finding them quaint and pointless however meaningful to these simple savages. And, he reasoned to himself, even the white man had his own, albeit superior, rites — baptism, communion, and the like. "But I am ignorant of such ways for my people no longer swim the dream-waters."

Man-from-the-River nodded, smiling, and pulled off the dark spectacles to reveal his eyes. He spoke to John, who also nodded.

"Man-from-the-River is glad to swim with you and hopes you will find the healing of your sorrow in the waters."

Lewis didn't know what to say. All his life, he'd wrestled with his moods but in public, particularly since the formation of the Corps, he'd bent his will to concealing the gripping melancholy. Certainly Clark knew — they'd been friends long enough — and on more than one occasion Jefferson had asked after his heart, but they, too, had years under the belt. Was it possible this man could see past his resolve in so short a time?

Lewis said nothing.

John half-stood. "I will return in the morning. You will need no further interpretation." He lifted the door to leave.

"I'd rather you stayed," Lewis said.

"It is not the way." He left, replacing the woven screen of branches. Lewis turned back to the old man.

Grunting in satisfaction, Man-from-the-River stretched a gnarled hand above his head and plucked a crisp green parchment. Laying it on a flat, smooth stone he reached behind and drew a bone knife. He duck-walked to Lewis and tugged at his pack, pointing at his bedroll and then at the corner of the hovel. Lewis unrolled it and stripped out of his jacket.

The old man ran the knife along his hand, not breaking the skin, to show Lewis his intentions. Familiar with the bonding ritual, Lewis nodded and winced as the blade sliced through his offered hand. A line of crimson beaded up and he watched it. Man-from-the-River cut his own hand and pressed their wounds together, chanting in a low voice.

After about five minutes, Man-from-the-River pulled away and drew a squirrel-skin sack from beneath his own bedroll. He carefully untied its strings, folded the green parchment in half length-wise and sprinkled a mixture of herb and powder into the valley it created. Then, he rolled the paper around it as if it were a cigar and ran his tongue around it to hold it shut. He twisted the ends and grinned up at Lewis with raised eyebrows.

Lewis smiled back, inwardly wondering what the contents of the medicine bag were and what effect they may have on his physiology.

Man-from-the-River dug a stick out of the fire and held it to one end while he puffed at the other. The room filled with a scent of old paper mingled with alfalfa. After drawing in a lungful, he grunted and passed it to Lewis.

He filled his lungs and burst into a fit of coughing. The smoke tasted sweet with just a hint of licorice. Man-from-the-River laughed and motioned for him to try again. He did.

They passed it back and forth for half an hour, each lungful stretching at Lewis' perceptions. The room began to vibrate slightly. It pulsated like a great beating heart. He could hear the rasp of his beard growing, could see the blood racing beneath Man-from-the-River's skin. Each time he moved, his surroundings moved with him. Finally, when the cigar was nothing but a glowing stub, Man-from-the-River re-opened their wounds, mingled their blood again, and waved Lewis to the bedroll.

He fell into it like it was the deepest of rivers.

Then, he swam.

IMAGES CROWDED HIS EYES, fleeting pictures that moved across a window set in the side of an ornate wooden box. He heard sounds, too, but they were far away. He sat in a strange chair, reclined in front of the box, drinking a weak beer from a light but somehow metal can.

WHOMP.

He saw a low black carriage without horses, surrounded by strangely dressed men. A man sitting in back with a woman suddenly jerked then slumped over.

WHOMP.

He saw a large metal box-like something that settled down from the sky. Men holding strange rifles, wearing green uniforms and helmets, scrambled from it into a jungle.

WHOMP.

He saw a man-shaped creature jump from a ladder onto a dusty, barren landscape, heard a crackling voice talk about small steps and giant leaps.

WHOMP.

He saw the flag of the United States, burning in the hands of a wild-haired, wild-eyed youth, and realized the handful of stars had become a crowded field.

WHOMP.

Suddenly, Lewis was somewhere else — a room crowded with young people dressed strangely. He stood behind a lectern, a stick of chalk held tightly in his hand. In front of him lay an open book. His own face stared back at him from one of the pages. Clark's face looked out from the other.

WHOMP.

The scene changed again to the comfortable chair and the window-box.

A black man in a suit led a mob of other blacks on a march through streets that looked vaguely familiar.

WHOMP.

"Miss, you'd better look at that note," he heard himself say in a voice not his own. "I have a bomb." He sat in a less comfortable, narrow seat with a briefcase on his lap. He opened it slightly, showing the indecently dressed woman a bundle of red sticks and wires. He sat in a tunnel-like corridor with humming in his ears. The other chairs around him, row on row from one end of the tube to another, were nearly empty. When he saw the windows, he looked out the one closest.

The first thing he saw was his reflection, also not his own. Instead, Man-from-the-River, thirty years younger, with short dark hair and dark skin, eyes hidden behind dark glasses.

The second thing he saw was the ocean of darkness above and below. He was flying.

WHOMP.

Now, weighed down by a pack and satchel, he stood by an open door and stairs leading down into the sky. Wind howled and tore at him. Outside, nothing but darkness and cold awaited him. A disembodied voice crackled near him: "Is everything okay back there, Mr. Cooper?"

"No," he said and jumped into the storm.

He fell faster and faster, eyes forced open, until something snapped and billowed. Something like the hand of an almighty, saving god jerked him upward, threatening to rip him asunder. A moment of pain, then he floated on the air. Lightning flashed. Frozen rain pelted. Above him, a metal bird rumbled away.

Below him, somewhere lost in a November night, a river awaited. Time opened its mouth and swallowed him whole.

Lewis slept.

"I WAS A TEACHER, BEFORE."

Lewis opened his eyes, forced them wide against the room's threatened collapse. A sharp pain lanced the front of his head and his mouth tasted like dry ashes. Man-from-the-River sat slouched in the corner, dark glasses bouncing back the flickering fire.

Lewis stretched and sat up as quickly as his head allowed. "You speak English?"

The old man chuckled. "Sometimes. How do you think JFK learned it?" JFK...John Fitzgerald Kennedy, Lewis realized. "Now *that* was a goddamn shame," Man-from-the-River said. "Oswald could have never pulled it off alone."

Lewis didn't know what to say. A dozen questions danced in his brain.

"Yes," the old man continued, "Teaching history, you see the unlikely, accidental heroes and the true ones. You were a true one, Meriwether Lewis, and one of my favorites. The tragedy is that you never saw it. And me? Well, I was never a hero...just a guy who wanted to be part of history, a guy tired of talking about it all the time." He nodded at the green papers overhead. "I suppose somewhere up there people still talk about both of us, too. Movies, books...God knows what else." He laughed and it became a wet cough.

Lewis shifted uncomfortably. "I don't know what you mean."

Man-from-the-River waved a hand and his outstretched fingers caught the smoke and dispersed it in gray tendrils. "You don't have to, Captain Lewis."

"Where do you come from?"

The old man coughed again. "Someplace I'll never see again." He pulled off the spectacles. He chuckled and then sang in a quiet voice: "We've all come to look for America."

Lewis leaned forward. "The United States of America? Tell me, I beg you, what you know?"

"Jefferson sent you. Your Great Father, right?"

He nodded. "Yes. The scrip...it's from our future, isn't it?" Lewis swallowed back a sudden queasiness in his stomach. "You...you are from our future, too."

Man-from-the-River smiled. "What do you really want to know, Meriwether? You've seen everything in the dream-waters. You know the Union shall prevail. Oh, they'll kill Abraham, Martin and John. Bobby, too. There will be wars and rumors of war. There will be peace and rumors of peace." He paused. "What do you really want to know, Meriwether?"

Sadness sprung into his throat. Water pried at his eyes. He'd held it back long enough, denied it long enough. Whatever squeezed his heart also muttered that his one moment of true honesty was upon him here in this lean-to, thousands of miles from home. Lewis choked, his voice a whisper. "But," he asked, "Will *I* prevail?"

Man-from-the-River looked away. "I am an old man. My remaining days are few and I have waited years for your arrival. Stay with me and I will teach you to swim the dream-waters alone. In time they will wash your sorrows as they have washed mine and those who came before me."

Yes, he thought. For years he'd wrestled his demon. He *could* stay; he *could* find some kind of peace here, away from the world. There truly was medicine in this place, with this old man. But duty nudged him. "Sir, I can not." Lewis's voice shook. "And you have not answered my question."

Man-from-the-River looked at him. Their eyes locked. "You will survive your expedition. You will be hailed a hero."

Lewis held his stare. "That is not what I mean."

"You are no coward. You are strong and hard to die. Remember those words well."

"And my melancholia?" A tear leaked out. "I fear sometimes it may be the end of me."

Man-from-the-River said nothing. Lewis waited but knew he had his answer. The knowing somehow gentled him. Hours crawled and Lewis drifted off again. He awoke with John Fitzgerald Kennedy gently shaking him.

The native pointed to a still, slumped figure. "He swims the deepest dream-waters now."

Lewis stayed to help build the pyre. Man-from-the-River had left detailed instructions with John and they carried them out. He resisted the strong urge to snatch one of the green papers, the scrip of a far-away time. Instead, they packed them into a battered satchel and placed them onto Man-from-the-River's naked chest.

Not Man-from-the-River, Lewis thought, but Man-from-the-Sky...Man-from-Tomorrow.

John Fitzgerald Kennedy lit the pyre and the kindling crackled to life despite the fine morning rain. "He wished for you to stay. He spoke often of you. He waited for your coming with great anticipation."

Lewis nodded, lost in thought. Soon, he would head south and find his small group of men. They would meet up with Clark and the others on the Columbia, wait out the winter on that western shore and eventually turn homeward. What would he tell his President and friend? How would he tell this part of his journey? Or should he tell it at all?

The fire grew and ashes lifted from the burning satchel like gray butterflies suddenly freed.

LEWIS SIPPED HIS BRANDY and watched the dancing flames in Jefferson's hearth. Every flame now a pyre. Every ash, a question he knew he could not answer honestly.

"Missouri will suit you well," the President said with a smile. "*Governor* Lewis." He raised his glass and Lewis did the same.

"Thank you, Sir."

"Anything for a hero of the Republic."

There was an endless march of parades and speeches and parties. Attentions from the highest of society and huzzahs from the basest. Lewis lived in a whirlwind frenzy.

Jefferson stood and went to a high shelf. He reached for a large book, opened it, and removed the familiar green scrap of paper from its pages. He held it in his hands. "What of our other matter, Meriwether?" the President asked.

Lewis had thought long on what to say. He'd waited politely for weeks, expecting the question to come at any time. He cleared his voice.

"I...I found nothing, Mr. President."

Jefferson remained silent, waiting for Lewis to elaborate.

"I did inquire. This medicine man — Man-from-the-River they called him — he died a year earlier of the pox, I'm afraid."

Jefferson sighed, turning the scrip over again. "Perhaps a clever hoax then," he said. "Still, wouldn't it be something to know. To really *know*."

Lewis closed his eyes. The brandy, the warm fire, wrapped him tight. Behind his eyes, despair lay at arm's length, appeased for now. "To know what, Sir?"

Jefferson placed the scrip in the book, closed it and replaced it on the shelf. He smiled, his voice suddenly merry. "How it all turns out, of course. Our great experiment in Democracy."

Lewis opened his mouth to speak, shut it, opened it again. "But..."

"Yes?"

His words tumbled like the waters in a hundred rivers he had crossed over the past few years. "But if we could know, Sir, exactly how it would all come out. If we could know for certain that we either would or would not prevail in whatever task we had set our hands to do...would it change anything? If we knew success was guaranteed, could that not lead to risks that might undo our own future?" Jefferson studied Lewis, caught in his words. "And if we knew that our failure was certain, wouldn't we still do what needs doing? In faith and in hope for something better?" He leaned forward now, feeling the heat in his face. The darkness stirred inside of him at the question, a cold lover rolling over in her sleep. "If you knew that you would fail, Sir, wouldn't you still try?"

Jefferson laughed. "Of course." He clapped Lewis's shoulder. "My old friend, I think perhaps you're a bit drunk."

Lewis smiled. "Perhaps a bit."

"I'll find us coffee."

Lewis again closed his eyes as his friend and President left the room. Sleep fell over him like a canopy of green paper bills. Images flashed against the inside of his eyelids. A door opening onto the sky. This time, no storm clawed and no darkness blinded him, but somewhere up ahead both waited. One day, he knew, they would take him. But not now. Instead, a clear, warm night met his leap. He spread his arms in supplication. Below, a river wound its way west throwing back moonlight and starshine, calling him towards some rendezvous he could not name. Once again, time swallowed him.

And he dreamed he was flying.

KEN SCHOLES HAS SOLD SHORT STORIES to Realms of Fantasy, Weird Tales, Aeon Speculative Fiction, Talebones, Polyphony 6, TEL : Stories, Best of the Rest 3 *and* Best of the Rest 4. *He is a winner of the Writers of the Future contest with a story appearing in* L. Ron Hubbard Presents Writers of the Future Volume XXI. *His first standalone project,* Last Flight of the Goddess, *is available from Fairwood Press. Ken lives in Gresham, Oregon, with his amazing wonder-wife Jen West Scholes, two utterly worthless cats, and a whole lot of books. By day, he works in government procurement and contracting. Visit his website at www.sff.net/people/kenscholes.*

WIZARDS' ENCORE

BY GEOFFREY GIRARD

IN 1856, THE FRENCH GOVERNMENT EMPLOYED POPULAR STAGE MAGICIAN Jean Robert-Houdin to travel to Algeria for a very special performance of deception. It was believed that once the Algerian natives saw that the 'magic' of the Frenchmen rivaled that of their own revered conjurers, the tribes' revolt within this important French colony would surely be broken.

—*Magic Revealed* by Sheldon Davis

AFTER HE'D DEFEATED THEIR KINGDOM, the French wizard came to speak to Kabir's father. The Frenchman wore a *burnous*, the traditional desert robe dark and long, a camel's-hair cord wrapped tight around his fat and large forehead. He had dead, white skin, his face bare and corpselike with hard sharp eyes of a stone, blue as the sky, gazing lewdly about the tent from under his robe's hood.

Djenoum, Kabir thought again. A demon. His father had told him this wizard, this Houdin, was not an evil spirit but only another powerful magic man. But Kabir had been to the arena and he'd seen the reaction of the others as this champion of France revealed his dark powers to the chieftains of their various tribes.

And though Kabir loved his father and treasured his word as the truth, as the French wizard stepped into their tent, he believed Houdin was indeed Shaitan himself. The very devil. Why else would his father have done it?

"*Salam aleikoum*," the Frenchman spoke easily in Arabic as if he'd used their language his entire life. Kabir's father returned the salutation in a somber voice, his hand upon his heart. He gestured and bowed, inviting the dark wizard full into the tent.

Kabir perched in the corner, afraid to move, focused against his thumping heart to vanish into the carpets or the lamp-cast shadows of the room. He was a thin, tall boy with light brown skin, bronzed with sixteen years of the Algerian sun. His dark black hair was both tousled and dusty from desert winds. He thought, 'If only I could become a snake and slip away.' But even as he did, Houdin's eyes settled upon him and fixed him with a stare that meant Kabir to stay exactly where he was.

"*Pourquoi?*" the wizard asked in French, turning to Kabir's father.

Kabir's heart jumped. Had the stranger read his mind? It was the one word, the one question which had also burned in his heart for hours. But as Kabir and his father hiked the several miles back to camp after the contest, he'd been too terrified, too hurt, to ask it. This Frenchman was *not* afraid and he asked again in Arabic. "Why?"

Kabir's father looked at his son briefly, pained, and then turned again to the wizard. "Have you not shamed us enough?"

Houdin's eyes went wide. "*Ana asif,*" he apologized, bowing deeply, with his hand to his heart. "I meant no disrespect. It is I who..." He paused and held out his hands, thinking.

It was to be a competition. The tribes' honored sorcerers, a group of magic men known as the Marabouts, against France's greatest wizard, Jean Robert-Houdin. Recently, several of the tribes had started a revolt in Algeria, hoping to overthrow France's colonial rule of the important African nation. The contest of magic was to show which of the two kingdoms had the most powerful magic.

And so, at the arena that day, Kabir's father and the other Marabouts had actually floated in the air for several moments, hovering like ghosts. They'd caught bullets shot from flintlock muskets with their very mouths. They swallowed thorns and hot coals and made live snakes spring from their fingers.

To those in attendance, a mixed crowd of tribesmen, everything from Moors, Kabyles and Biskri, to Mozabites and Arab Jews, this demonstration was enough. But Kabir knew that his father could also turn himself into a desert jackal, that he could raise the dead to walk the desert nights again, and call enormous monsters from out of the sand storms. Kabir cringed. He could think of a hundred other enchantments his father knew that would have made the horrible Frenchmen weep as babies.

But his father had not cast these spells. He had simply quit the competition and walked away with the other Marabouts. And because of that, all of Algeria now knew of the defeat, and was lost to the French. And so, the French devil now had the same question Kabir did. *Why?*

Houdin asked specifically. "Why did you not reveal all today?"

Kabir's father growled. "You toy with words to mock me."

"That isn't my—"

"Bah!" his father spat. He lowered his head and tapped the top of it in misery. "Even the boy saw through your performer's tricks."

The wizard turned to Kabir again and the boy gulped, staring back bravely to somehow convey and confirm that what his father had just said was true. But in truth, Kabir did not yet understand what he'd had seen. He only knew that he had seen something at the arena that terrified him still. His own father's fear.

The French wizard had made shadows bleed, and several tribe warriors vanish before the stunned audience's eyes. With the wave of something-he-called a wand, he'd paralyzed a massive dark-skinned Moor, the very *Caid* of the Beni-Salah, with weakness. Then, with another turn of his bone-white wrist, Houdin had made the same man scream in total agony and drop to the ground. The other tribal leaders, the *caids*, *agas*, and *bash-agas*, in attendance howled in fright and amazement. And even then, Kabir was not afraid.

But then his father and the other Marabouts had stopped. They had, *his father had*, accepted defeat and turned without another word, quitting the competition. Kabir couldn't understand. He still did not.

Houdin's strange eyes blazed in interest. "If you knew my demonstrations were only 'performer's tricks,' why did you not simply expose and defeat me?"

Kabir's father glared. "Your insult was quite clear. We are not equal to you and so, as I would not lower myself to challenge that boy in the corner, you will not compromise yourself to a true contest. You give us 'tricks.'"

The wizard leaned back, seemingly truly astonished by the direct accusation. "No. No... No..." he whispered. The Frenchman's eyes narrowed and a thin smile broke across his dead lips. "I see. You wonder why *I* did not 'reveal all.'"

Kabir stirred in his spot, shaken. *Had his father sensed something in Houdin — some stronger magic not revealed?*

His father crossed his arms. "Why are you here?" he demanded.

"France asked me to perform a service for my country. And so I have! After a simple magic demonstration, the rebellion is over. And there will be no need for further bloodshed. We saved many lives today by settling matters on a stage instead of a battlefield."

"As it pleases Allah," Kabir's father allowed, crossly.

The sorcerer nodded in agreement. "But now that that has been accomplished, I wish to tell you something of the future."

"That your people will enslave Algeria. That French will rule all of Africa!" Kabir's father hissed. "What of it?"

"That is not our concern now," Houdin shrugged. "You know what I speak of." Kabir's father looked at him sideways, uninterested. "How much longer will your people believe?" the French wizard asked. "How long before the magic you rely on for your conjurations is all but gone? I tell you that it has already left my world." His eyes widened, daring. "But while the people of my land may no longer hold faith in enchantments and spells, they believe strongly in other arts. Arts that categorize, sort, grade, count and prove with base facts even the simplest of minds will eventually accept. *This*, this 'science,' is where their *belief*, the power we must draw upon for our spells, has moved."

The tribe's magic man listened, face reddening in anger.

"So now, too, must you. As I did years ago. As many others have before when it became necessary. Da Vinci, Franklin, Galileo, Zu Chongzhi... You must find and study with engineers and chemists. Surgeons and —"

Kabir's father shook his head.

Houdin ignored him. "The men today vanished with simple reflections, refractions and dispersions of light. I used large mirrors and sunlight to make this magic work. Your warrior lost his strength because the box he lifted was made of steel and I'd secretly charged the metal floor beneath him with electricity. It is called an electromagnet and quite simple, actually. It magnetized the metal floor and made it impossible for *anyone* to pick up that metal box. With it, I also sent an electric charge through his feet, a simple shock, that knocked him unconscious."

"You *are* a demon!" Kabir's father gasped. "A demon who fills my mind with foolishness." He stood tall again and marched in front of Houdin. Kabir's heart leapt. The white-faced wizard would surely kill his father for this insult. Yet he continued still. "Perhaps I *did* misjudge you. Perhaps the power I sensed in you was false and you truly are nothing but stage tricks and '*science*!'" He sneered the last words, clenching his fists, charging. "No more, Frenchman. I do not want to hear your lies anymore. Be gone!"

The French wizard watched Kabir's father silently for a long while before speaking again. "Very well," he finally said. "I will leave you now. I apologize again for the appearance of insult today and I am truly sorry that I could not better advise you tonight." He looked directly to Kabir. "As one magic man to another." He turned then and vanished through the tent's flaps into the night.

Kabir's father shouted half-hearted curses after the man, then dropped his head into his hands, mumbling angrily. He stood still for several minutes, rubbing his temples with his fingers, trying to work out both the French wizard's intrusion and the ache from the day's spells. Each year more difficult to cast, more painful. Eyes closed, he listened to the sounds of the camp just outside their tent, sounds of the women cooking, the soft rhythm of an arab drum, a camel's snort. He looked up suddenly, irate and hot. "Kabir," he growled. He spun around the tent. "Kabir?" His eyes narrowed, thinking.

Kabir was gone.

"STOP!" KABIR SHOUTED, springing from the darkness of the rocks into the open desert, the fearless moon providing only shadowed light.

"I thought I might see you again," the wizard said calmly, stopping. He turned to him. "I *hoped* I would."

Kabir stopped himself. The burst of anger that had lured him from the safety of his camp to chase after the wizard, had been replaced again with complete fear. He stood now alone before a powerful sorcerer, one who had apparently bested his own father and the other tribe's magic men without even a fight. And now that he'd caught the wizard, he had no idea what to do with him. Kabir straightened his shoulders and stood tall before the dark sorcerer. "My father is more powerful than you could ever be," he snapped defiantly. "It wasn't a true challenge." *But father sensed something in this man,* Karib thought suddenly. *Something…*

"We'll never know for sure," Houdin shrugged. "Your father's decision aside, no one else in your kingdom thought to challenge me either." He waited. "Isn't that right?"

He knows, Kabir realized suddenly. *He knows that too.* "Very well," he gulped, running the back of his hand nervously across his mouth. "If my father will not fight you, then…"

"Yes?" Houdin said, eyes widening in curiosity.

"Then I will," Kabir finished boldly, hoping the wizard couldn't hear the tremble in his voice.

The Frenchman only smiled.

Kabir ignored the sorcerer and closed his eyes. He took several slow breaths and gathered his thoughts as his father had taught him. When he opened his eyes again, they were focused and stark. He was ready.

Beetles dropped from Kabir's dark fingertips. They sprang free, fat and wet, tumbling to the ground as if thick drops of blood gushed from his hands. The bugs splattered in a heap of a dozen, a hundred, now a thousand, at his feet and scurried the short distance across the desert floor, scampering over the French magician's robes.

They crawled over each other, wings and legs clicking, mouths cracking hungrily as their ticking and chittering filled the night in a surprising uproar that brought Kabir's hands to his own ears.

The dark form of united insects advanced quickly above Houdin's waist and continued to rise like black pitch up to his shoulders as he calmly lifted his arms above the turmoil and grabbed hold of his own throat as if to choke himself.

Insects now vomited from the man's mouth. Large flies of some kind pouring from the gaping black hole, squeezing past his white teeth. His jaws stretched wider, a stream of the horrible creatures rushing forth. Bigger than any Kabir had ever seen, like thin locusts. The roar of the beetles' clamor was replaced with a more horrible sound. Like the high-pitched prayers and wailing of a million men all at once. Quick and maddening, the insects rushed about the desert air. How many, Kabir would never know. He expected to be attacked and killed by the creatures at any moment. He had failed.

Instead of attacking him though, the new infestation swarmed about the Frenchman, covering the wizard in a second layer of insects and plague. Houdin stood still, his body building in shape and darkness, the insects, both beetle and the alien flies, running over his shoulders and coating his entire face and body. He truly had become Shatian himself. And Kabir now understood clearly that Houdin, too, had not fully shown his true powers during the performance earlier.

The darkness receded some, the insects bit by bit drawing away from the top of Houdin's hood and face. Lowering to his shoulders. Now to his chest. The beetles dropping in a pile about his feet. His flies were literally killing Kabir's enchantment, picking them away from the magician's body one by one. The beetles kicked and wallowed at the Frenchman's feet, and Kabir could now clearly make out his chest and waist. His legs became a swirling dervish, a sandstorm of black shapes and lunacy. The twitching beetle shells piled higher at the wizard's feet until only the devil flies remained roaring in a circle about him.

The wizard then waved his hand and the flying insects vanished into the night. Kabir trembled, his body shaking as if in fever from the casting. He ignored the ache in his body and thought quickly of another spell. Kabir punched two closed fists together, pushing out towards the cloaked man. The darkest shadows of the night at once pulled into themselves, drawing back from the corners of the desert's floor, pulling away from the night and into the available moonlight. All that was shadowed light had become total darkness, and all that had just been night now sprang to life in bright magical radiance.

Kabir could no longer see his own hands. They had become as drops of sunlight sprinkling to the ground, the ground shining, stretching across miles beneath him, endless. He had become as a thin white light that moved rapidly across the desert floor in circles of impossible daylight. The Frenchman was now a black shadow, bulky and contorted. Frozen in the enchanted light's brilliance. It was a wonderful spell his father had taught him the previous summer. Houdin was trapped for sure!

But then the blackshape that was Houdin waved its hands across the space before them and the night cleared of Kabir's spell. With a quick motion, Houdin blew the very air toward him, a cool stream of mist that flowed around Kabir like a blanket.

Suddenly, the French wizard's head expanded to the size and shape of a camel's face, both comical and gruesome at the same time. The eyes pushed out to the sides, the big sloppy jowls, giant camel teeth growing from out of the hood. Kabir smiled. Houdin looked ridiculous. Horrifying, truly, but mostly *silly*. The dark wizard now looked like a big, stupid French camel.

Kabir started to laugh. He could picture the magician returning home with his giant camel head. He marveled that Houdin was still standing at all and wondered how long it would take before the weight of his oversized head knocked him over. Kabir held his hands over his mouth to hide the laughter but the harder he tried not to laugh, the funnier Houdin looked. He wondered how long the Frenchmen could go without water and how many humps he had, and the laughs came out louder. Suddenly, he was very sleepy and he sat down in the sand, giggling until his sides hurt.

It was only then that he realized what had happened , and he looked away from Houdin. Kabir fought through his own laughter and quickly cast another spell. Enchanted winds roared above him suddenly while he stayed in a heap to the ground, clinging to the earth and sanity. Hard sand flogged his eyes and mouth, biting.

Kabir's breathing was ragged, hard. He was only sixteen but felt now as one of the tribe elders. So very tired. He forced himself to look up.

The French wizard, however, looked at ease, as tranquil and composed as he had at his performance earlier. As if he had done no more than pull on his sandals. "Now do you understand?" Houdin asked in Arabic.

Kabir roared in response, shouting ancient words he had never used before. Strange words that were not Arabic taught to him by the other Marabouts. His very bones hurt.

Slowly, in front of him, the thing took shape. It lifted from the ground, rising larger with each passing moment until it stood taller than both of them. It was of sand but resembled a pile of rocks, a man of boulders with legs and arms and a thick, squat head. Rocks that moved quickly and easily, sliding in the shape of rounded muscles the color and texture of wet sand. The thing stepped before Houdin and grunted in a grating dry sound. *Fenughil*. What the Arab Jews called Golem. Kabir made this.

But Houdin made his own beast. It too rose from the sands just in front of him, his hands lifted out. The creature expanded outward, taking a form Kabir soon recognized. A snake's snout rose from the sand. But it was not of sand. It was of water! The head rose, flickering in fluid, flowing motion as only water can. And it was no snake. It grew, a fang-filled snout, long flowing hairs as fire running behind its head like the mane of some great lion. The long neck emerged from the desert floor, twice as high as the golem. Its shoulders and wings now appeared. Kabir had never seen one but he knew that this must be a dragon.

Earlier, they'd not had enough water to properly wet their camels. Kabir beheld now a dragon of water higher than any building he had ever seen.

It crashed down upon his *fenughil*, the sand creature slowly raising its hands in hopeless defense. The great lizard fell and, just as quickly as Kabir had created it, the man thing vanished again into the sands. The dragon elevated itself again, its neck and jaws craning towards the startled moon, wings outstretched blocking the stars, while the rest of the beast laid just beneath the ground. Its head turned each way, looking, and caught Kabir square in its monstrous eye. Then, it too dipped back down into the desert sands, vanishing in a brief eruption of cool spray and foam.

Kabir collapsed at the wizard's feet. He coughed and clawed at his mouth, fighting for air. His body shuddering in the cool desert air.

The French magician stood straight and wiped a single line of sweat from his white forehead. "You are, clearly, already a powerful sorcerer. I sensed this even today at the arena." Kabir looked up. "But the world is changing," Houdin said. He pulled something from inside his robe and brought it to Kabir as he crouched against the ground. He held his pinched fingers together down for him to see. "This is a wasp," he said. "Interesting scents, called pheromones, can control much more than insects. This works in *all* worlds. Because I can show people how it is done, they believe it is so."

He took hold of Kabir's arm, showing him that it was healed again and that there were no machines or scorpions inside him. "The laughter 'spell' I put upon your mind?" He shrugged. "A gas mixture of ammonium nitrate and water, a simple concoction called nitrous oxide that causes mild illusions and laughter. One that can be put together in any lab with some tubes and a little patience."

He helped pull Kabir to his knees, the young man too drained from the magic to stand on his own yet. "An ample supply of that," the wizard explained. "And in the process, I'm not locked away as a witch or madman. Far, far from it in fact," he explained suddenly. "I'm treated as a King. And…" he whispered, leaning in. "While my inspiration may still come directly from the supernatural, from the real magic within me, I now find the strength of actual creation in that which they believe in now. This… This Science."

"And the dragon?" Kabir heard his own voice ask. Its shape still partly visible in the dark, wet sand.

Houdin smiled. "Your noble father and your kingdom deserved better from me earlier this day. I hope I have amended by showing *you* my powers."

He held up a finger. "But know that that same dragon could not be conjured in Paris. I could not… There are fewer places in this world that can provide that which is needed for such a thing. Far too few. That is why your castings take so much out of you. Why it becomes more difficult each year for your father and the other Marabouts. And for you." He watched Kabir. "And as the civilized world continues to touch your tribes and land, it will become even more difficult to cast your spells. In fact, one day, it may even kill you."

"Is that why you came to see my father?"

"To a merchant, gold is given. To a warrior, arms are offered. To both you and your father… To men such as we, I reveal the means to keep that which you have always had. And perhaps you can accept and utilize what your father would not. As one age ends, another must surely begin." He paused, thinking. "The key to any trick, to the sleights-of-hand I employ, is simple misdirection. Getting the audience to look at one hand as you do whatever you wish with the other." He looked at Kabir carefully. "Powered with technology, by the people's belief in hard science, and yet not completely without our special gift either. Understand that, understand the greatest misdirection trick ever performed, and you will begin to understand how men such as we may continue to exist and create in a modern world."

Kabir reached out and took hold of the wasp in Houdin's hand. He turned it in his fingers, studying the strange insect and thought. "I think I understand," he said.

The Frenchman bowed a final time, most sincerely, and, disappearing into the darkness, was never heard from by Kabir again.

HIS FATHER STEPPED OUT OF THE NIGHT. He had clearly seen and heard all.

"I'm sorry," Kabir said. "I needed to see for myself."

"And what did you see?"

Kabir thought. "I…" His head dropped. "I don't know." While Houdin's words raced through his mind, he felt that even *remembering* them was somehow a betrayal of his father's way, of the magic he'd grown up with and loved. He stood silently, unsure. "I will have to think about it," Kabir replied.

His father nodded, clearing his throat with a low gruff.

Kabir dropped his eyes to the desert floor and they started walking, silently, back to camp. He was tired, still nauseated and wobbly from the castings and every step to keep beside his father was difficult. He hoped their camp was closer than he remembered.

His father spoke suddenly beside him. "The French have built a new school in Algiers," he said quietly. "A university." His father's pace slowed.

"There is a great library there and... " He stopped now. Silence fell between them, the desert's winds cooing across the night. His father scratched at his beard thoughtfully. "Perhaps... Would you like to go there some time?" he asked.

Kabir turned to look up at his father, the greatest sorcerer he would ever know.

"Yes," he said. "I think I would like that very much."

CAREFULLY STUDY BEFOREHAND and see to it that all fits naturally into place, helping to conceal the real workings of the trick. A good magician directs the audience's attention to what he does not do; he doesn't do what he pretends to do; and to that magic which he actually does, he is careful not to arouse the audience's attention at all.

— Jean Robert-Houdin

GEOFFREY GIRARD'S WORKS HAVE APPEARED IN SUCH VENUES as Writers of the Future *(a 2003 winner),* Apex Science Fiction and Horror Digest, Aoife's Kiss *and the horror anthology* Damned Nation. *His first book,* Tales of the Jersey Devil *(a collection of thirteen tales based on the myth), was published in 2005 and* Tales of the Atlantic Pirates *arrived in '06. Born in Germany, shaped in New Jersey and currently teaching in Ohio, Geoffrey is also a musician having released an album of piano songs he composed and recorded. Upcoming publications to include two more* Tales Of... *books and a fantasy series. More info at www.geoffreygirard.com.*

THE DISENCHANTMENT OF KIVRON OX-MASTER

BY ELAINE ISAAK

"OH, YOUR MAGNIFICENCE," the musk ox began, endeavoring to sound pleasant despite her gasping breath. She took a few more waddling steps and stopped, lowering her shaggy head until the swooping horns almost touched the sand.

"I wish you wouldn't call me that, Mei-ling," Kivron the Enchanter of Xian-ho sighed for the hundredth time.

"What better title for the one who gave me the world, Your Magnificence?" Mei-ling lumbered up beside the camel, her sides heaving.

The camel snorted, shaking its head and rolling its eyes.

"We're almost there, Mei-ling, can you make it a little further?" Kivron pleaded. His journey, begun in excitement and urgency, had slowed to the pace of tired ox, unfit for such travel. From his perch between the camel's humps, he could at last see the tents of the Conjerum in the canyon below, round gers of felt turned red from the sand that blew between them, their shapes shifting in the setting sun.

Raising her head, she gazed at him from dark, adoring eyes. "I follow you, Your Magnificence."

The camel whuffed out a few times, and Kivron realized it was laughing.

Resolutely, the musk ox plodded forward, and, after a few steps, began lowing softly, adding a few clicks of her teeth at careful intervals.

The camel drooped its lower lip, showing its teeth. Kivron whispered, "She's singing — a dance tune from our home in Xian-ho. I think she has a talent for remembering tunes."

"More talents," the camel grumbled. "I think she is a silly beast."

Recalling his earlier resentment, Kivron said, "Maybe so, but she loves me."

Silently, the camel plodded on into the desert, every step drawing them nearer to their goal: the Flaming Cliffs, and the annual sorcerer's Conjerum where he hoped to be accepted for membership — and to find out what the Grand Master meant by her mysterious summons. *"I have heard of your thrilling talent and am anxious to meet with you."* No more anxious than he was to finally meet people like himself, who would understand the glories and burdens of magic. His enthusiasm sprang once more fully to his heart and he nudged the camel a little faster.

The two beasts stumbled their way down a slope of red rocks, blazing in the long, late sun. White tents, stained about the edges with the dust, dotted the slope before them, filling the space from there to the towering cliffs opposite. Where the valley narrowed, a curtain blocked off the end, the backdrop to a dais of stone where someone addressed a crowd lounging on cushions and rugs. Kivron urged the camel down among the tents. These were the sorcerers, born with talents and willing to share them. His people.

As they neared the gathering, a man dressed all in black approached. "You are late, Brother," he called out, then drew closer still, and stopped short, his long mustaches quivering. "This is a gathering of learned people," he snapped. "We don't have room for vagrants." He turned to go.

"Wait, sir!" Kivron kneed the camel, who lowered him unceremoniously, though without unseating him as it usually did. The young sorcerer fumbled in his satchel to come out with his precious letter. "This is the Conjerum? I've been invited. The Grand Master says—"

The other snatched the letter and unrolled it, scanning it with a speed that Kivron envied. Perhaps he was unworthy to be here. This was a meeting of masters who would not wish to waste their time with an illiterate farmer's son. Mei-ling thrust her moist nose against his side, and he absently scratched her between the eyes.

The man peered from under his brows. "You are Kivron the Enchanter?"

"Of Xian-ho. Yes."

He scanned the letter again. Two narrow black lines like deft brush-strokes, his mustaches hung down past his waist. "I am not familiar with you. What is it that you do?"

"He brings speech and spirit to lesser beasts, Your Honor," Mei-ling said, attempting a bow on her forelegs, her rump thrusting up into the air.

The man snorted, and nearly smiled. "Ventriloquists and trained animals are not welcome here."

Kivron frowned. "Mei-ling speaks for herself."

"I'll vouch for his talent, if you'll rid me of it," the camel put in.

"My master has enchanted many, and freed them from their small herds to seek the deeper meanings of the world," Mei-ling added.

"Well, Kivron Ox-master, I will report your arrival and take this to the Grand Master. She will decide what's to be done." He whirled and hustled back around the tents toward the carpets.

Had he come so far, only to be turned aside, run back into the wilderness? Kivron kicked the dirt, glaring. Mei-ling lowed at him, and leaned her shoulder against his side, careful not to gore him with her horns.

"You will find someone to dis-enchant me, yes?" the camel inquired.

"I'm sure one of the other sorcerers will know how," Kivron said. Since childhood, he had been burdened with half a talent — that of bringing human awareness and speech to any living thing. It had taken a few tries for him to realize he could not undo what he had done, and the novelty of talking animals wore off quickly for the villagers who couldn't bring themselves to eat the enchanted creatures, especially after a group of goats began to worship the local deity. Besides which, the Sorcerer's Conjerum decreed that the individual sorcerer had direct responsibility for the use of his talents, so that Kivron spent much of his time tending the needs of his enchanted herd. So far as he knew, they would remain so until their death, or his, when his magic slowly ebbed away.

"You do not sound sure," the camel commented, cropping a mouthful of coarse desert grass.

Sweaty, tired, and increasingly annoyed, Kivron snapped, "If you didn't want to be enchanted, why did you come forward when I asked for a volunteer?"

The camel let out a whistling breath and looked away. "I don't recall."

Kivron folded his arms and leaned gently against Mei-ling's wooly side. "I don't believe you."

"If you must know, " drawled the camel, "I was going to spit on you."

"What?"

"In my tribe, that's what we do to people like you." The camel examined him, and shook its head so that the thick ruff at the base of its neck swept up little dust devils.

Kivron self-consciously ran a hand over his deep red hair. He wore it in seven braids, tied behind, as his father's people had done. He had also inherited his mother's almond eyes and darker skin, but the long red hair ensured that herders and townsfolk snubbed him whenever possible, and sometimes went so far as to run him into the wilderness rather than sell him food or supplies. He'd never imagined this attitude would trickle down to their animals, however. "I am a man as any other," he growled. "You could have told me of your contempt, and I would have found another way."

"You told me," the camel said archly, "that you had a responsibility to me, once having enchanted me, unless I found another home. What herder would take a camel defiled by a sorcerer, and a foreign sorcerer at that!"

Kivron flinched and tried to frame an answer, but stopped himself, listening. Staccato voices rose, growing nearer, and a tall figure burst from around the tent, followed by the man in black and a handful of curious sorcerers. The leader, a woman, ended the argument with a quick gesture, and stopped to study Kivron. She wore a silk robe embroidered with dragons. Brass dragons adorned her throat and ears, and the sticks which held up the thick knot of her raven hair. She stared at him openly and walked forward again, pushing the broad leaf hat from his head with a firm gesture. She frowned in a way he took to be focused rather than angry. Again, her pale hand shot out, lifting his bundle of braids, and pulling them over his shoulder, so that he had to turn his head slightly.

"Your Honor—" Kivron started.

"Ah!" She cut him off with the single syllable.

He waited, and Mei-ling pushed against him. The woman smelled faintly sweet, a curious whiff of honey.

Her fingers worked into the braids, and stroked along them, plucking at the leather thongs which tied them. "Is all red hair so coarse?"

"I don't know. Mine is not so coarse when washed."

"Yes, and the desert is harsh." She pushed his hair back over his shoulder. "I did not expect that." She indicated his hair.

Unsure what to say, Kivron shrugged a little in acknowledgement.

She turned from him to Mei-ling. "Ox, why have you come here?"

"Your Honor, my Master, who is a great enchanter, came by invitation of the Grand Master. I was proud to bear him to the desert, and to follow him even here, to gather with the sorcerers." She bowed again, with only a little more grace. The on-lookers chuckled, and shared glances, but the woman nodded gravely.

"You are faithful to him because of his responsibility to you."

"Oh, no, Your Honor. He has given me the gift of humanity."

More chuckles greeted this statement, and the man who had met them stepped forward, waving Kivron's letter. "Here's his map, I say we return him to wherever he came from."

The camel reached out and grabbed the paper in its yellow teeth. Carefully it chewed up the letter, grinding it with cool patience.

"What have you done?" Kivron demanded, pulling the corner back. Only a few lovely letters remained on the pulpy mass.

"We will not go back until I have been thoroughly disenchanted." The camel glowered down at Kivron.

"Then your talent does not extend to its own removal?" the woman inquired.

"No, it doesn't. I hope someone among the Conjerum has that skill, and maybe I can learn it."

"No regret, please. You have a remarkable talent, Kivron." She offered a tight-lipped smile which nevertheless crinkled the corners of her eyes. "I'm glad you came, for I have great need of your talent."

"Shenchya—" the mustached man started, stepping up beside her — "I'm not sure about this. At least we should discuss it. He may even be an imposter — a spy!" He spoke in a whisper, so that the lingering crowd could not hear him.

"A rival would have sent someone less conspicuous, Luzo. Your fears belittle my strength. Besides, I will not have dug in the sand these two years in vain, not when I may avail myself of Kivron's expertise."

Once her attention returned to him, Kivron placed his hands together and bowed low. "It would be an honor, Grand Master, to be of assistance to you in any way." Shenchya the Animator — he should have recognized her immediately from her bearing, and the dragons which bedecked her. Even in his home at Xian-ho, where little news of sorcerers ever came, Shenchya's love of dragons was well known. That, and the rumor that she was concubine to the emperor himself.

As if she also had a talent for mind-reading, Shenchya raised an eyebrow to him. With a flick of the wrist, an ivory fan slid into her hand, and she waved it gently toward her face. She let go of the fan, and it continued to flap before her like a butterfly's wing. "I must tell the assembly of your arrival. Luzo the Recaller can show you to a tent to refresh yourself."

Luzo glowered, his mustaches quivering.

She turned and walked back toward the lecture space, with the ivory fan fluttering in her wake, pulled inexorably after her. The little crowd parted for her, then trickled after, leaving Kivron and Luzo, and the two animals.

Now that she had gone, the weariness of travel descended upon him again, and Kivron decided she had been wise. Sweat streaked his face, and darkened his clothing. Why had they met in the desert? Surely the other sorcerers were even more used to comfort than himself, yet they had come here, a hundred miles from a proper bath.

"The Grand Master is beautiful, Your Magnificence. I do not think I have seen such a beautiful woman before," Mei-ling remarked.

"If you like them without humps," the camel snorted.

Luzo bristled, and pushed past them. "Follow," he barked.

Kivron hurried up alongside him. "You're a Recaller? I haven't heard of that talent before."

"I can cause complete recollection of any event or lifetime."

"That would seem a welcome gift."

He softened a little, and squared his shoulders. "The Emperor himself has asked my services to recall the joy of his childhood. And I have been called upon to assist witnesses in remembering every detail of a crime."

"Are there any Disenchanters here?" the camel interrupted. "I don't wish to be like this any longer than necessary."

Luzo glanced back at the camel. "I do not know of any, but I may ask. Why would you want to return to the life of a dumb beast?"

"I can recall the company of my herd, and the pride of my work. Now I've been cursed by this foreigner with speech and reason, I'll never feel those things again."

"Unless he were to pre-decease you." With a brief, tight smile, Luzo stopped before a large, round tent with drifts of red sand lapping all around it as if it had stood there a long time. "A basin and water are inside. The well is to the east."

"Your Honor," Kivron said carefully, "can you tell me why the Grand Master was so eager to have me here?"

"She will tell you." Luzo spun on his heel and left them.

"Not a friendly sort," the camel grumbled.

"Great men have many things to think about," Mei-ling offered.

"Like Shenchya, I'll bet." Luzo had been jealous of the attention she gave him, perhaps belying the rumors that swirled around her. Could he, Kivron, really be a threat to anything those two shared? Luzo apparently believed it. Kivron touched his red hair as she had done, and grinned to himself.

"She did show you her rump," the camel observed. "Will you initiate mating with her?"

Kivron giggled. "She was just walking away, and besides, that's not how people go about it."

"Clothing must make it difficult in any case."

"Oh, no," Mei-ling put in, "people simply shed that, then they—"

"Why don't you two go find a drink and some shade." Kivron, blushing, pulled his belongings from the back of the camel.

Mei-ling nudged him with her head, and turned back to the camel as they picked their way between tents. "They also don't reveal it as openly as we do," she was saying as they moved out of sight.

Kivron ducked into the stifling interior, and rolled back two flaps to encourage a breeze. A thick pile of carpets and furs lay heaped against one wall, opposite a low table with a large pitcher of water. A plate of fresh fruits sat beside it, and Kivron set-to hungrily, letting the juice run down his grubby fingers. He licked them off anyhow, reveling in the sweetness, then pulled off his beige robe, and splashed himself with water. He reached for his bundle to find his formal robe, shrugged into it and fastened the rope buttons. His robe, dark blue, bore his mother's poor embroidery on the back: a portrait of Mei-ling she had stitched for his appearance here. Still, the cloth was good, even if it could not compare to Shenchya's gold-worked dragon gown. Ox-master, Luzo called him. This robe would prove it to all who saw; it would have to do, though, for his only other still stank of the journey.

As if arriving upon the breeze, Shenchya appeared in the doorway glittering in her golden robe. "Are you ready, Enchanter?"

"Ah — yes." He scrambled to his feet, smoothing the robe as if he could wipe away the wrinkles or the shabbiness of the garment

"Have you ever enchanted bones?" She stepped back, inviting him to pass.

"Bones?" he repeated, still flustered by her appearance. "No, only living things. And one time—" he broke off, remembering.

"One time," she prompted.

"A dog we had taken for dead. It had just stopped breathing, and I held out my hands to it. I wanted it to live." He looked away from her. "When I enchanted it, it begged for death because the pain was so great. It was my responsibility, and I had to watch it die."

"Do you think you could enchant a skeleton?"

"I don't know. I doubt it."

She frowned. "You do wish to join the Conjerum."

"Yes, with all my heart!" Who then would dare to sneer at him, to chase him out of town?

"I have addressed them about you, and they are skeptical. You must undergo the audition, as any other sorcerer would, but they will be even more critical of you. Therefore, your talent must be so clear, so strong that they cannot deny you."

He heard a whuffling breath, and saw Mei-ling watching him from the entrance.

"A talking ox and camel will not be enough to convince them you are no charlatan. But I believe you can help me, and if you will, then the proof will be before them, and no one will deny that you are worthy of us."

"And you wish me to enchant a skeleton."

She nodded once.

"What if I fail? I won't be accepted in the Conjerum."

"True." Her dark eyes remained steady and earnest. A slight breeze stroked the dragons that hung at her ears. "Yet if you succeed, your fame will perhaps outshine us all. This deed I ask of you is a gift, and a weapon, a symbol to shatter our enemies and earn the admiration of the emperor himself."

"By enchanting a skeleton?"

"You will see." She drew him from the ger with a firm hand. "And you will believe."

They wound between the tents, with Mei-ling clumping along behind. Kivron's stomach growled, but Shenchya's intensity overcame hunger, and they soon reached the open space of the lecture. Two sorcerers circled the rugs, placing flames of glowing magic to light up whatever was to come. Sunset cast its final crimson hue over all, and the stars were beginning to appear.

"We are meeting now so that the Dragon will be high above us as we work. It is very auspicious." She pointed to the first of the faint stars.

"Is this the traditional meeting place, Grand Master?"

Shenchya laughed silently. "Oh, no. Former Grand Masters have brought us to palaces and temples, or even to the mountains. No, this place is very special."

She led him to the stone dais. Rugs and cushions radiated out before it, leaving an open space of sand behind it leading up to the curtained place he had noticed before. The curtain still concealed the narrow canyon from view, but ropes attached to it ran down to pulleys where a few servants waited. Shenchya's plan must involve revealing whatever had been hidden there. Kivron frowned, recalling her whispers about the emperor and Luzo's fear. The desert night grew cold around him, and he hugged himself tightly. What did she have in mind? Would she humiliate him before the people he hoped would be his peers? She seemed too eager for that to be her motive as she waved him to a seat just at the foot of the dais. Then the Grand Master slipped off toward the curtain. Luzo emerged from the darkness there, snorting at Mei-ling just as the camel might have done. Mei-ling only folded her legs beneath her, preparing to settle beside him.

"Mei-ling," Kivron started gently, "you must be very tired. You should rest by the tent."

"Thank you for your kindness, but I wish to be here when these people recognize Your Magnificence for the great sorcerer that you are."

"It won't be very interesting for you," Kivron hinted. Sorcerers moved through the strange light to find their places, and stared at the man talking to his ox.

"You do not wish me to be here," she said, freezing with her rump still in the air. Her shaggy head lowered, then she heaved herself up. "I understand, Your Magnificence," she murmured.

He scrambled up. "Oh, Mei-ling, it's just—" he waved an arm at the gathering sorcerers.

"You should be friends with men, not just with foolish animals."

"You will always be my friend." He wriggled his fingers into her thick hair.

"Then you probably don't want me, either," the camel said, ambling up behind.

"What are you doing here?"

"Looking for a Disenchanter. No luck so far." The camel brought his head down beside the musk ox. "Why don't we go toward the well? I saw some beautiful shrubs, and you could even sing for me."

Mei-ling lifted her head to blink at the camel. "That sounds very nice."

Kivron gave her a last pat, and she moved away, carefully maneuvering her bulk between the blankets. The camel swiveled his neck to look back at Kivron. "I won't enjoy this. You had better find me a Disenchanter soon."

"I will. Thank you."

The camel flicked its tail, and followed Mei-ling toward the well. Laughter erupted in the wake of the beasts' passing, and Kivron felt himself grow red. He was glad of the dim light as he sat back down.

"How touching," Luzo remarked, stroking his mustache.

Kivron bristled. "I take my responsibility very seriously."

"You will tonight, unless you fail, of course. In which case, your animals can comfort you."

"Of all the things you recall to people, I'm sure most of them would rather forget meeting you," Kivron snapped.

"I had rather it be so than that I present such an unforgettable appearance as yourself. Kivron the Entertainer, and his Amazing Talking Cattle. How about dogs? Do you enchant them as well? Kivron and his Cussing Curs?"

"Most of the curs I meet are already human." He stared straight ahead.

Luzo shut his mouth and stood as Shenchya returned. He gave a little bow, smiling up at her.

Kivron, on his feet after the last remark, bowed also.

"We are all together in this, Luzo, Kivron. Please do not kill each other just yet."

They eyed each other and did not respond.

The sound of a gong rolled through the canyon, and the last few sorcerers took seats among the crowd. Shenchya mounted the stone platform. Kivron and Luzo stiffly sat down again as she began.

"Many of you questioned my asking you to come to the desert for this session of the Conjerum. The Grand Master is mad, summoning us to ride through the heat and sand, miles from anyplace. And, more maddening still, she will not tell us why. Tonight, you will find out why all of this has been necessary. For two years, I have been living in this canyon, working toward my greatest accomplishment, which will soon be revealed. Luzo the Recaller has worked with me, another great puzzle. You knew as well that I awaited the arrival of a young sorcerer who is not even a member of the Conjerum.

Tonight, your questions will be answered." She raised a commanding arm, inviting Luzo and Kivron to come up. Sharing a glare, they did so. "Luzo the Recaller, a long esteemed member," Shenchya said. Then she turned to Kivron, "And Kivron the Enchanter—"

"Ox-master!" called several voices, to the general amusement of the audience.

Shenchya's sudden glare quieted the audience. "Kivron comes to us from Xian-ho, where foreigners have mingled with our people. He does not look like us, but he is the peer of every one of you in the realm of magic. In a few moments I believe you will acknowledge this. Esteemed colleagues, I give you the Dragon."

She stood rigid, radiating a kind of excitement Kivron had never known. Shenchya gracefully raised her arms, and the curtain behind her whooshed back. He turned to see the narrow end of the canyon, and found only darkness revealed. Shenchya's hand clenched into a fist, and the sound began. Something in the dark rumbled like a avalanche, far away at first, then growing louder. Stones ground on stones. The earth shook so that he nearly fell. Shenchya stood firm, with Luzo beside her, the only two not peering into the darkness. Luzo's mustache shivered, and his eyes were shut.

Eddies of dust rose into the air, and pebbles atop the dais bounced with the trembling earth. The terrible rhythm grated nearer — footfalls! But what—?

A head emerged from the dust clouds, towering over the curtain. An enormous skull, with great black pits for eyes, gazed down on them. The thick vertebrae of the neck pushed down the feeble rope holding the curtain, and the servants cowering by the cliffs fled.

The Dragon came on, its forelegs held up at the ready. Claws longer than Kivron's arm clacked together as it came. The knobs of its spine formed a spiky ridge. Its ribs thrust out like the pillars of a palace, broad enough to contain his family's house, with half of their cattle. It stood erect on power-ful legs, each bone taller than any man. The taloned toes spread into the sand, leaving huge tracks. Its tail hovered above the ground, a massive chain of bones nearly as long as the rest of the Dragon.

Between the reverberating footfalls, Kivron heard the furtive scuttling of the sorcerers as they crept back from the creature. His knees trembled so much that it required all his strength not to collapse to the stone. He gasped desperate breaths as the Dragon approached.

The terrible creature slowly closed the distance between, then took a last earth-shaking step. It loomed above them, and swung its head down toward the dais. Its claws came together as if it were bowing to Shenchya. With a moan of long-still joints, the mouth opened, revealing a row of vicious teeth, but no sound emerged. Then it drew itself erect, and froze.

Shenchya gradually let down her arms. Sweat poured down her face, soaking the loose strands of her hair. She breathed deeply for a time, unclenching her fists. Her fingers trembled. Beside her, Luzo raised his head, and blinked his eyes open, swallowing hard. Murmuring into the heavy silence, the audience crept forward again, keeping their eyes on the skeleton. They dare not pass the dais to look closer.

"I bring you the Dragon, the ancient symbol of power and wisdom, a gift for the glory of the empire, and a formidable weapon to win the respect we have so long deserved," Shenchya said. "But I am a mere Animator. I have spent two years finding and repairing what you see before you, digging it out of the rock in which it lay imprisoned. I give it motion, but I cannot give it life. Even now, simply holding the creature together requires my conscious will. Luzo the Recaller, though, can make it remember what it was to be alive. Today he set his hands upon it, bringing forth its memory. Perhaps even now, it yearns again for life." She turned to Kivron. "And I believe this Enchanter, the first Enchanter among us in a hundred years, can endow it with human spirit, with speech, reason, and will."

Slowly, Kivron shook his head. "I don't know that. I can help animals become more human, but this." He gestured toward the towering bones. "How long has it been buried in stone? I can't bring it back," he whispered urgently.

"If you cannot, then no one can," Shenchya said. "But are you not sorcerer enough to try?" She stretched out an inviting arm toward the Dragon. "If you do this, Kivron Dragon-master, your name will never die."

He gazed up at the terrible jaws. A Dragon — a thing without flesh — given speech and reason. Was it possible? Could he walk away not knowing? Already, he could hear their laughter as he passed away from them in his ox-embroidered robe. No worse than if he tried and failed. And if he succeeded...? He could dare any man to spit on him then. "I will need to place my hands upon its head," he said quietly.

Luzo flashed a quick glance at Shenchya. "Have you forgotten what I saw?" he hissed, "The memories of blood?"

Ignoring him, she clenched her fist again, and slowly drew it down; the huge skull lowered to the sand, leaving the tail high and stiff above them.

Kivron stepped down from the stone and stood a moment, then strode forward. Despite the cold night, sweat trickled down his neck amongst the braids. The skull, even resting on the ground, was nearly as tall as he. The pits of the eyes and nostrils swallowed light. His mind flashed back to Mei-ling, to laying his hands upon her small head, just below the swooping horns. She had looked up to him with dark eyes, but a warm, damp darkness, trusting, not hollow.

He placed his sweaty palms under the eye sockets, stretching his arms as if embracing the head of the Dragon. He looked deep into those absent eyes, and drew the strength into himself. The tendrils of talent within him stirred, reaching and twining out, seeking to touch life. At first it drew back, receding from the cold stone of the skull. He mastered his will, and called forth the talent again, coaxing its heat down into his hands. His arms began to tremble, then his entire body shook with the channeling. His heart raced, and awareness flowed into him. His fingers suddenly knew every pore and crevice of the bone beneath them. In flashes, he saw it stalking a dense jungle, tearing the flesh from a huge lizard, nudging a tiny Dragon emerging from its egg. Still, he kept his eyes to those pits. He scarcely breathed.

A vibration ran through the stone; or did his own shaking deceive him? Something flickered in the darkest hollows. He sank down so that his head and chest lay upon the muzzle of the beast. *Come*, he urged it. *Live*. Again, the skull quivered, and he clutched the edges of the eyesockets. A surge of power burst through him. The head reared up, lifting him from the ground, then stopped. Not breathing, he glanced down.

Shenchya stood with her fists clenched. She controlled it, then; he had failed.

Her fists shook, and she stared back up at him. The head swiveled with a sound like thunder. Would she shake him off, try to pretend the enchantment had worked? He clung tighter, then started to creep forward, locking his fingers into successive hollows, trying to reach the spine and scramble down. He had only moments before the exhilaration of the magic vanished, and dizziness would overcome him. "Just let me down," he called. "No one will believe—"

The head jerked to the side, and Kivron gasped. Shenchya gasped as well, then flung up her hands. She shook all over. The head wavered, then slashed violently through the air. Shenchya sank to the ground, her limbs spasming.

The skeleton trembled all over, with an echoing clamor of stone. It sagged toward the earth. The tip of its tail shook loose and tumbled from the sky. The shuddering grew in waves, then abruptly ceased.

A new sort of rasping began. Kivron popped his eyes open.

He scrambled earnestly toward the neck, wrapping his arms around the rough bones as the skeleton reared up into the air. A blast of wind stung his fingers as the creature roared. Without a throat of flesh, the roar rumbled with the voice of the earth itself, a cold, stony sound which deafened Kivron for a long moment. Blood rushed to his head as he dangled there. His strength ebbed, and abruptly vanished. He watched in numb horror as his fingers loosened, and he fell.

Kivron lay in the sand, choking. Pain lanced through his right arm. With muffled ears, he heard the creature roar again. Its footfalls shook him. He raised his head, blinking furiously. Silhouetted by the moon, the Dragon stood over him, its head swaying from one side to the other. The neck groaned downward, and the terrible blackness of its eyes picked him out.

Suddenly, a bellowing boulder separated itself from the cliffside. It caromed toward him, full tilt, then veered off, skittering in the sand. A shaggy boulder with drooping horns. "Over here!" cried the ox as she danced madly in the sand.

The Dragon's roar reverberated from the cliffs, and it lunged forward. A massive, bony foot slammed into the sand just beyond Kivron, then the other followed, and the tail cracked over his head. The monster pounded away. Kivron let out a long breath.

Flat teeth suddenly clenched into his shoulder. When he yelped in pain, they let go, and took a firm bite of his robe. The camel snorted moist breaths into his neck as it dragged him across the sand. Human hands grabbed him. The camel relinquished its hold, and followed the sorcerers into a cave at the base of the cliff.

They leaned him against the wall. Rough hands slapped the sand from his eyes and mouth. "Wake up! Wake up and get us out of this!" Luzo snapped.

"Where is the Grand Master?" grumbled another voice. "This is no symbol of strength, but of madness."

Kivron coughed and frowned. "Mei-ling?"

"Still outside," the camel said.

"I have to go—"

"You have to stop that monster!" Luzo insisted.

"Mei-ling needs me." He struggled to rise, but his legs would not obey him. His right arm hung limp, and sticky with blood.

Shenchya's face loomed out of the darkness. "You are responsible." Her beautiful face was streaked with tears and the dragon-sticks were gone, letting her hair trail over her shoulders.

"Not alone," Kivron stammered. "You, both of you, made this happen. We must find a way—"

Luzo shook his head. "We never should have gone through with it! I warned you against this. The two of us might have controlled it, but—"

Shenchya cut him off with a hiss, still glaring at Kivron. "This is why we have him. We did not give it life. We didn't release it to terrorize our fellows. That thing must be stopped!"

"That thing is your Dragon," Kivron replied.

"Your Dragon, now, Ox-master." She squared her shoulders, shaking back her hair. "If you subdue it, I may yet be able to take control."

Outside, the Dragon thundered across the canyon. Straining, Kivron thought he heard an ox's angry bellow. "Some things are not for you to control."

"The Enchanter is right, Shenchya," said another sorcerer. "He may be responsible, but your ambition has done this just as surely. Would you have us die in these caves?"

Luzo's hand fell to his belt and drew forth a long dagger. "There is more than one path to disenchantment."

Kivron's throat worked, but his mouth felt dry. Shenchya, Luzo and the other sorcerers watched him with vulture's eyes. "Camel?" he waved his arm.

The camel leaned down to him. Kivron clutched its neck, and pulled himself to his feet. "You said I would be a member, Grand Master," he paused, glancing at the huddled sorcerers, "well, I quit."

He turned to the canyon. "Stay here," he told the camel, releasing it. As he took a tottering step, the camel pushed its head in front of him.

"You can barely walk. Get on." It knelt down smoothly, and Kivron clambered up. He ducked over the front hump as the camel carried him out.

The tents and blankets of the Conjerum lay strewn across the sand. The Dragon's tail lashed. Its nostrils searched the air, then it sprang forward again, wobbling a little in the rough footing. The dark lump rose up before it and scrambled away. Mei-ling's sides heaved as she entered the circle of magic lights. She had feinted around the dragon, and now dashed for the caves and safety. Even as she drew nearer, her tired hooves flew out from under her, and she slid sideways, letting out a terribly human scream merging with the bellow of an ox about to meet its death.

The camel galloped, bouncing madly. Kivron held on one-handed, cursing the pain which jolted through his arm.

In four bounds, the Dragon loomed over Mei-ling.

Kivron could see the whites of her eyes, and her lolling tongue. "No!" he screamed. "No!"

The Dragon hesitated. The great head rotated and a low growl rumbled in its empty ribcage.

"No," Kivron moaned again. They stopped beside the fallen ox, under the very nose of the Dragon.

Still it waited, and the ominous rumbling grew.

The camel let him down gently, and he knelt beside Mei-ling, stroking her hot velvet nose. "You do not need to kill," he said, tilting his head to look up at the creature. Mei-ling's throat jerked beneath his hand. Tears trickled from his eyes.

The Dragon took a ponderous step back, then leaned down until it looked him full in the face. Though its eyes were empty, he felt the intensity of its gaze. The mouth gaped at him, showing teeth as big as his hand.

"You're not fighting any more," Kivron said. "You're not hungry any more."

"How do you know what I am not?" The voice, like a breath of mountain wind, echoed around him, raspy and cold.

The camel sank down to its knees, laying its long neck over Mei-ling's flank.

"I know you. I touched you and gave you something you have never had before."

Its tail flicked back and forth, sweeping down one of the remaining tents. "I lay down in the mud and could not rise. When I awoke again, such strength filled me. There was one—" The head swiveled back to study him. "That one sought to force me down again. Was it you?"

"I don't have that power. What was mine, is yours."

"He lies," said a voice from the darkness. Shenchya stood tall, her robe fluttering around her though there was no breeze. "He would force you to serve his own ends, oh Mighty Dragon. He's responsible — he would tell you that himself."

The Dragon drew itself up, towering above them, and Shenchya's eyes sparkled.

"Are you trying to get me killed?" Kivron demanded.

A trace of a smile touched her lips and she bowed.

With a roar that shook Kivron from toes to teeth, the Dragon lunged. One forearm snatched Kivron off the ground and he screamed, the sound frail and pitiful in the blast of the Dragon's fury. The claws wrapped his body and carried him upward, wind whipping his braids about his face. Kivron clamped his hand around the hard, cold bone and called upon his power, the only thing he had, the only thing he knew.

He rose up into the air, the jaw groaning open to receive him. Teeth flashed silver in the moonlight over his head.

Heat rushed through Kivron's body. If ever he had need of disenchantment, it was now. He begged, he pleaded.

For a moment, the Dragon stilled. Wind sucked down through the gaping jaws. With a crash of stone on stone, the beast drove downwards and its jaws slammed shut. Bones crunched. Blood spattered Kivron's face.

Shenchya's shriek rebounded from the stones. She flung out her arm as she fell, her face obscured by blood. With a whisper of wind, her robe unfurled beneath her and swooped away, bearing the Grand Master into the shadows.

A low rumble echoed around Kivron. A fierce desire shot through him, cold as the bones that held him, but the blood touched only on memory, and a longing welled up that touched Kivron's eyes with tears. He thought of the dog that died beneath his hand, and the Dragon's rumble fell low.

The Dragon's claws lowered Kivron to the ground beside his animals. Their breathing, harsh and moist, filled his ears and, for a moment, Kivron shut his eyes.

"I felt your touch, little thing," the Dragon said.

Carefully, he opened his eyes again, to find the Dragon staring back at him, its skull nearly touching the ground. "Thank you," Kivron whispered, wondering if he could be heard over the pounding of his heart. He worked his fingers into Mei-ling's thick coat.

The Dragon slowly gazed about the canyon. "I do not know this place. There were trees and water where I fell."

"You slept for a very long time. This place has changed since then."

"I do not like it much."

Kivron blinked up at the Dragon. "Neither do I." Beneath his hand, Mei-ling's breathing eased.

"I could still kill you," the Dragon mused. "That has not changed." A few drops of blood fell from its teeth.

Kivron swallowed. "But you would know what you had done."

Its spine carved bites of bone out of the distant silver moon as it stood as still as stone. At last, the Dragon turned its head to peer closely at Mei-ling, who stared defiantly back. "You are quick for a turtle."

"I am an ox," she replied quietly.

"Ah." It tilted its head to look at Kivron. "And you are responsible for me?"

Kivron stared back, the black pits of its eyes strangely no longer hollow. "Until I have found a home for you," he gulped, "yes."

The Dragon raised itself to its full height. The moon shone between its bones, rimming them in silver. The Flaming Cliffs looked like cliffs of ice. "There is no home for me here, I think." It looked down to him. "Are there other places with trees, water? Lizards, perhaps?"

"I have heard of jungles," Kivron said, "which may be like that."

"Mmm." The Dragon gave a soft rumble, like the start of a bonfire.

"Another journey, Your Magnificence?" Mei-ling asked.

"You might be better off at home, Mei-ling."

"Home is where you are, my Master."

Kivron patted the camel's neck. "I promised to find you a Disenchanter, and I failed. The sorcerers may yet know someone—"

The camel spat into the sand. "If it comes to going back to those cowards, I would rather be enchanted."

The Dragon sniffed loudly. "You are bleeding, little thing."

"I broke my arm in the fall."

Mei-ling raised her head in alarm. "You should clean and set it, Your Magnificence."

"I can carry you to the well," the camel offered, then lifted its head wearily, and added, "I think."

"Allow me, if you will," said the Dragon, lowering the thunder of its voice. "You are as delicate as hatchlings." It burrowed its nose into the sand.

Over the top of the skull, Kivron could see the shadowy figures of a huddle of men, their eyes round, all upon him. His name would never die, Shenchya said. Slowly, he rose to his feet and mounted the Dragon's skull. Accompanied by the moan of the wind and the ancient percussion of stone, the Dragon bore him up into the sky.

Far below, the sorcerers gasped, and stepped a little back.

Kivron caught his breath, looking down to Mei-ling and the camel. The musk ox pushed herself onto her feet, and nodded.

As the Dragon carried off her master, Mei-ling turned to the camel. "You must admit the herd was never like this."

"No, indeed. I may yet accept living outside the herd."

As they plodded off in strange procession, Kivron heard Mei-ling's voice drift up among the bones. His faithful ox was singing.

ELAINE ISAAK DROPPED OUT OF ART SCHOOL after two and a half years to found Curious Characters, designing original stuffed animals and fun small-scale sculptures, and to follow her bliss: writing. She is the author of The Singer's Crown *(Eos, 2005), and sequel* The Eunuch's Heir *(Eos, 2006). She currently resides in Seacoast New Hampshire, in a town so small, it doesn't even have its own post office. Visit www.elaineisaak.com to find out why you do not want to be her hero.*

SISTER OF THE HEDGE

BY JIM C. HINES

TALIA STOOD AT THE EDGE OF THE WOODS, both excited and repulsed by the sight before her. The Accursed Hedge was an enormous mound of brown and purple that blocked all but the snow-dusted tips of the distant mountains.

Talia shouldered her pack and hiked onward. The land around the Hedge had been cleared long ago. Rotting, insect-infested stumps dotted the field. Farther on, the ground turned brown and barren, as though the fairies had drawn an invisible line past which grass could not grow.

A cluster of buildings sat amidst the field of brown. Four long, wooden dormitories sat to either side of a tall church: The Church of the Iron Cross. From here, she could barely make out the dull gleam of the cross atop the roof. Harnesses bound two tiny figures to the steeple as they scraped rust from the cross

Talia hadn't set foot in a church for five years.

A man and a girl walked out to meet her. They both wore the rough, handspun robes of the church, but the man's clothes were adorned with gleaming brass buckles, and he wore a long hunting knife strapped to his waist A wooden cross with iron bands on the ends hung from a silver chain around his neck.

"Impressive, isn't it?" he asked, once he was within range. He yanked Talia's head down and tied a small wooden cross around her neck with a leather thong.

"Yes," she said tightly. Years of restraint kept her still as his fingers pulled the knot tight.

He snapped his fingers. "Impressive and evil. Look hard, girl. Never forget this Hedge is the work of the Devil."

What right did he have to talk down to her, like she was a mere child?

"I am Brother Samuel." He stared at Talia, taking in every detail, from her ragged black hair to the clumsy, hand-sewn repairs on her leather boots. "This is Lilly. She will show you to your cot and answer any questions you have about your new life." He started to turn, then paused. "I trust that is why you've come? To join the church and serve the princes?"

"It certainly wasn't for the pleasure of your company."

Samuel sniffed. "You've an arrogant air about you. No doubt your family hopes you'll learn some humility."

"No doubt," Talia agreed. She waited until Samuel started to walk away, then added, "I certainly understand why *your* family sent you away."

Lilly let out a yelp of surprise as Samuel whirled. His fingers were like claws, reaching for Talia's head, but then he caught himself. Voice low, he whispered, "Despise me if you like, girl. But you will show me proper respect as a member of the church and a servant of the princes, or I'll have you thrown upon the thorns. Understand?"

Talia clenched her jaw. She couldn't afford to argue, not if she was to survive here. She lowered her eyes. "I apologize for my rash words."

Still muttering, Samuel stalked away, leaving Talia alone with Lilly. Talia adjusted her pack. "Well? Aren't you supposed to show me where I'm to live?"

Lilly nodded quickly. "He wouldn't really throw you into the thorns, you know."

Talia's blood still thrummed through her veins. She kept both hands wrapped around the straps of her pack so Lilly wouldn't see them shake.

"I'm so glad you're here," Lilly went on. "You'll be able to see me take the Oath of Servitude next week. You have to serve for thirteen weeks before you can take it. Thirteen is a sacred number here, you know."

"Yes, I know." Did she think Talia had spent her life in darkness? Thirteen weeks, thirteen fairies. Twelve good, one evil. The good fairies had supposedly gifted Princess Aurora with beauty and grace beyond measure. One, the spurned fairy, had cursed the princess out of hatred and spite.

"You don't act like you want to be here." Lilly's mouth was pursed, almost a pout. Then she smiled. "Silly me. You've had a long journey. I doubt I was all sunshine and smiles when I arrived in the spring."

Talia didn't believe it. She had known girls like Lilly, blindly cheerful through any circumstances. If Lilly were burnt alive, no doubt she would babble merrily about the warmth and the beauty of the flames.

"My uncle brought me," Lilly went on. "We came from the north. I spent nine days in his old wagon before we reached town. The front left wheel squeaked like a mouse with every turn, but it was worth it to serve the princes and live amidst such a battle between God and evil…"

They reached the edge of the field, and now Talia could see why grass didn't grow around the Hedge.

Dry, tangled vines blanketed the earth. While the Accursed Hedge itself was a deep purple, these secondary thorns were a dull brown, with spots of tiny, dark green leaves.

"Don't worry, these aren't enchanted like the Hedge," Lilly assured her. "Samuel and the others have tried to kill the overgrowth, but there's just too much."

A few steps later, Talia's foot caught in one of the vines, and she fell. Thorns scraped her legs and palms, like dozens of tiny knives. She yanked up her right hand, but that put more weight on her left, driving the thorns deeper.

"Oh no!" Lilly grabbed her shoulders and helped her up. "You have to learn to walk here. Take high steps, like soldiers marching." She used the hem of her shirt to dab at the blood on Talia's forearms. "I'm so sorry. I should have warned you. Especially in your condition."

"What condition?" Annoyed, Talia yanked her hands away from Lilly's inexpert care.

"The twin boys you carry in your womb."

Talia nearly fell again. "That's impossible!"

Lilly's round eyes filled with shock and chagrin. "I'm sorry. I didn't mean...sometimes I see things. It's the Devil in me, I know, but I've never been wrong. My parents hoped the church could drive it from me. Talia, I...Talia? What's wrong?"

Talia pulled away so hard she nearly sent Lilly sprawling into the thorns. "Say nothing of it. *Nothing*!"

Lilly started to cry. "I wouldn't. If they knew what I could do, they might send *me* away, too."

Talia clenched her fists so tightly that new blood dripped from the scratches. Without another word, she walked onward.

TALIA DIDN'T SPEAK TO ANYONE until the following day. A few girls tried to talk to her, but Talia ignored them, and they didn't try very hard. She spent the night in a crowded longhouse with the rest of the Initiates, and followed them to church before sunrise.

The Church of the Iron Cross was different from any church Talia had ever seen. Dried vines bordered every window and doorway, held in place by heavy, square nails. Candles flickered in nests of thorns.

Beyond the altar hung an enormous cross, the ends capped in iron. Brittle vines surrounded the cross, but at a distance, as though the cross had driven them back.

Four tile mosaics decorated the floor in the middle of the nave. The first showed an infant being embraced by a king. In the second, a young girl sat at a spinning wheel. The third depicted a purple mountain beneath a dark sky: the Accursed Hedge. The final mosaic foretold hope and redemption: a young man led the princess forth while the Hedge burned behind them and angels sang from the clouds.

Talia shivered. The stone walls leached the heat from the air. This was a cold, hard place, more like a fortress than a church.

Alien though the church might be, the mass itself was familiar. Even after so many years, the Latin phrases still came automatically to her lips. As the service progressed, Talia found her attention wandering back to the first mosaic. The baby Aurora, her picture nothing more than a scattering of tile, made her queasy.

Maybe Lilly had been mistaken. Maybe she had lied, a way to test or taunt the new arrival.

Even if Talia had believed Lilly to be capable of that kind of cruelty, one look at the girl would have changed her mind. Lilly kept glancing back at Talia between hymns. Dark shadows marked her bloodshot eyes. She had spent the whole night in the chapel. No doubt praying for deliverance from her curse. Clearly, Lilly believed in her visions.

Deep down, so did Talia. It was all she could do to keep from crying

After the mass, Brother Samuel called the Initiates to him. "After morning mass, we bathe our charges." His eyes never left Talia. He seemed annoyed at having to explain. Of course, the rest of the girls knew all of this already. "You are about to enter the presence of royalty. You will obey any order given by one who wears the iron cross." He fingered the cross around his neck, still watching Talia. "Disobey the rules or disrespect the princes, and you will be punished."

Spinning sharply, he led them toward the Hedge.

There were no paths among the thorns. That morning, Talia had found a pair of wood-soled sandals at the foot of her cot. They were uncomfortable, but they protected her feet better than the thin boots she had worn before. She concentrated on walking like the others, and managed to make it to the Hedge without stumbling.

The wind shifted. Talia wrinkled her nose

"The smell of Satan," Samuel said, spotting her expression. "The smell of evil."

Talia rolled her eyes. Human waste and rotting flesh. Unpleasant, but hardly evil. Or if evil was to be judged by scent alone, Talia had known many a peasant who was in league with the devil. She noticed Lilly staring at her again, and deliberately turned away. Why couldn't everyone leave her alone?

"Do not touch the thorns," Samuel said. "A slip in the field will leave you scratched and bloody. A slip at the Hedge, and you will be scarred forever." He pushed back his sleeves, to reveal deep, dark lines about the wrists and elbows. "I was fortunate. I attempted to follow my prince, to save him. I spent months abed before I recovered."

Talia swallowed. Up close, the Accursed Hedge drove all else from her mind. The vines rose like a wall twenty times the height of a man. Near the base, many were thick as trees. The lowest thorns were spears as thick as her arm.

Yet it wasn't the solid wall she had expected. Even at a cursory glance, she could see gaps among the purple vines. She had already noticed at least four places where someone her size could slip between the thorns.

They walked around the Hedge, circling toward the rising sun. After a while, Lilly whispered, "He must be taking us to Prince Jerome."

Talia said nothing.

"I'm sorry about what I said." Lilly bit her lip. "You really didn't know?"

Her face tight, Talia shook her head.

"You should tell Brother Samuel. It's bad luck, here. The curse doomed Princess Aurora as an infant. It could do the same to your babies. The fairies will come for you, and—"

"Have you ever seen a fairy?" Talia snapped.

"They stay away. The church drives them back. But then, no infant has ever been allowed near the Hedge."

Thankfully, they reached their destination before Talia had to endure much more. Samuel brought them together in a half-circle, facing the Hedge

A crate sat beside a square wooden platform. A full water barrel nested in the vines next to the crate. On the platform, a Sister stood maneuvering a pole into the Hedge

"Prince Jerome was in his fourteenth year when he came to free the princess," Samuel said. "He was slender and quick, and sought to slip between the thorns. He made it deeper than many before the Hedge seized him." He bowed his head in quick prayer. "Lilly, would you take over for Sister Margaret?"

Joy suffused Lilly's face, but her voice remained humble. "Thank you, Brother Samuel." Her hands trembled as she stepped onto the platform and took the pole.

Talia moved away from the other girls, trying to see. The best view seemed to be from beyond the water barrel. She crouched and peered through the tangles.

Talia thought she had prepared herself. She had seen animals slaughtered before a feast. She had watched executions in the town square. How much worse could this be? She gasped when she spotted the prince.

He was naked and emaciated, his skin tight as canvas on tent poles. Either the Hedge had torn his clothing away, or the Sisters had done so. Talia guessed the latter. Given his situation, clothes would have quickly become an added torture.

He stood sideways, one leg extended as if the Hedge had caught him in midstep. Two thorns pierced his thigh. Another pinned his left arm to his side. Only his right arm was free. The bicep rested on a young vine that curled back on itself. Bloody scratches marked the arm. Older scars criss-crossed the skin, nearly the same shade of purple as the vines. His head twisted to face the girls. Water matted his tangled brown beard.

He squinted at Lilly. "You're a pretty young thing, aren't you?" His voice was harsh, and he made whistling noises when he spoke. Talia could see where a needle-like thorn passed through his throat. "How would you like to come back later, to dance for a prince? What's your name, girl?"

"Lilly, m'lord." She finished fastening a brass bowl to the end of the pole. Adjusting her grip, she struggled to dip it in the water, then began to slide it through the Hedge.

The prince leered. His manhood hardened and brushed against a narrow vine. One of the girls giggled nervously. "Don't be shy," he called out. "You can all dance for Prince Jerome!"

Talia's fists clenched. She wanted to reach in and drive a thorn through his tongue.

Suddenly he grimaced, as if in pain. Several girls gasped. Samuel's face was stone, and Sister Margaret simply began pulling rags from the crate.

With an odd whistling groan, Prince Jerome defecated onto his leg. Lilly's hands began to shake, and Talia lunged to catch the pole. One of the thorns stabbed her forearm.

It stabbed her too quickly to hurt. She could see the thorn lodged beneath the skin, a dark line beneath an inch-long bulge of flesh. And then Samuel was yanking her away from the Hedge while Sister Margaret withdrew the pole.

Talia watched, dazed, as Samuel took another rag from the chest and wound it gently around her arm. Sister Margaret had unscrewed the brass bowl from the pole, replacing it with a narrow metal loop. She threaded the rag through the loop, wrapping and tying it off so that none of the metal was exposed. Then she slid the rag into the Hedge and began to clean the prince.

Prince Jerome was sobbing like a child. So was Lilly. "I'm sorry," she said, over and over.

The prince started to scream. "Go away. Leave me! All of you, *leave now*! *At once!*"

"Of course," Sister Margaret said calmly, pulling the shit-stained rag from the pole.

As Samuel herded them back toward the church, he turned back toward Talia. "You bear the agony well. Few can endure the bite of the Hedge without screaming."

"Thank you," Talia said, still dazed. In truth, there was no pain, only a gentle throbbing in her veins.

"This is the life you've chosen. A life of blood and filth and servitude before God. Are you certain this is what you want?"

Talia shrugged and rubbed her bandaged arm. She thought of the babies in her womb. Why should she serve a God who had turned his back on Talia so long ago? At that moment, Talia's sympathy lay with the fairies who had left princes like Jerome to suffer. If only…Talia bowed her head and said nothing.

Samuel took that as assent. He clasped her shoulder. "Give your strength and will to God, child. In the end, he *will* destroy this abomination."

THAT NIGHT, TALIA DREAMED SHE WAS THE PRINCESS AURORA. She stood near a narrow window, watching from her room as Prince Jerome waded through the thorns. Naked and soiled, the prince fought his way into the courtyard.

Jerome approached the castle. Suddenly Talia found herself abed, unable to move. She lay frozen as the door creaked inward. Her body was heavy as stone. Even her breathing slowed, too quiet to hear.

From the corner of her eyes, she watched the door swing silently inward. Prince Jerome fastened a long blade to the end of a pole. She tried to shake her head, to beg for mercy, but her body failed. She couldn't even close her eyes.

The pole jabbed her belly. Twin infants wailed from her womb, but she couldn't move her head to see them.

The prince tossed the pole aside and wiped blood from his hands. Talia tried to get away, but thorn-covered vines grew from the mattress to pin her in place. His body blocked the light. Ever so slowly, the prince leaned closer, a faceless shadow in the darkness.

Talia lurched awake.

Moonlight gleamed through cracks in the walls and doorway. Moving as quietly as she could, Talia grabbed her sandals and crept over the sleeping bodies of the other Initiates.

Once outside, she slipped into her sandals and sucked the cold air into her lungs, trying to regain control.

"Are you all right?"

Talia jumped. She hadn't seen Lilly standing there in the shadows. "What are you doing awake?"

Lilly shrugged. "Praying for forgiveness. For my mistake today. For my curse and my sins. And for you. Talia, the Hedge *wants* you."

Talia shivered at the conviction in Lilly's voice. "Why?"

"I don't know." Lilly looked away. "Your children, I suppose."

"The Hedge can have them, for all I care. The thorns can send them back to God."

"You don't mean that." Lilly crossed herself. "You shouldn't say such things here. Brother Samuel says that each sin gives new strength to the evil."

Lilly was right. She didn't mean it. It only made her angrier. "You know nothing of evil," she snapped.

She could see a pair of Sisters walking alongside the Hedge. One carried a small oil lamp, the other a large, woven basket.

"Herbs for tea," Lilly explained. "To help bring sleep for the princes. Many of them can only sleep for short stretches of time. Night is a constant battle between pain and exhaustion." She touched Talia's cheek. "You're as young as I am. Why are you so sad and bitter?"

Talia swallowed, frightened by an upsurge of emotion. "I...I came here to find safety. Like a fool, a part of me still hoped God would look after me."

"But He will!" Lilly said excitedly. She stood, pulling Talia to her feet. "Come with me to the chapel, and we can pray together."

Talia freed her hands. "Has God helped you? Has he done away with your 'curse,' or done anything at all to protect you from the visions that haunt you?"

"He will," Lilly said again. Her eyes were wide. "My faith isn't yet strong enough. I watch Brother Samuel go forth each day without doubt or confusion. He helps me see my own weakness. But someday—"

"Someday, what? Brother Samuel will discover your visions and cast you out?"

Lilly stiffened. "If that is God's will."

Talia gave up. "Very well. I'll join you as soon as I've dressed in something more modest."

But as she left, she found herself turning away from the church and walking instead toward the Accursed Hedge.

TALIA WALKED FOR A LONG TIME, keeping her distance from the Hedge so she wouldn't be bothered by the men and women working through the night. Eventually, she reached Prince Jerome. Glancing around to make sure it was safe, she moved closer. She wasn't sure how she could tell this bit of Hedge from any other, especially in the moonlight. The platforms for the princes were identical. Somehow she simply knew, just as she knew she would find traces of dried blood on that thorn in front of her, from when she had injured herself.

Jerome was a dark shadow. Darkness hid his face, but his chest moved slowly, and he didn't react to her presence. Asleep, then.

Talia went closer and rested her hands on a fat, gnarled vine. Flakes of purple skin fell away beneath her hands.

The vine was warmer than she would have guessed. It felt alive. Was this the feel of fairy magic? No doubt Samuel would say it was fueled by the fires of Hell.

Jerome gasped and shifted his head. Talia heard his whistling hiss of pain, but he didn't seem to awaken.

In sleep, he was nothing more than a man. No different from Brother Samuel or any other. Only days ago, Talia had thought to spend her life in service to men such as this. The idea of joining a convent had come to her the first night away from home, as she lay shivering and hidden in a chicken coop. A convent would bring safety and security. Better yet, her family would never expect it of her.

Her mother would have laughed at the thought of Talia willingly serving any man or woman. But then, Talia's mother had been dead five years.

Talia banished those thoughts before they could lead any further. Instead, she concentrated on Jerome. She watched him for a long time.

Why this convent? Why the Church of the Iron cross? It wasn't until now, after seeing the princes, that she began to understand her own motives.

Perhaps she had come to see the kinglings suffer.

BROTHER SAMUEL CAME TO HER THE NEXT MORNING, as she and the other Initiates watched Sister Petitia tend Prince Aaron. Talia saw Samuel arrive, but he said nothing. Nor could he speak, until Sister Petitia finished shaving the prince.

Nearly fifty years old, Prince Aaron had spent half his life trapped in the Hedge. He never spoke, and barely moved at all, except to eat and drink whatever was placed in front of him. It had been two years since his hair was last cut. In that time, it had grown long enough to snarl and knot around the thorns.

Sister Petitia delicately slid the pole back and forth, sawing the razor-sharp blade through a lock of beard caught on a thorn. She was one of the few servants trusted to wield a blade this close to a prince, and she had made it clear that *nobody* was to make a sound until the blade was fully removed

from the Hedge. Anyone who distracted her could be banished, no matter what the excuse.

Inside the Hedge, sparrows chirped and fluttered about, collecting fallen locks for their nests. Prince Aaron might as well have been a statue for all the notice they took of him.

Eventually, Sister Petitia finished. Before she could speak, Samuel grabbed Talia's shoulder. "You were out last night. You went to see the princes."

Talia shot a quick glare at Lilly. Had she told Samuel? "I went for a walk. To clear my head. I have trouble sleeping."

"You went to Prince Jerome. He saw you, but wouldn't say what you did."

So Lilly hadn't betrayed her after all. Several of the girls giggled. A furious look from Samuel silenced them. She knew what they must be thinking, though.

"I did nothing about your prince's...*desires*, if that's what you're asking. I thought he was asleep."

Sister Petitia cleared her throat. "Initiates aren't allowed to wander the Hedge alone, dear."

"You could be banished," Samuel added.

"On the other hand," Sister Petitia went on, "I recall a young boy who snuck out every night to talk to his dying prince, even before he took the Oath."

Samuel's cheeks turned red. He looked like he wanted to shout at the elderly Sister, but didn't dare. From the way his neck muscles were moving, it was a close thing. Finally, he scowled and said, "Very well. As punishment, you'll remain here to scrub and repair the platform."

"Thank you." There was true gratitude in Talia's words, and she hated it. So what if that trumped-up clod threatened to send her away. She could always go elsewhere.

But the mere thought of leaving left her throat dry and her hands damp. After only two days, the very idea made her ill. Her arm throbbed, and she glanced at the Hedge.

Lilly said the Hedge wanted Talia and her unborn children. For the first time, Talia started to take that warning seriously.

THAT NIGHT, TALIA WOKE SUDDENLY. She kept perfectly still until she identified the sound that had awakened her. There...the scrape of a bare foot against the floor. She turned. It was too dark to make out the girl's features, but Lilly's careful, hesitant movements were unmistakable.

"I couldn't sleep," Lilly said. "I dreamed of your children, beautiful as the sun and the moon. I saw them taken from you, Talia. Broken and left to die." Her voice broke. "The Accursed Hedge is fairy magic. Fairies have always taken human children. You're in danger!"

"Is it?" Talia whispered. "Fairy magic, I mean. According to the stories, the twelfth fairy laid her curse upon the princess. The thirteenth used her magic to combat the curse and save the princess's life. But none of the songs say who created the Hedge"

"Of course it's magic. It's obviously not natural."

"Have you ever met a fairy? Has anyone ever tried to find them, to ask their aid in destroying the Hedge?"

Lilly shook her head. "That's blasphemy, Talia!"

"Perhaps it is. Or perhaps it's common sense!" But why would the fairies create the Hedge in the first place? Why would they then abandon their creation? She sighed. "Even in the wildest tales, I've never heard of a fairy changeling swapped while the babe was still in the womb. I should be safe for a while. Safe from the Hedge, at least."

"I guess." Lilly touched Talia's arm. "But what will you do when the babies come?"

"It doesn't matter." For some reason, she found it easier to talk in the darkness. "My father will find me. He has woodsmen who can track a gnat's flight at midnight. He'll bribe or torture every villager for miles if he has to."

"How? Surely he can't—"

"He can." Talia had known all along, really. Tonight was simply the first time she had allowed herself to recognize the truth. She would never be free. "Kings can do anything they wish. Just ask your precious Brother Samuel."

She heard Lilly suck in her breath. "You're a princess? Talia, you have to go now! The curse was laid upon a princess. You're twice endangered."

Talia shook her head. "It doesn't matter. I'm no more likely to escape my father than Prince Aaron is to break free from the thorns. If he can't find me by conventional means, he'll hire witches and sorcerers. He would even deal with the fairy folk if he had to."

"Any father would want his daughter back. And when he discovers his grandchildren, he'll—"

"He'll destroy them." Talia closed her eyes. "They're in greater danger from him than from the Hedge. He will come for me, like a hunter chasing a prize stag. He'll never stop looking, especially once he learns of my children."

"I don't understand."

Perhaps it was the darkness that loosened Talia's throat. "He can't afford to let me go. Not with twin boys to prove what he did to me."

Lilly gasped and crossed herself. "You mustn't speak of such things."

"It's the truth. If you can't hear it, go away and let me lie in peace."

The mattress shifted as Lilly stood. "I'll pray for you, Princess Talia. Maybe God will show you a way out."

Talia snorted loudly, then winced. But she heard nothing from the other girls. Hopefully they still slept. "God has never taken much interest in protecting me," she said.

"So you turn your back on Him?"

"He turned his back on me. Just like he turned his back on Aurora. Who is the more heartless?" Talia rolled over on her side, away from Lilly. A few minutes later, she heard Lilly slip away, leaving her alone.

THE INITIATES WATCHED AS LILLY SERVED PRINCE HUMPHREY, a pompous, angry block of a man who cursed and swore at everyone who passed.

Lilly and Talia hadn't spoken since the other night. Talia wasn't surprised. Lilly had probably decided Talia was damned, and was trying to distance herself as much as possible. Whether for the children in her womb or because she had "turned her back on God," Talia wasn't sure. Probably both.

"Look at that bird," said one of the younger Initiates, a skinny thing with a high-pitched squeal of a voice. "It's beautiful."

Talia didn't look. She was busy watching Lilly struggle with Prince Humphrey. The prince had seized the end of the pole with his good left hand and refused to release it. Lilly looked close to tears, but she kept trying to gently pull it back.

"Damn you, woman!" shouted the prince. "Feeding me this miserable slop." He yanked the pole, nearly breaking it out of Lilly's grip. Oatmeal sloshed over his arm. "Miserable bastards can't even make a palatable meal. Get this ugly bitch from my sight!"

"I'm sorry, m'lord," Lilly said. She had given up trying to retrieve the pole, and was now simply holding the end so Prince Humphrey wouldn't pull the whole thing into the Hedge.

"Flush anger and despair from your heart," Samuel whispered to Lilly, too low for the prince to hear. "Prince Humphrey has spent years in agony. Forgive his harsh words, and pity him his fate."

Lilly nodded and held on, but Prince Humphrey only yanked harder.

"It looks like a hawk." said another girl. "It's flying toward us!"

If Talia hadn't been distracted, she might have been able to intercept the bird. She might have had a chance.

Instead, she stepped closer to Lilly and took the pole from her hands. Brother Samuel started to protest, then seemed to change his mind.

"I'm sorry, m'lord," Talia called. She gave the pole a sharp twist. "Lilly didn't understand how much you desired to keep the bowl for yourself." A few more turns, and the end of the pole came unscrewed from the bowl. Talia pulled the pole back before the prince could grab it.

"Stupid wench!" The prince had dropped the bowl, and oatmeal covered his hip and leg. "Look what you've done!"

"My humblest apologies, m'lord," she said. She shoved the pole into Lilly's hands. "I suggest you use the hook to retrieve the bowl. You'll need a rag to clean him up as well. Or perhaps you expect God to take care of it?"

Then she took a deep breath and turned around, readying herself for the tongue-lashing Brother Samuel was sure to give.

Brother Samuel was paying no attention. A large blue and red bird perched on the edge of the Hedge. Samuel raised one arm. The bird, well-trained, flew to Samuel and waited, wings spread, while Samuel untied the message tube from its leg.

Talia stopped breathing.

"What kind of bird is that?" Lilly asked.

"A western blue-tailed hawk. An exotic messenger bird from across the ocean," Talia said. She glanced around, wanting to run, but it was too late. Samuel was already staring at her.

Talia looked down and added, "My father collects them."

THE TRUTH ABOUT TALIA'S IDENTITY brought at least one blessing. As a princess, she no longer had to obey Brother Samuel. The lines of his face tightened each time she gave him an order, but he never complained. He would do anything she asked, except allow her to leave.

"Remind me when my father's men are due to arrive," she said.

"Two days, according to his note."

They stood at the back of the church, watching as Lilly took the Oath of Servitude. The Brothers and Sisters of the church filled the front rows. Townsfolk crowded around the edges and near the doors.

The priest was a small man whose wild red hair made him look younger than the Initiates. He raised his voice, surprisingly deep for one so skinny. "Children of God, we come to recognize our sister Lilly as she dedicates herself to a life of servitude."

Lilly had spent last night in solitude, sleeping in the open. For her bed, she had nothing but the thorns on the earth. For warmth and comfort, she had only a thin robe and an iron-banded cross, the same cross she now clutched in her hands.

Talia glanced at the healing scar on her forearm. "Samuel, why do you make Initiates sleep among the thorns?"

"So they may understand the agony of the princes trapped by the fairy curse. I spend one night a week in the thorns, so I do not forget." There was no boastfulness in his words.

Talia nodded. "But the fairy didn't curse the princes. She cursed Princess Aurora." At least, that was what the stories said.

The priest motioned for Lilly to kneel. "Do you promise to serve in sickness and health, forsaking all earthly bonds? Letting neither pain nor desire sway you from the light of God?"

"I do," Lilly said loudly.

Talia stared at the mosaic on the floor, the young man leading the princess from the thorns. "Do you believe God will overcome the curse?"

"I have no doubt," said Samuel.

"Then why has it taken so many years? Why have so many princes lost their lives?"

There was no answer.

"Why is your God so weak?"

"God is all the princes...and myself...have left." Samuel walked out of the church. Talia knew he would be waiting just beyond the doors, to make sure she didn't try to escape.

"We believe in one God, triumphant and almighty," the priest said. "We believe in salvation, and the fall of evil."

"Amen," whispered Talia.

TALIA GRIPPED LILLY'S ARMS and whispered, "I need you to look into the Hedge."

Lilly blinked. "You can see as well as I—"

"No," Talia said. "I need you to *look*."

Lilly paled. It had taken Talia the entire day to make an opportunity to speak with Lilly. She was Sister Lilly now, but even Sisters rarely attended the princes alone. To make matters worse, Samuel still shadowed Talia like a hound. It hadn't been until evening, when a wagon arrived from town, that Talia found her chance.

Lilly was helping to prepare bread for the princes' evening meal, tearing away the hard crusts for those who no longer had their teeth. Talia had sat down to join her, muttering, "If I'm forced to remain, at least allow me to feel useful." Grudgingly, Samuel had agreed. He now stood with the other Brothers, helping to unload sacks of flour and wheat while keeping an eye on Talia.

"Why would you ask me to do that?" Lilly said quietly. "I've sworn my life to God."

"Because I need your help," Talia said. "Because if you don't, my children will be executed by their own father." She waited to see how Lilly would respond, if she would flee like last time.

"Would he really…" Lilly bit her lip. "They're innocent. How could anyone–"

"Innocence doesn't matter." Talia pointed to the Hedge The sun was setting, and the thorns shone in the orange light. "They're as innocent as the princess was when she was cursed to death."

Lilly swallowed. Her fingers slipped as she tried to crack another loaf of bread. "What do you hope to see?"

"I want to understand. The stories…they make no sense. I want to know the truth about the Accursed Hedge."

"What truth? The Hedge is wicked!" Several people glanced their way, including Samuel.

"Don't make me beg," Talia whispered.

Lilly stared at the bread for a long time. "No, I wouldn't do that."

"Then help me. Please."

Lilly nodded. "I…I had a dream last night. I didn't want to speak of it."

"Was it a vision?" Talia pressed.

"I don't know. I saw the Hedge. It had grown into an enormous mockery of a cathedral, enveloping everything. The church, the town, everything was gone." Her eyes shone as she stared at Talia. "It came for *you*. I told you the Hedge wanted you, Talia. I mean, Princess."

Talia clenched Lilly's hands so tightly her fingers whitened. It made no sense! The Hedge…the church…there was something more. Something important. Why couldn't she figure it out? "Lilly, I need you to do something else for me."

"I can't help you escape, Princess," Lilly said.

Talia ignored her. "I need you to meet me before morning mass. I want you to come with me to the Hedge, one last time before my father arrives. I'm not allowed to wander alone, but if I have to be guarded, I want my guard to be a friend. Also…" She lowered her gaze. Pride warred with desperation. Desperation won. "Also, I want you to pray for me."

SEVERAL MORE HAWKS ARRIVED the following morning, announcing the pending arrival of Talia's father. Most of the Brothers woke early to patrol the Accursed Hedge. Those who circled the Hedge itself carried long spears. Others went into town to guard the roads. Another group shouldered short, powerful bows and disappeared into the woods. Lilly said this was how the Brothers reacted to any visiting noble.

"It's their job to keep the princes safe," Lilly said. "While they're here, they're sacrosanct. No kingdom would violate the safety of the Hedge. But there are always individuals, assassins, and others, who might try. The Brothers protect the princes with their lives."

Morning dew glittered on the thorns along the ground, and the Hedge shone like dark metal.

"What are you going to do, Princess?"

Talia kept walking. "In your vision, you said the Hedge became a cathedral and overwhelmed the land."

"That's right," Lilly said quietly.

"How could fairy magic overcome the might of God?"

"I don't know." She was walking quickly to keep up. "Talia, please stop."

Talia halted.

"I can't let you run away. I know you don't want to go back, but—"

"I said I wanted a friend, Lilly." Talia turned. Her eyes searched Lilly's round face, trying to read the thoughts behind her eyes. "Did you pray for me, like I asked? Did God tell you to betray me?"

Footsteps crunched behind her. Talia guessed who it would be. "Good morning, Brother Samuel."

"Lilly told me about the children within your womb," Samuel said. He planted the butt of his spear amidst the vines. "Infants are forbidden here. They endanger us all. I don't know why you abandoned your husband, but—"

"*Not* my husband."

"You were married in the eyes of God," Samuel said firmly. "Your sin brings evil to this place. Your presence strengthens the fairy magic and delays God's triumph."

Talia took a step toward Lilly, who backed away, eyes wide. "What happened to Aurora's family?"

Lilly blinked. "They were cast into sleep with the princess."

"Why? The fairy curse was laid upon Aurora alone."

"She was the most precious thing in their world," Samuel said. "I'm certain they would have chosen to join her in her curse. It was the noble thing."

"Noble?" Talia shot him a look so scathing he actually took a step back. "Her family invited fairies to her birth. They bribed those fairies to give her beauty, to transform her into a prize doll to be won at a summer festival.

"*Nobility* treats Aurora as a treasure to be won. You think Prince Jerome came to rescue a sleeping maiden? Or is he simply a man who *preferred* his women unconscious. And what of your own prince, Brother Samuel? Did he truly quest to rescue the princess? Was it selfless love that drove him into the thorns? Or did he, like the rest, come in pursuit of his own glory?"

Samuel drew back a fist, then caught himself. "You know nothing of my prince."

"I know royalty," she snapped. "I know how kings use sleeping maidens, and I know what your princes would do to Aurora."

"You *must* go." His face was dark. "For years, the fairies have avoided this place, driven back by the might of God. By bringing your children here, you call to them. You'll bring them down upon us all."

Talia hesitated. There was no denying the way the Hedge longed for her. In her dreams...the way it had reacted to her touch... "I won't go back."

"You must." Samuel moved forward, so they formed a triangle. No matter which way Talia ran, Lilly or Samuel would be able to intercept her. She took a step back, and they followed.

"You knew I planned to run?"

"You deceived us from the day you arrived," Samuel said. "I can't believe you would change your ways now."

Talia shook her head. "What would God say to that, I wonder? Wasn't it God who sent his own son to teach forgiveness?"

"You've not asked for forgiveness, nor have you repented your sins," Samuel countered. He took another step, backing Talia closer toward the Hedge and blocking her escape with his spear. "Believe it or not, Princess, I've prayed for you. I've prayed for an end to your unhappiness. It's not my place to judge you. That is for God."

"You're right," she said slowly. "Tell me, Samuel, are you *certain* the Hedge is cursed? Are you *certain* that curse was placed by fairies, and not by another?"

Before he could answer, she spun and ducked between the thorns, into the Accursed Hedge.

Lilly screamed.

"Princess, no!" Samuel dropped his spear and lunged for her, heedless of the bloody cuts he received in the process. His fingers caught the sleeve of her gown. Thorns scratched her skin as she struggled. She forced her arm toward a vine so the thorns pierced the sleeve. There was a tearing sound, and Samuel stumbled back, a ragged scrap of cloth in his fingers.

Talia stepped deeper. Thorns tangled her hair. One pricked the back of her leg. She had to step over an enormous vine, then duck and pull her hair with both hands to rip it free.

"Lilly, get the pole and the hook! Quickly!"

Talia glanced back. By now, she was nearly ten feet into the Hedge. She could see Samuel clutching his arm. Blood trickled through his fingers.

Lilly was crying. "Talia, you've seen what the Hedge will do to you. I know what you've endured, but you have to put your faith in God to save you."

"I think that's what I'm doing," Talia said.

"Lilly, go!" Samuel shouted. "Others have made such progress into the thicket. Each one came to regret his decision to forge onward. Or have you struck a deal with Satan, that he will protect you from his foul magic? If so, you have my pity, for you'll be damned beyond redemption."

Talia straightened as much as she could. So long as she kept her shoulders hunched and her head tilted to the left, she could rest without the thorns touching her skin. "The songs say the Princess Aurora was the most beautiful maiden in the world," she said.

"Your point, m'lady?" Samuel asked. He glanced at Lilly. "Retrieve the pole, Sister!"

"My point?" Talia asked. She rested her fingers on a thorn. "What greater curse could the fairies have given, than such perfect beauty? Perhaps there is one who will look upon her as a person rather than a prize, but if so, that one hasn't yet come."

Talia clutched the small Initiate's cross at her neck. "And until then, God will protect her, just as He will protect me and my children."

"You blasphemous—"

Lilly caught Samuel by the arm. "Brother, what if she's right? What if this is God's way of sheltering her?"

Samuel jerked free and hurried away, no doubt going for the pole.

"Thank you," Talia said to Lilly. She wanted to reach out and squeeze Lilly's hand, but she had already waded too deep into the Hedge. She turned and squeezed sideways, dropping to her knees to crawl through a gap. The thorns continued to scratch her skin, but none of the vines closed round her. She glanced back. "Lilly...if the Hedge is a gift from God, couldn't the same be true of your own gift?"

Lilly stiffened, but nodded grudgingly.

Something tickled Talia's cheek. A single red bloom, barely open.

She could hear Samuel thrusting the pole into the Hedge, but when she looked back, she relaxed. The hook had caught in a thick knot of vines...a knot which hadn't been there before.

She wondered if anyone would believe the tale Samuel and Lilly told. More likely Talia's father would assume she had fled, and somehow bribed or bewitched them into telling such an outlandish tale.

It was darker up ahead. The orange light grew heavy, like the sunset. Her body felt warm and numb.

How long would the "curse" last? Years? Centuries?

She fought a yawn. It didn't matter. She, like the Princess Aurora, would be safe.

Talia barely noticed when the ground softened beneath her feet, or when her face fell to rest on gentle green moss instead of sharp thorns.

JIM C. HINES HAS SPENT THE LAST SIX YEARS as a state employee, using his union-regulated lunch break to write about everything from zombie amusement parks to butt-kicking octogenarian warrior women to a nearsighted goblin runt named Jig. His humorous fantasy novels Goblin Quest *and* Goblin Hero *were both published by DAW Books, and he's hard at work on a third book in the series. He lives in Holt, Michigan, with his wonderful wife, two amazing children, an overly hairy dog, and 2.75 cats. Online, he can be found at www.jimchines.com.*

RAMPION

BY MARY ROBINETTE KOWAL

AS THE WARRIOR GUIDED HIS HORSE BACK HOME, Sybille pondered what the future might hold. She brushed a strand of her golden hair, still sweat-damp, back from her face. Tracing a path to her belly, her hand came to rest above her womb.

If his seed failed to quicken, her cuckoldry would be for nothing. Her yearning for a child ran deep, winding through her bones and into the secret places inside. Sybille had seduced the man for one purpose — to get her the child Roland could not.

She turned and went into the cottage she shared with her husband. If the man chanced to look back, she did not want to be standing in the doorway, watching like a girl at a barn dance. Stripping the linens off the bed, she carried them to the pile of laundry waiting in the garden. When Roland returned from his fool's errand, she wanted him to find nothing more than his wife doing the washing.

As she banked the fire under the cauldron, Sybille fought the sadness simmering below her surface. Mother Gothel, the witch on the far side of the village, had said Sybille was not barren. Poor Roland. She loved him for his gentle ways, but he could not give her what she wanted most.

So, when the band of warriors came to the village, Sybille realized how she might bear a child.

She let down her long hair and seduced the man who looked most like her husband. And though she had come to Roland as a chaste bride, she invited the man to her home. To her bed.

Sybille wanted to burn the sheets.

Before the man arrived at the cottage, she had sent Roland in search of rampion, knowing it was too late in the year to find the green. She claimed to be ill from craving it.

Roland had believed her.

She closed her eyes against the memory; she had never lied to him before.

Plunging the linens into the cauldron, Sybille tried to wash her guilt away with the soil on the sheets. As she worked over the boiling water, new sweat beaded her skin despite the October air. A droplet trailed between her breasts, reminding her of the man's hand. She wiped furiously at it; Roland would be home soon.

Sybille hung a shirt, which she had made for Roland shortly after their marriage, over the line. She imagined hanging a girl's dress on the line beside it. In her mind, the dress had tiny pintucks and delicate lace at the hem.

She smiled, fingering the sleeve of Roland's shirt. The autumn sun lit the linen, seeming to bleach it back to a new white, but she knew that when she pulled it from the line, eight years of toil would still tinge the fabric. How long would her guilt tinge her mind?

The sound of footsteps, running along the path, reached her ears before Roland burst into the back garden. Beneath his sandy hair, his face was flushed red as maple leaves.

Her heart seemed to race in answer to his haste. Sybille turned from the line, conscious of the perspiration still between her thighs. "Roland?" Had someone seen the man come to her?

Roland ducked past the laundry and wrapped his arms around her, pressing her to him. His shirt was damp and heat radiated from him even though the autumn day was cool. His breath was ragged in Sybille's ear as he clung to her.

"I love you." He kissed her cheek. "I love you."

She squeezed Roland back, her fear of being caught replaced by concern for her husband. "I love you, too."

He smoothed her hair as he released her. "I don't know if you still will."

"Roland, what's wrong?" Fear seemed to form a bubble at the top of her throat, stopping her breath.

In answer, he knelt and swung the strap of the basket off his shoulder. He lifted the lid. A sweet peppery tang floated from the greens within. "I found rampion."

Sybille sank to her knees beside him. She reached into the basket, plunging her hand into the cool green leaves. Scattered across the top were stems covered with purple flowers. It was too late in the year for rampion to grow. Far too late. Mesmerized by the green, she pulled out a leaf and placed it between her lips. The flavor exploded on her tongue with promises of hot summer.

She lifted her eyes to Roland and leaned across the basket to kiss him gently on the lips. "Thank you, my love."

He pulled away from her and shook his head. "They were in the witch's garden."

The taste in her mouth turned to ash. The witch. Mother Gothel, who had told Sybille her womb could bear a child. "What—?"

"She caught me." His eyes were huge, like a little boy's. "I had to promise —I thought it would be all right, because it's been eight years and—"

"What did you promise her?"

"Our first-born child."

His words seemed to silence every sound from the surrounding forest. His lips continued to move, but she heard nothing he said. She staggered to her feet and stumbled away from him. Racked with sudden nausea, she clutched her stomach and vomited, bright green flecks spattering the dirt.

She felt Roland's hands on her back. "I'm sorry. When she demanded a child, I thought I wasn't giving anything away . . . We had tried so hard."

He could not know the truth. Wiping her mouth with the back of her hand, she said, "You had to get away from her." Roland could not know how she spent the afternoon. "And we can't have children, so you've promised her nothing."

A moan of despair ground out of him. "After I promised, she said you would have a child, a girl." His voice dwindled to a whisper. "We're to name her Rapunzel, after the rampion I stole."

Sybille straightened slowly, with her hand over her womb.

Roland hovered by her, tears coursing down his solid face. "I didn't think we could have children."

"I know." She looked away from him, at the sheets hanging over the line. "I tried everything."

MARY ROBINETTE KOWAL IS A PROFESSIONAL PUPPETEER who moonlights as a writer. Originally from North Carolina, Mrs. Kowal lives in New York or Iceland. She is a graduate of Orson Scott Card's Literary BootCamp. Visit her website, www.maryrobinettekowal.com, if you'd like a list of where her other stories appear.

SALT OF JUDAS

BY ERIC JAMES STONE

OSBERT PEALE DID NOT PAINT PORTRAITS when he sat on his stool beside the Avon. He painted Tewkesbury Abbey or one of the footbridges over the river. Sometimes he portrayed the boatmen on the water or passersby on land, but those people were merely parts of the landscape. Only in his narrow rented room above the butcher's did he paint portraits, and those he never showed to anyone for fear they would laugh.

Every portrait was of *her*. He'd begun to paint her portrait even before he discovered that her name was Amelia. He said that delightful name occasionally to himself as he drew in charcoal the curve of her neck or used the painting knife to soften the glow of her cheek. But in his mind she remained most often "her." And though he often whispered — to himself — that he loved her, he knew that a wealthy landowner's daughter like her would never love a humble artist like him.

As he sat beside the river, palette in one hand and knife in the other, creating landscapes in oil, he always watched for her, since she often strolled along the footpath with her companions. On occasion she would stop and look at his work in progress, and Osbert would then find it difficult to breathe as he painted with trembling hand. But except in his imagination she had never spoken to him, nor he to her. His love for her was a secret he kept from all the world.

He was using the blending knife to darken the shadows of an overcast sky on his canvas when a deep voice came from behind him.

"I understand you paint portraits."

Osbert turned his head to look up at the stranger. The man was bald as an egg, and under the darkening sky his skin seemed Lead White with a touch of Ultramarine Blue. He wore a red vest — Cadmium Red darkened perhaps by Burnt Sienna — over a white silk shirt, black breeches and white stockings. The buckles on his shoes glinted gold even without direct sunlight. Although Osbert had been in Tewkesbury less than a year, he thought he knew everyone of consequence in the town. This man must be a wealthy traveler, perhaps brought here by the convergence of the Avon and the Severn rivers.

"You are mistaken, sir. I am only a landscape painter."

The stranger nodded slowly. "Where do you buy your oils?"

"From Barber the apothecary. He has a shop on Church Street."

"From now on, you will buy them from me." The stranger spoke as if stating an obvious fact.

"But Barber has always—"

"Barber has sold his shop to me. I am the new apothecary."

"Oh." Osbert did not know what else to say. Barber had been a friendly fellow, quite unlike this brusque man. But possibly the new apothecary would become more amiable in time.

"Soon you will want to bring life to your portraits. Come to me then." The apothecary turned and strode away.

"I don't paint portraits," Osbert called after him, but the bald head made no acknowledgement.

IN THE DIM MORNING LIGHT that came through his one small window, Osbert looked at the latest portrait of her. She was tilting her head inquisitively, and her lips were pursed slightly, as if she were about to ask a question.

"You wish to know my name, milady? I am Osbert Peale, at your service. Or perhaps you wonder what it is I will be painting today? I believe I shall attempt once more to capture the spirit of Tewkesbury Abbey.

"Or do you merely wish to inquire whether I think it will rain? Yes, that must be it, for the weather will do quite well as a subject of conversation with someone when you have nothing else in common."

He fell silent. This piece was his best, seeming to catch a moment before motion rather than an eternal pose.

Soon you will want to bring life to your portraits. Come to me then.

What had the apothecary meant? Could he have known of Osbert's secret portraits?

What would it be like to touch her, to feel the softness of her skin? Osbert reached out and gently stroked her face. His fingers came away wet with paint.

THE WOODEN SIGN SHOWING A MORTAR AND PESTLE still hung over the door, but someone had painted over the name Barber and replaced it with Dyer. Osbert hesitated before opening the door and walking into the shop.

"Ah, the young artist." The bald man rose from his seat behind the counter, ducking his head to avoid various bottles that hung from the ceiling beams. "I knew you would come."

"I need linseed oil."

"That is all you wish?"

"Yes." A sudden sweat broke out on Osbert's brow, though the air was cool in the darkened shop.

The apothecary rummaged around under the counter, clinking bottles together. "How is your portrait work progressing?"

"I paint landscapes."

"So you said. So you said." The apothecary rose from behind the counter and held out a corked bottle. "I'll put it on your account. Barber said you paid him monthly without fail. I like a man who keeps his bargains."

"Thank you." Osbert took the bottle and quickly exited. Once he was sure the man could not see him through the shop windows, he shuddered in relief. He didn't like the way those dark eyes seemed to look past his own.

AS DAYS BECAME SHORTER AND THE WEATHER COOLER, Osbert saw her less frequently on her walks. And since there were fewer daylight hours for painting landscapes, he spent more time in his cramped room painting portraits by the light of an oil lamp. Often he would paint through the night: a portrait of her smiling coyly or laughing or merely looking to the horizon.

Over the past three nights he had experimented with painting a sequence of small portraits capturing different positions as her head turned until her eyes seemed to look into his. Now as he looked from one painting to the next in order, it was almost as if she moved. Almost.

Soon you will want to bring life to your portraits. Come to me then.

Three times he walked past the apothecary's door before he went inside.

"Ah, the young artist." The apothecary rose to his feet. "More linseed oil? Some White Lead, perhaps?"

"What did you mean?"

The apothecary raised a dark eyebrow. "I am surprised, however, that you are running low on supplies so soon, since the weather is not generally fit for painting landscapes."

Osbert pointed his index finger at the man. "You said I should come to you if I wanted to give life to my portraits. What did you mean?"

The apothecary nodded. "Now you are ready."

"Ready for what?"

"Ready to give life to your work. Are you a religious man, Master Peale?"

Osbert blinked. "I… I'm a God-fearing man, if that's what you mean."

"God-fearing. A good word." The apothecary smiled, his teeth gleaming in the dark shop. "I, too, am God-fearing, you could say."

"Enough of this. What do you know of my painting portraits? What do you mean by 'give life'?"

"You paint portraits of a young lady, perhaps? Someone you desire, but who remains forever beyond your reach?"

Osbert couldn't think what to say. The apothecary seemed to know him intimately.

"You paint her portrait till you know her face better than your own. But you do not know her voice, her touch. She is no more alive to you than a stone." He tapped the stone pestle on the counter. "But there are…other arts beyond the art of painting."

"You practice the arts of witchcraft," Osbert said in astonished realization. He knew he should denounce the apothecary to the Church immediately, but curiosity restrained him.

"Those who fear its power may call it witchcraft. It is nothing more than knowledge, and knowledge is neither good nor evil. 'Tis the use that makes it so."

"Yet you talk of giving life to the creations of men. Surely that is blasphemy, as only God can create life."

The apothecary smiled again. "You are wise for one so young. But I speak not of creating life, but of giving it. Tell me, what is it that makes a man live?"

Osbert pressed his lips together as he thought. "The spirit — the soul."

"And if a painting had a soul?"

"But how is that possible? A soul comes from God, and He would not give one to a mere painting."

"There are heathen tribes who believe that a painting steals the soul of the person portrayed. That is not true — to steal someone's soul into a painting requires the application of magics far beyond their primitive superstitions." The apothecary waved a hand dismissively, then pointed at Osbert. "However, you have a soul. If you are willing to give up part of yours to make the painting live, that is within my power."

Osbert stepped back. "You want me to give you part of my soul? So you can drag me down to damnation piece by piece?"

"No, you would not give it to *me*. You would give it to the painting, give life to the portrait."

Though the response allayed Osbert's suspicions somewhat, he asked, "And what benefit do you receive from this, then, that you would risk hanging as a witch?"

"What benefit? You would pay me, of course."

"I'm not wealthy. I have but twenty pounds a year bequeathed by my uncle. It is enough to live on, but painting is my one luxury." Osbert hoped someday to paint well enough to sell his work, but that day was still to come.

"I will not charge much. The ingredients I require are not costly, excepting the salt. Shall we say, eight shillings?"

Almost half a pound. But to have her speak to him, to be able to touch her would be worth that price. "How do I know I will get my money's worth?"

"You are a man who fulfills his bargains; so am I. I will add the cost to your bill. If you are not satisfied, you can merely refuse to pay."

With such an offer, how could the apothecary possibly swindle him? What suspicions could remain? "How is it done?"

"We will need to cut off a piece of your soul and grind it to a powder you can mix with your paint. Then whatever portrait you paint will be given life."

"The soul is immaterial. How can it be cut or ground?"

The apothecary sighed. "Not everything the Church teaches you is to be believed. The soul is not immaterial; it is a material more refined, more pure than base matter. That is how it can occupy the same space as your body. The trick is to get part of the soul to separate itself from the body, so it can be removed without harming the flesh."

The apothecary turned and reached for a metal saltcellar on the top shelf behind him. "Salt is a symbol of purity because it prevents corruption. That's why it's used for protection against evil spirits. The purity of salt has power."

Osbert nodded.

"But the salt I have here is not common salt. During the Last Supper, Judas Iscariot knocked over a dish of salt. That salt became cursed for all eternity. And I have some of it here."

Skepticism returned to Osbert's mind. "I cannot believe you have the very same salt that was at the Last Supper."

"It matters not what you believe. The power of the salt is real." The apothecary smiled. "But you are a clever young man to see that this is not the very same salt. The spilt salt was collected by one who recognized its power. And when that cursed salt is mixed with uncursed salt, the curse spreads. As it says in the Bible, 'If the salt has lost its savour, wherewith shall it be salted?' So this is known as the Salt of Judas or Traitor's Salt. The grains may not be the same, but the curse is."

Osbert stared in fascination at the saltcellar. "What does the curse do?"

"As normal salt is repellent to an evil spirit, Salt of Judas is repellent to a good spirit, only far stronger in its effects. Place your left hand on the counter here, fingers spread apart."

Osbert did as he was told.

The apothecary reached out and gripped Osbert's wrist with fingers hard and cold as iron. "This will be painful, but no real harm will come to you."

"Painful?" Osbert almost tried to pull his arm back, but the apothecary's grip held him fast.

"It will not last long." The apothecary sprinkled salt onto Osbert's little finger.

Osbert's knees buckled as he felt fire spread across his hand and into his forearm. He exhaled a choking scream, then found himself unable to draw breath. The apothecary's icy fingers tightened on his wrist. His vision blurred with tears, but he thought he saw a wavering tendril of fire rise from the knuckle of his little finger.

"There it is." The apothecary's voice was calm. He had put down the saltcellar and now held a pair of shears. Deftly he snipped the tendril of fire just above the knuckle. The tendril writhed on the counter, leaving scorch marks where it touched. "Looks very much like a salted slug, does it not?"

Still unable to breathe, Osbert tried to yank his hand away, but the apothecary did not let go.

"Oh, yes. The pain." The apothecary pulled Osbert's hand several inches away from the tendril, then poured some water from a bottle onto Osbert's little finger. "Holy water, to wash away the salt. The pain should subside." He finally let go of Osbert's wrist.

Clasping at his finger to make certain it was still there, Osbert realized the pain was easing. He was able to breathe again, and he took several deep breaths to steady himself before shouting, "What did you do to me?"

"Just what I said I would. I sprinkled Salt of Judas on part of your body to force your soul out of that part, allowing me to clip it off." The apothecary used tongs to pick up the tendril of soul and drop it in the mortar. He added some dried leaves, which burst into flames. "The salt also corrupted it enough that we can see it and even touch it." He took a pestle and began pounding it in the mortar. "There are many who say that the curse on the Salt of Judas is the curse of Hell itself, and that the pain you felt is what a damned soul will feel for all eternity, but I don't know that is so."

"You have damned me." His vision dimmed as despair filled his heart. "I have been touched by the curse of Judas."

The apothecary laughed. "You are a good man, Osbert Peale. If your soul were not good, the Salt of Judas would not cause you pain." The apothecary looked in the mortar, ground the mixture a little more, then removed the pestle. "Now, take this powder—" He tilted the mortar and poured an ash-white powder onto a sheet of paper, which he expertly folded. "—mix it with linseed oil, then blend it with the paint on your next portrait."

Osbert looked at the packet but made no move to take it.

"Come now. Are you going to waste all the pain you've suffered? Take it."

Osbert slowly reached out his hand.

THE GRAY LIGHT OF DAWN DIFFUSED FROM THE WINDOW, blending with the yellow from the oil lamp. Still wet, a portrait of her stood lifeless on the easel. On his palette, still unused, was some of the soul-paint.

Osbert feared it would not work. And he feared it would. The events of the night before were becoming confused in his mind. Was the apothecary a charlatan or a puissant witch? Osbert rubbed the little finger of his left hand. It had felt a little numb during the night, then prickly, but seemed almost normal now. Perhaps it was getting accustomed to missing its soul.

He took his blender and dipped it in the translucent soul-paint, then carefully began applying it to her face. Now that he had started, he worked feverishly until there was none of the substance left on his palette.

On the canvas, nothing had changed: her eyes still looked to the distance, her serious expression remained frozen in oils. The pain, the fright, his work — all were for naught. Osbert threw down his palette and painting knife, then stretched himself out in exhaustion upon his cot.

He would deal with the fraudulent apothecary later.

WHEN HE WOKE UP, the first thing he saw was her smile.

A WEEK LATER — SEVEN PORTRAITS LATER — Osbert hurried into the apothecary shop and closed the door. "I need to make more soul-paint. And it needs to be stronger."

"Soul-paint? Apropos." The apothecary's teeth glinted in his smile. "Run out already, have you?"

"She smiles at me. She gazes into my eyes. But she doesn't talk, and when I try to touch her, I can sense her movement but she still feels like paint."

Nodding, the apothecary said, "Yes, a higher concentration is needed to give the portrait more vitality. But that would require a larger portion of your soul. Are you willing to give it?"

The pain hadn't been too much to endure, had it? And it had been over quickly, had it not? "How much would I need?"

The apothecary bobbed his head back and forth in thought. "For talking and touching, let me see…Perhaps, to be on the safe side, we should take the whole hand."

Osbert clenched his left hand into a fist, then opened it again, looking at it carefully. "Will it make a difference to my hand, not having a soul? My finger felt strange that first night."

"Oh, my dear boy! Is that what you thought?" The apothecary laughed. "You do not have a soulless finger, nor will you have a soulless hand. The rest of your soul extends to fill the empty parts. It is the same with fat men — they do not have more of a soul than thin men; their souls just stretch to fill their bulk."

Osbert's relief at this explanation made him realize how much he had feared having a part of his body without a soul. He rolled up his sleeve and put his left hand down on the counter.

THREE DAYS LATER HIS TONGUE WAS STILL SORE from having bitten it during the agony of the salt on his hand, but he was otherwise recovered from the ordeal. Nonetheless, now that he had a sufficient supply of the soul-paint, he was glad he would not need to go through that again.

Osbert glanced at a portrait he had finished the previous week. Her face smiled at him, and her eyelashes fluttered demurely. But that portrait was imperfect, flawed.

He would create a new portrait. This would be his best work, perfectly capturing her eyes, her hair, the flush of her cheek. And this one would speak to him.

"BACK AGAIN, MY YOUNG FRIEND?" The apothecary rose to greet him.

"Her portrait has stopped talking to me. She still smiles, but the earlier ones no longer smile. They are utterly lifeless!" Osbert gripped the edge of the counter.

Running a palm over the smooth dome of his head, the apothecary said, "Interesting. The ground-up soul must be gradually escaping the paint."

"How do I stop it?"

"It is returning to its natural state. I do not think it can be stopped."

Osbert looked at his hand. "Is it coming back into me?"

"I doubt that. You voluntarily surrendered it, so it no longer pertains to you."

"What can be done? I need her."

With an appraising eye, the apothecary looked him up and down. "Perhaps an arm? Just from the elbow down? We'll have to do it piece by piece, though, to fit in the mortar."

THE BANGING ON THE DOOR ROUSED OSBERT from sleep. The afternoon daylight cutting into the room hurt his eyes. He stumbled to the door and opened it a crack.

It was his landlord, the butcher. "Peale, I'm giving you till Saturday to come up with two months' rent, or you'll have to leave."

Desperate confusion swirled in Osbert's mind. He was two months late with rent? "You'll get the money. It's just that my mother's sister is ill, and the leech—"

"I thought you said it was your father's sister."

Had he said that? "This is a difficult time. Illness sweeping through my family's village." He coughed. Why did his chest hurt so?

The butcher took a step back. "You don't look well yourself."

"I'm fine. You'll get your money. Just give me some time."

"Hmph." The butcher turned and went down the stairs.

Osbert sat down on his cot.

"You seem ill, my love." Her voice was melodious, and Osbert felt better just hearing it.

"I'm just tired, is all." He lay back and closed his eyes. Late with the rent? Lying to his landlord? What was wrong with him?

He felt her palm on his forehead. "You're burning up. It's a fever. You need help."

A fever? The apothecary could help. Yes, he must go to the apothecary.

He staggered down the stairs and out onto the street. He was exhausted by the time he reached the apothecary shop, and once inside he allowed himself to sink to the floor.

HE AWOKE IN A STRANGE ROOM, surrounded by portraits of her. One of them smiled at him as he sat up.

"Where am I?" he asked her.

Her shoulders shrugged slightly, but she did not answer.

Osbert walked unsteadily to the door, opened it and looked out. The scents of the apothecary shop met him. "Hallo?" he called out.

"Ah, you are recovered at last," said the apothecary from below. "We were quite worried about you."

"We?"

"The young lady of your portraits and I. Gave us quite a scare, you did."

"What am I doing here? What are my paintings doing here?"

"When you fell ill, you came to me. I then discovered that you were unable to pay the rent for your prior room, so I had everything brought here."

A fog seemed to lift from his mind. He walked down the stairs to confront the apothecary. "That was your fault. I couldn't pay the rent because I spent all my money on soul-paint."

"It does no good to blame me. It was all by your choice. How was I to know you were spending too much?"

Still weak in his legs, Osbert sat down on the floor.

"But you have no worries now, my boy. You can stay here with me, as I can spare the room."

"Thank you." Did he really want to stay here? Where else could he go? Then he remembered her. "The portraits! She didn't talk to me, she only smiled."

"Yes, it's been too long. The power of your soul-paint is fading."

"I need more."

The apothecary smiled. "You are sure? Your soul is stretched so thin I estimate we'd need to take both legs now to have enough."

"Yes, I'm sure." She'd help nurse him back to health, so he owed it to her to bring her back to life.

The apothecary reached up for the saltcellar.

"I THINK I WOULD LIKE TO SEE ONE OF YOUR LANDSCAPES," she said one morning.

"What?"

"You used to paint landscapes, did you not? I should very much like to see one. You have such a talent for painting."

"Then see one you shall. I'll go out and paint one today."

She smiled brightly. "Just for me?"

"Just for you."

He scraped an old canvas, removing one of her lifeless portraits. After gathering his paints, he went downstairs.

"Going somewhere?" asked the apothecary, who was putting on his coat to leave.

"I'm going to paint a landscape."

The apothecary frowned. "Are you sure that's wise? The spring weather is rather damp, and you are still weak. There is illness about — I am going to treat someone even now."

"It's for her. She wants to see a landscape."

"Ah, well if she wants it, how can you refuse? Just don't stay out too long."

HE SAT ON HIS STOOL on the bank of the Avon. The canvas before him held only a half-hearted charcoal sketch. It had been so long since he had done a landscape that nothing seemed right.

"Trouble painting?" A man's voice came from behind him.

Osbert turned to see an elderly monk from the abbey. "Yes, I'm afraid I'm somewhat out of practice."

The monk nodded. "I recall having seen you painting many a day last year, but not in recent months."

"I've been ill."

"Ah."

The silence stretched. Osbert raised his charcoal to the canvas, then brought it back down. He turned to look at the monk again. "Is it a sin to paint a portrait of…of a young lady?"

The monk raised his eyebrows. "I've never been asked that before."

"Is it?"

"The Muslim believes all images of people are prohibited. And I've read of primitive tribes that believe an image can trap the soul of the person portrayed. But portraiture in itself is not against the laws of Christ."

Osbert nodded gratefully, though the talk of souls trapped in images came uncomfortably close to his secret.

"But this young lady whose portrait you paint — is there perhaps more to it than that? Is that what troubles you?"

Suddenly Osbert no longer wanted to talk to this monk. He stood up. "I've been outside too long. I must get back. My health, you understand."

The monk nodded. "May God speed your recovery."

IN THE MIDDLE OF THE NIGHT Osbert awoke to pounding on the door of the shop. He heard the apothecary call out that he was coming.

"I wonder who is ill tonight." Her voice was concerned.

"I'll find out," he said. Rising from his bed, he opened the door and crept out to sit on the stairs and eavesdrop.

A man was speaking, an edge of desperation in his voice. "—grows ever weaker. It's as if the very life were being drained from her body."

The apothecary's voice was sympathetic. "I don't know what else is to be done but help her sleep better. This illness is beyond my power to aid."

"I don't understand it. My daughter was always a picture of health, until last autumn."

"It is most mysterious."

"Is there nothing in your books? Please, you must help my Amelia. I'll pay whatever you ask."

"I am sorry," said the apothecary. "Take this powder to ease her rest. That is all I can do."

Osbert barely heard the door of the shop shut. His mind was awhirl. Amelia. Was this coincidence? No. His portraits of her were somehow harming the real young woman, drawing the life out of her. He tried to reject the thought, but he remembered the primitive belief the monk had mentioned about images trapping the soul of the person portrayed. The apothecary had mentioned it, too, Osbert recalled now. It had to be true — he was the cause of Amelia's suffering.

He rose to his feet and descended the stairs. The apothecary was sitting in his chair behind the counter. On seeing Osbert, he rose to his feet.

Clenching his fists, Osbert said, "What have you done to Amelia?"

"I've done nothing to the young lady."

"It's me, isn't it? My portraits are stealing pieces of her soul."

"You imagine things, dear boy. Go back to bed and get some rest." The apothecary didn't look him in the eye.

"How do I set things right?"

The apothecary sighed. "You can't. By painting her image with the soul-paint, you have robbed that girl of most of her soul, binding it permanently away from her. she will die shortly, and it is your obsession that has killed her."

What could Osbert do? "I'll destroy the paintings. Burn them all."

"Ignorant child. You are dealing with magics of the soul. Mere flames cannot break such bindings."

Osbert lunged forward and grabbed at the apothecary, who broke the grip with ease and pushed him to the floor.

Tears of hopelessness welled in his eyes, then began to flow down his cheeks. "Dear God, what have I done?"

The apothecary laughed. "Yes, now you call out to Him. Far too late, of course."

Wiping at the tears on his face, Osbert realized he was damned. Step by step, he had brought ruin upon himself and Amelia.

And then as he licked at his lips, he tasted his tears. Salt. The Salt of Judas.

He rose to his feet. The apothecary had moved to the doorway and was bolting it shut. Osbert climbed up on the counter and grabbed the saltcellar from the top shelf behind it. The apothecary spotted him as he climbed down from the counter.

"What are you doing? Give that back!" The apothecary's voice was angry.

Osbert ran up the stairs to his room, locked the door and pulled off his nightshirt.

"Stop!" yelled the apothecary from below.

Ordinary flames might not burn the paintings and release the pieces of Amelia's soul, but perhaps the magical fire of his burning soul could. He hurriedly piled the portraits of Amelia in the middle of the room as the apothecary banged on the door. He could hear the voice of the portraits asking what he was doing.

Lying back on the portraits, he unscrewed the top of the saltcellar and spilled the salt upon his chest.

His body spasmed as gouts of pale fire spread from his chest. The pain twisted his mind and all reason fled. All that remained was the desire to destroy the portraits. Flames surrounded him and then all went dark.

AS HE RETURNED TO CONSCIOUSNESS, he felt a burning sensation over most of his body. The scent of smoke filled his nostrils. This must be hell, his eternal destiny. As he opened his eyes, though, he saw the old monk leaning over him, not a devil.

"He's awake," said the monk to someone outside Osbert's view. "Be still, young man. That you are alive is a miracle, though you have some burns on your body from the fire."

Osbert tried to speak, but at first could not find a voice in his dry throat. Finally he managed to whisper, "Where am I?"

"The infirmary at Tewkesbury Abbey. Be still."

"Where is the apothecary?"

The monk shook his head. "He must have been consumed by the fire. We did not find his body."

Osbert found it hard to believe the apothecary was truly dead. "And my paintings?"

"They are destroyed. The entire building burned to ashes; there is nothing left. But you must rest. Go back to sleep."

PROPPED UP ON HIS BED IN THE INFIRMARY, Osbert drank the broth that was supposed to restore his strength. It was no use, he knew — his strength was gone because he had given up most of his soul, not because of his injuries.

The one real comfort he had was that Amelia still lived, and was said to be recovering slowly. At least her death was not on his conscience.

The old monk arrived and sat on a stool by Osbert's bed. "I have something for you." He reached into a sack and brought out the saltcellar.

Osbert nearly spilled his broth. "Where did you get that?" he whispered.

"You were clutching it when we found you. It is a symbol of the miracle that saved you."

Saved? He could not be saved. "What do you mean?"

"After the fire burned out, no one thought anybody could have survived. But then you were found in the midst of the ashes, still alive, with a pile of salt on your chest and this saltcellar in your hand." The monk smiled. "I know salt is a preservative, but I didn't think it had quite so much power."

"That salt had magical properties." For what evil fate had the Salt of Judas saved him?

The monk laughed. "It is but ordinary salt." He opened up the saltcellar, dipped his finger in, and dabbed some crystals on his tongue. "See?"

Osbert held his breath for a moment, but nothing happened to the monk. "It cannot be. I saw it. The apothecary…"

The monk raised an eyebrow. "The apothecary claimed it was magical salt? I had my suspicions the man was a fraud."

"He was no fraud. At least, not the way you think." What purpose was there in hiding the truth? Osbert felt as if a burden lifted from his shoulders as he quietly began to tell the monk what he had done.

"SO I TRIED TO RELEASE AMELIA'S SOUL by burning the paintings with the magical fire, and that's the last thing I remember before I awoke after the fire," Osbert finished.

During Osbert's narration, the monk had not interrupted, although he had frowned at several points. Now the monk leaned forward and stared into Osbert's eyes. After a few seconds, he said, "You do not appear to be either a madman or a liar, and I cannot see why you would concoct such a tale. I believe you."

"Thank you." It was a relief to be believed. Osbert looked at the saltcellar still gripped in the monk's hands. "But I still don't understand why the Salt of Judas didn't burn you when you touched it. What happened to the curse?"

The monk looked up to the ceiling of the infirmary. Osbert followed his gaze, but he could see nothing.

The monk looked back down to Osbert. "The salt lost its savour through an act of betrayal. Perhaps it took an act of sacrifice to let it be salted again."

THE CANVAS BEFORE HIM WAS NEARLY COMPLETE. The image of Tewkesbury Abbey was ethereal, wreathed in morning mist, though the actual mist had vanished hours ago. Osbert paused as he carefully considered where to add a little more shadow.

"You paint very well," said a voice over his shoulder.

He knew before turning that it was Amelia. She had recently begun taking walks again as she had recovered from her illness, and he had seen her every few days over the past month. But this was the first time she had spoken to him.

"Thank you, Miss." He turned back to the canvas.

"Perhaps one day you could paint a portrait of me," Amelia said.

"I only paint landscapes."

ONE OF ERIC JAMES STONE'S EARLIEST MEMORIES is of seeing an Apollo moon-shot launch on television. That — plus his father's collection of old science fiction — might explain his fascination with astronomy and space travel. Despite taking creative writing classes in the 1980s, Eric did not begin seriously writing fiction until 2002. In 2003 he attended Orson Scott Card's Literary Boot Camp. Since then, he has sold stories to the Writers of the Future Contest, Analog, *and* Intergalactic Medicine Show. *His personal website is www.ericjamesstone.com.*

BUTTON BY BUTTON

BY E. CATHERINE TOBLER

SHE HAD KNOWN HIM FOR FIVE YEARS and he was leaving her.

Alice Oxbridge stared into the watery depths of her tea, sweeping the silver spoon around again. Lord Covington was a gracious host, yet he left much to be desired when it came to measuring sugar.

As Covington rambled about his latest excursion to Africa, Alice's attention wandered to the tall arced window at the end of the room. It looked out onto a garden, much like any other garden she had seen in her lifetime. Now, her mind drifted backward in time five years; her eyes grew heavy and the wave of the leaves took her away.

Edward O'Brien had been in her garden that day, tall figure bent, his nose pressed into a ruffled geranium. Alice had studied him for the longest time, finding the cut of his suit odd and the shine of his boots nonexistent. Was he lost? Had he come to call on her younger sister? Alice did not recognize him; he was no one she had seen in London.

When he didn't leave, Alice had gone out to him. If he needed assistance, she would give what she could. Perhaps he was looking for Covington.

"Sir?"

He hadn't turned around; he continued smelling the geranium, fingers brushing the broad leaves. Alice could imagine the smell of them, dusty and peppery, making her sneeze.

"Excuse me, sir?"

Again, nothing. Alice was annoyed; what business did this man have in her garden and why wasn't he willing to share? Alice had taken another step toward him and had begun to reach for the sleeve of his jacket when he turned. His eyes were like vapor over a pond, then they settled into an ordinary brown. Alice blinked, certain she had imagined it.

"Madam, do forgive me," he said, reaching for Alice's hand.

Then he stopped, holding her hand and staring in what Alice could only define as awe. He turned her hand over and back again, fingers running over hers, then over the multitude of buttons that ran up her wrist and arm. His fingers pressed at the gray material, wrinkles amassing at her wrist. One button popped open, revealing pale skin.

"You're an odd construct," he said, looking up at Alice, who withdrew her hand and hid it behind her back.

"And you, sir, are rude. What business do you have in this garden?"

"I came to see the widow Templeton, but am I to understand she is no longer in residence?" He looked toward the house in the distance. Alice looked as well, seeing nothing remarkable in the red brick or the white shutters.

"The widow Templeton lives a mile east of here, sir," Alice said as he went back to the flowers. A frown creased her brow and she followed. "I can't understand how you mistook this place for hers. Her brick is ivory, while mine is red."

"The garden," he said. "There are so many here — I mistook your geraniums for hers, though yours are better tended." He looked at Alice. "Forgive my manners. I'm Edward O'Brien." He extended his hand, but Alice did not take it. He withdrew the hand and turned back to the flowers.

"You don't look or sound Irish," Alice said, following him as he walked along the flowerbed.

"I'm not," Edward said with a wide grin.

"What game do you play, sir?" Alice looked toward the house; there was no sign of her sister. If they were late to tea at the Bain's—

"No game. I'm not Irish." He stood up again from the flowers. "I lived in Ireland for a time, though; took my name from the people."

"Took your name? Didn't your parents name you upon your birth?" A pain began to bloom in Alice's temple and she lifted a hand, pressing. Edward's eyes followed her hand, focusing on the buttons of her glove.

"They did," he said, nodding, "but it wasn't a proper name for this place."

"This place?" Alice looked around the garden.

"Earth."

Alice turned away from Edward. "You can find the widow Templeton on Cross Street, sir. Good day to you."

She walked as quickly as could, but feared she might stumble when she reached the courtyard. She drew in a breath and realized she was shaking. When she looked back to the garden, the man was gone.

So began her relationship with Edward O'Brien.

TWO WEEKS LATER, ALICE SAW HIM AGAIN; he lingered beside a cherry tree, long fingers trailing over the leaves. The gnarled trees made a rough border around the building. Though pretty in the spring, they stood like men in the winter, hunched and thin. Alice left her sister to the church ladies. Edward's eyes lit up when he saw her.

"Looking for the widow Templeton again?" Alice gestured to the church steps. "She's there, with Father Brandenburg now."

"No, no," Edward said in a hushed tone. "Not looking for her. Came to look upon these old trees."

"I asked her about you," Alice said, circling the tree to get a closer look at Edward. His features were almost feminine, lashes long, nose straight, mouth full. "She said she didn't know any Edward O'Brien."

"Then you have caught me in a lie." Edward pressed a hand against his chest. "It seems I am always asking your forgiveness. Would once more be too much?"

"Yes, unless you explain yourself." Alice clutched her Bible in her hands, waiting. When Edward made no move to speak, she continued. "You said you took your name, that the one your parents had given you was not right for this place, meaning Earth. Explain yourself."

"I said all that?" Edward withdrew a handkerchief, patting at his brow. "You did."

"One would think after all my time here, I would learn to hold my tongue in certain matters. Miss — It occurs to me that I don't know your name."

Alice straightened, determined not to give it to him. At that exact moment, her sister bellowed.

"Alice! We're leaving without you if you don't come directly!"

"Alice," Edward said, making the name a sigh.

Alice said nothing, turning and walking away from the trees, and Edward, and every question she wanted to ask. The man made no sense; there was no reason to continue.

"I shall call on you, Alice," he said.

Alice turned, but again, he had gone.

TWO DAYS LATER, HE CAME TO CALL.

Swathed in her veil-draped hat and thick gloves, Alice dipped her hand into the hive, bees swarming around her. She didn't know Edward was there until he cleared his throat. She looked up at him, surprised at the way the bees seemed to be avoiding him. He cut a path right through their saffron cloud and came to stand beside the hive. The hum from the insects increased.

"You're frightening them," Alice said, withdrawing a hunk of honey-comb. "They don't know what you are." I don't know what you are, she thought, angry that she was attracted by the mystery. She loved mysteries and now, she had a great one.

Edward stepped back, letting Alice work. The bees calmed. She shoved the honeycomb into the jar she'd brought, brushing an errant bee on its way. Edward was roaming the garden by this point. Alice set the jar of honeycomb aside, stripping her gloves off and brushing her veil back; retrieving the jar, she set off in search of Edward.

She found him admiring a stand of lilac bushes, his nose buried in a large purple bunch of the flowers. Alice smiled, amused by the sight of the large man enjoying the simple scent of a lilac.

"They are my favorites."

"I can understand why," he said, moving along the line of bushes; his hand brushed the leaves as he went. "Walk with me, Alice?"

She fell into step with him, sneaking glances at him as they went. He was handsome, there was no denying that, but it was the mystery about him that attracted her. Her sister and aunt had not heard of Edward O'Brien. He had appeared out of nothingness, whole and mysterious.

"Who planted this garden?" he asked as they stepped onto the flagstone walk that led to the goldfish pond.

"My great-great grandmother."

"Your people have been here a long time then."

"Quite," Alice said. "I suspect the garden would have been planted earlier, but no one had the energy Margaret had. How long have your people been here?" She should have been shocked by the question, that she had the courage to ask it, but Edward smiled.

"Longer than that, Alice." He looked at her, eyes vapor, then normal. "You are the first one I've told and the only one to see me slip for even a moment. My time here has been long, though I haven't done enough, seen enough."

Alice looked away from him, disturbed by the admission. She didn't know what to make of it. How could this man not be of this place, of Earth? She watched Edward walk to the edge of the pond; he kneeled and stroked his fingers across the surface of the water.

"What is that in your jar, Alice?"

She looked down at it, having forgotten she was holding it. "Honey and comb," she said, holding it up to the light. It looked like the comb was melting, honey running like liquid gold into the jar.

"Have you ever had any?" she asked. When he shook his head, Alice removed the lid from the jar, breaking off a bit of the honeycomb. She brought it to Edward, pressing it to his lips. His mouth opened and she popped it inside; his eyes closed as he chewed. Alice withdrew her hand, honey dribbling on her skirt, on the stones. All around her, the air was alive; it seemed to vibrate with Edward's happiness.

Alice couldn't help but smile.

TWO MORE WEEKS PASSED. Alice was exiting the church when she spied Edward's coattails vanishing into the garden. Slipping away from the crowd on the lawn, Alice followed.

"Edward? Are you— Oh!"

Edward's hands fell to Alice's cinched waist, pulling her backward, turning her to face him. She smiled up at him as he handed her a small package.

"You gave me the great gift of your honey," Edward said, "and I thought to repay you."

Alice looked down at the box, shaking her head. "That really wasn't necessary." How would she explain such a gift to her aunt? "I can't—"

"I've been here long enough to have seen women enjoying these things." Edward took the box back, prying it open. Inside lay a delicate gold bracelet. He picked it up and held it out to Alice.

"My glove will have to come off," she said, shaking her head again. "Edward." She looked over her shoulder, but no one had followed.

Palming the bracelet, Edward stepped forward, grasping Alice's glove. "I don't know how this works."

"The buttons," Alice said as he extended her left arm. Edward's finger ran over the long line of buttons and he nibbled his lip in consideration.

As the first button came open, Alice squeezed her eyes shut. This wasn't proper. No man save her husband should be unbuttoning her gloves, yet Alice felt the glove come apart, button by button, and then felt Edward's fingers on her skin. She opened her eyes to see the astonishment in his.

"Why do you hide your hands?" he asked, reaching for the fingers of the glove.

"They—" Little finger. "Protect." Ring finger. "And keep me—" Middle finger, index. "Ladylike." Thumb. The glove came away in a gray twist and Alice knew then how foolish they were. Gloves did nothing but confine.

Alice stretched her fingers, Edward wrapping the bracelet around her wrist. When done, he stepped back, and smiled, pressing her glove to his nose. Alice flushed. "Oh Edward, I–" He stepped forward again.

Finger by finger, he replaced her glove, pulling the fabric over her wrist and arm. "No one has to know."

But I will, Alice thought, feeling the line of the bracelet and the whisper of Edward's fingers as he fastened the glove, button by button.

"**WHY DO YOU ALWAYS HAVE TO BE SO CONTRARY,** Alice? It's an evening in the park; you enjoy those."

Alice shook her head. "Not tonight." She didn't need to look up from her book to know her sister was wearing a frown that would have made a man's knees weak. Anne Oxbridge had a dozen suitors; Alice wished she would settle on one.

Anne left the study with a huff and Alice smiled, Anne's heels thundering on the marble floors. She would be going to Cook now, telling her to unpack Alice's food from the picnic basket. Alice stretched out on the sofa, her book falling into her lap.

She closed her eyes and listened as Anne made a noisy exit from the house, doors slamming. With her temper it was no wonder Anne hadn't received a proposal from her suitors.

Good marriages had been the only thing their parents had wanted for them. Though their parents were five years dead, the wish clung; good marriages to strong men who would support them for the rest of their days. Anne saw nothing wrong with that, though Alice didn't want to be supported. She wanted to fly on her own.

Alice fell asleep on the couch, waking when the moon was high and the sky star-scattered. She closed her book, wondering if Anne was home yet. The house was silent. Not even the grandfather clock ticked. Alice approached it, frowning. The hands and pendulum were still.

She walked through the darkened rooms. "Anne?" she asked, looking up the staircase. Silence replied.

"Anne?" Her voice trembled now and tried to tell herself she was being foolish, but the air didn't feel right; it seemed as though someone would walk up at any moment and touch her shoulder.

Alice turned, pressing her back to the banister. She saw that the outer study door was open. She moved from the foyer to the study, the rustle of her skirts breaking the silence. Grasping the edge of the door, Alice realized with a moment of panic that anyone could have come inside.

And then, she saw Edward on the small porch off of the study. He was leaning over the moon-splashed roses, smelling them. Had he opened the door?

"Edward?" she asked.

He turned and smiled, extending a hand to her. "Alice, come enjoy the night with me."

Alice looked back over her shoulder, feeling as though every nerve in her body had been rubbed with ice. It was silent and cold in the house, though the outside air was warm and sweet. Alice went to Edward, placing her ungloved hand in his.

It had been another two weeks since Edward had given her the bracelet. Alice smiled at the memory, but after that incident, he had vanished again.

"Where do you go when you aren't here?" she asked as his bare fingers closed over hers. She looked up into his dark eyes, starlight seeming to hang there.

"There is always somewhere to go," Edward said, "something new to explore."

"Then why do you come back?"

Edward smiled Alice's hand. "Perhaps that is the true question."

He tucked her hand into his bent arm and they walked off the porch, into the cool grass. As Alice's skirts caught on the rosebush, she turned, only then seeing the moths suspended in flight.

"Edward, what have you done?" She reached out and touched them, but they didn't move; their wings were frozen silk.

"I've given us a piece of time, Alice." He smiled and pulled her along. "Come on!"

He laughed and she followed, running as he ran, striving to keep up through the moonlit garden. Edward was a dark shape ahead of her, the tails of his coat flying out behind him; Alice could have sworn that they weren't coattails at all, but wings — and maybe they were.

Alice followed, but began to tire; her breath caught in her throat and she slowed, calling for Edward to wait. He turned and in one smooth motion, swept her into his arms, continuing their flight through the gardens.

Widow Templeton's peonies burst apart as they rumbled through, a shower of pale pink and magenta petals whirling as if in a storm; Lord Covington's daisies didn't stand a chance against the wind they created, "he loves me, he loves me not" seeming to echo in their wake. Delicate lilacs came apart, mixing with leaves, and rose petals, and the ever-present scent of tilled earth.

"We don't have flowers on my world," Edward said later, plucking petals from Alice's hair. They sat atop the pavilion in the park, looking at the still people below, at the fiery stars above. He crushed a lilac bloom in his hand and inhaled. "I wish that I could become flowers, that I could be this scent."

"No flowers," Alice whispered, leaning back against his chest. She shook her head, finding it impossible to imagine. What did they have then? Was his world at all like Earth? "Is that why you came here?"

"We came to study everything," Edward said. "For me, flowers were a bonus. You should see some of my companions — they are allergic to everything you can imagine. Flowers, felines, everything."

Alice smiled. "There are humans like that as well."

"Perhaps why we blend so well." Edward brushed a lock of Alice's hair back over her ear, separating a peony petal from the simple hairpin she wore.

"Do you stop time when you study things?" she asked. "If you have, I've no memory of it."

"We prefer studying your world in motion. This moment is ours alone because I wished it so. Those of my kind still study."

Alice turned in Edward's arms, her eyes searching his. "How many of your kind are here?" she asked, fear skipping down her spine.

"Only five. Six if you count me. We're a small team. There are others throughout the galaxy, busy with other worlds." His hand came up, seeming to brush against the sky.

"Other worlds." Alice looked up. She had never considered there could be worlds other than this one, that the stars were anything more than pretty light. "That scares me," she whispered. "How many others? How many studying us like bugs?"

"Not bugs, Alice." He squeezed her cool hand. "We just want to understand different creatures."

"Earth is nothing more than a jar you look into!"

"No," Edward insisted. "Alice — we aren't supposed to interact with others and perhaps this is why. But when I saw you in your garden with your gloves — and, oh, those buttons. You captivated me, Alice."

"All this time on Earth and you hadn't seen gloves?"

"All this time on Earth and I've not spoken with another human like this," he said. "We stay as separate as we can. No one had confronted me as you did. We learn from a distance, interacting only when we must." Edward squeezed Alice's hands. "You were different. I shouldn't have been caught in your garden, but there you were. I shouldn't have come back, but I did. And here we are."

Alice looked over the still people in the park. Somewhere down there was her sister, perhaps frozen in a kiss with one of her many suitors. Somewhere down there, a man had taken a bite of a sandwich and waited to swallow. The entire world was draped in ice, until Edward freed it. The power terrified Alice.

She shook her head, looking back at Edward. "You scare me, Edward," she said. "Take me home."

And so, he did.

WINTER ERASED AUTUMN AND EDWARD STAYED AWAY. Alice took to her rooms, withdrawing from her sister and aunt. Ice coated the trees and Alice wondered if Edward had snow on his world, or trees at all. Though he was not at her side, he occupied a great deal of her time.

Had he returned to his own world? Was he in the southern hemisphere studying the flowers there? Were those flowers like any she knew here?

Edward's abilities scared her, but being alone was even more frightening. Alice realized she had lost a good friend. Edward had trusted in her to keep his secret, had told her things he hadn't told another human, and she had pushed him away.

What was it like, she wondered, to travel to another world, six alien people amid millions of others? How difficult had it been to stay apart from everyone except the other five with you? And how brave had Edward been to reach out to her at all?

A pounding on her door roused Alice from her thoughts. "Alice!" Anne called. "There is a man at the door."

"Open it and ask what he wants," Alice said, closing her book, waiting for Anne to go away.

"I mean — he's lurking there, Alice, like a thief or something. He hasn't rung the bell or called. I think he's studying the wreath!"

Alice opened her door, looking at Anne's panicked features. "I'll handle it," she said, brushing past Anne.

Alice's heart seemed to be in her throat. She swallowed hard. A man studying the wreath. She reached for the doorknob, then hesitated, peering out the leaded glass window beside the door. The man was turned into a watery shape, nothing solid at all. Alice scowled and opened the door. Edward stumbled forward, his finger sliding along the wreath. He bit out a word that Alice took for a curse, pushing him back to the porch as she came outside.

"What are you doing here?" she asked, looking at Edward's hand. He had caught his finger on the holly wreath and was now bleeding. Alice pulled the handkerchief from his coat pocket, wrapping it around his finger.

"Winter brings its own share of mysteries," Edward said, breath fogging. "What is this?" He reached out, plucking a red berry from the glossy green leaves.

"Holly," Alice said, knotting the handkerchief. "But don't–" Before she could warn him, Edward had popped the berry into his mouth. "They're poisonous — to humans."

"Delicious," Edward said.

"Why did you come back?" Alice's hands curled into the arm of his coat. The air was cold and bit at her skin; she wondered if he would like to come inside for tea.

"I lost a good friend," Edward said, his eyes warm and genuine, "and I was hoping to find her again."

"Come inside." Alice tugged on his arm, opening the door. "We'll have tea and something to eat. Something that isn't poisonous."

"With honey?" he asked as the door closed behind them.

"...**AFTER ALL, I DIDN'T WANT TO FIRE** and ruin the pelt. Miss Oxbridge?"

Alice looked at Lord Covington, managing a smile. "Whatever did you do?" she asked as though she had been paying attention the entire time. Are there roses in China?

"Climbed up the tree and..."

His words faded again as Alice rose from her chair and went to the long table against the wall. She added more tea to her cup, the hot rush of fresh liquid dissolving the sugar that clung to the bottom. What sort of gardens must Egypt have?

Alice sipped, looking at Covington's clock. It was almost time to say goodbye. Behind her, Covington's laughter rumbled and Alice turned with a smile. "You are the clever one." She looked up at the lion's head above his fireplace. What birds had those eyes seen? "When do you leave again?"

"Soon. Africa calls, I must go."

"And so must I," Alice said, setting her teacup down. "Anne and I have plans this evening."

A smile spread across Covington's weathered face and he kissed Alice's cheeks before letting her go. "A beautiful spring evening should be spent with your beau."

"He's not my beau," Alice said, though it was a tired argument. Half the town believed she and Edward had secretly married.

She left Covington's home and headed for her garden, which had only grown more beautiful over the past five years. Edward had helped tend the flowers and trees and loved spending time feeding the goldfish. He stayed away from the bees, but Alice gave him honeycomb whenever she came from the hives.

Above her, thunder rumbled and Alice felt the first touch of raindrops. She hurried through the garden, picking flowers as she went. Alice felt as though her hands were overflowing, but still that it would never be enough.

She found Edward where she had met him, bending over a geranium. Edward breathed, never removing his nose from the flower and Alice smiled.

"Sir?" she asked, much as she had on that first day. He didn't turn her way. "Excuse me, sir?"

Now, Edward turned and Alice shivered when she looked into his vapory eyes. They were like mist over a lake, calm and still, somehow soothing. He blinked, but the reality didn't fade and for that, Alice was thankful. Did he have wings tucked under his coat? Were his clothes real at all? There were too many questions left unanswered — he couldn't possibly leave.

"Edward," she said, her voice breaking. "I don't even know your real name." She blinked tears away. "Oh, I promised I wouldn't cry."

Edward closed the distance between them, wiping her tears away. "I've got to go, Alice. There are so many things to see."

"Will you come back?" she asked, afraid now of the answer.

"I always do," Edward said with a grin, kissing Alice's cheek. A poppy fell from her grip and he bent to pick it up, smelling the orange bloom.

"You don't even have flowers where you're going." Alice pressed all she held into Edward's arms, making him look like he'd caught a bridal bouquet.

Edward tossed the flowers into the air and as Alice watched, time stopped. Edward coated each petal and stem in ice, shaping them into a ball which he placed in his pocket. "Now I do," he said, brushing a kiss over Alice's cheek. He smelled like peppery geraniums and Alice sneezed against his lapel.

Edward left without saying goodbye, rushing headlong into the gardens, coattails blurring into wings. Alice wanted to move, but she felt rooted; lilac petals clung to her dress, and she remembered the night five years ago when Edward had taken them from her hair; daisy pollen coated her fingers, and "he loves me, he loves me not" echoed all around her.

Alice could feel the air tingling with his happiness and she turned in a wide circle, stretching her hands to the sky. When she stopped, Edward had vanished, but the world around her seemed to keep moving.

This was what Edward relished, and Covington when he traveled. This was what made them feel alive and frightened in the same instant; the endless possibility that lay beyond the walls of this garden and so many others.

The images she had seen in books were more than flat photographs; those places existed in a hundred shades of color, not in sepia, black, and white. Somewhere, someone like Edward smelled foreign flowers, perhaps standing knee-deep in mossy water do to so. Women with bare hands worked the earth, feeding and nurturing it so more flowers would come. Dirt under nails, hands browned by the sun, trousers soaked with mossy water.

"Take it button by button, Alice," she said. She had stayed in this place all her life, but it was time to breach the garden walls. There were, after all, so many things to see.

GIRL FRIDAY BY DAY, WRITER BY NIGHT, E. CATHERINE TOBLER still dreams of being a pirate. Her fiction has appeared in Scifiction, Realms of Fantasy, Talebones, *and* Lady Churchill's Rosebud Wristlet. *She lives in Colorado. For more visit www.ecatherine.com.*

 BLACK BOXES

BY MATTHEW S. ROTUNDO

"**MR. SABLE, MY NAME IS JEREMY ALDRICH.** I'm a public defender. I've been assigned to represent you in court."

Sable sat cross-legged on the concrete floor of his cell, arms folded, rocking himself. A small sound escaped his throat.

"Mr. Sable, do you know why I'm here? Do you understand that you've been charged with murder?"

Jeremy's voice echoed hollowly off the cinder block walls. Sable gave no reply.

"Mr. Sable, do you know why you're here?"

Sable paused in his rocking. "Little brother is watching you," he whispered. "Little brother is watching." Jeremy frowned. He sat on the edge of Sable's cot, opened his briefcase, and dug out a yellow legal pad and pen. At the top of the paper, he scribbled the words Sable: First Interview. On the next line, he jotted *little brother — contact family* and added a question mark.

The alleged killer was smaller of frame than he would have thought. The arrest report listed him at five foot eight and a half, a hundred and twenty pounds. Triangular face, thinning brown hair, eyeglasses, sallow cheeks. Dressed in an orange inmate singlesuit. Identified as Franklin Lee Sable. The accused.

A fairly intelligent man, according to the file. Degree in electronics engineering. He had lost his job about a year ago… right around the time the murders began.

The Black Box Killer, the pundits called him. Fourteen murders.

Fourteen mutilated bodies. Jeremy, who had sat in on more homicide cases than he cared to count, had been sickened by the coroner's playbacks.

He cleared his throat. "Mr. Sable, would you like to discuss the details of your case?"

Sable resumed his rocking. His lips moved silently.

"The...ah, remains found in your trash barrel have been sent to the pathologist. The report isn't back yet, but I think we should prepare ourselves for the worst."

Jeremy paused for a reply, got none. "Mr. Sable, our conversation is protected by lawyer-client privilege. None of what I save on my personal recorder can be used as evidence in court. Your black box is protected in the same way. You may speak candidly with me."

"Black box," Sable said. "I'm a black box. Black box." Jeremy leaned forward for a closer look at the man's eyes, waving a hand in front of his face. Sable rocked, unseeing.

Jeremy scribbled more notes on his legal pad: *psych exam...competency hearing?*

Angry red scars stood out on the back of Sable's neck, a jarring contrast to his pale skin. The wounds were self-inflicted, according to the arrest report. Jeremy scratched absently at the back of his own neck; the skin around his output jack was dry and irritated. He wrote *possible suicide attempt* and added another question mark.

He remained in the cell for another hour, making notes, outlining the beginnings of a defense strategy, trying to get Sable to talk. The alleged killer remained unresponsive. When he had seen enough, Jeremy stuffed his pad back into his briefcase and stood. "I'll be back, Mr. Sable. If you need to get in touch with me, let the guard outside know."

He lingered a moment longer, staring down at the scrawny man on the floor — the enigma he had been assigned to decipher.

The guard unsealed the cell door and showed him out.

HE STAYED LATE AT THE OFFICE that night, watching playback on a wall monitor in a darkened conference room until his eyes burned in their sockets. Papers from the case file lay scattered across the table before him.

Every second of the arrest had been dutifully recorded: from the moment officers had arrived on the scene to investigate reports of a disturbance to the discovery of Sable lying in a fetal position on the living room carpet, the back of his neck slicked with blood, a scalpel clutched in one hand. He was surrounded by scattered components from a television and stereo that had been smashed. On tape, both arresting officers made mention of an awful stench permeating the house, which had led to the search. In the garage, they found a taser gun, a crowbar, and trash bags full of blood and what appeared to be brain matter.

Jeremy reviewed the attempted interrogation of Sable, carefully watching the chrono readouts for any unexplained gaps or other signs that the playback had been spliced. He detected none, nor did he find any improprieties in the questioning. As he had with Jeremy, Sable responded to the interrogation by rocking himself and muttering nonsense.

A knock came at the conference room door, and Anna Sullivan stepped in. "Sorry to interrupt, Jeremy," she said. "I got your memo. You wanted to talk to me?"

Jeremy stopped the playback. The wall monitor went dead; the lights brightened. He squinted as his tired eyes tried to adapt.

Anna sat down across the table from him, glancing briefly at the papers scattered on its surface. Her smartly curled hair and her business suit — still neatly creased even after a long day's work — clashed with Jeremy's rumpled shirt and disheveled appearance. "Working late yourself, I see," she said.

"Yeah. Unfortunately." He pulled a tiny bottle of moisturizer from his suit pocket and squeezed a few cooling drops into each eye.

"What did you want to see me about?"

Jeremy massaged his temples. "It's becoming clear that the Sable trial is going to demand all my time. I don't suppose you have any room in your caseload, do you?"

Anna laughed incredulously. "Are you kidding? There isn't a lawyer in this office with room for another case, Jeremy."

"Sorry. Stupid question, I guess. But I had to ask, and you have the most seniority."

Anna studied him for long moments before responding. "You know, you shouldn't be throwing so much of yourself into this case. What's the point? Sable's going down."

"Not necessarily. I still have an insanity defense."

"No, you don't. The guy destroyed evidence, Jeremy."

He sighed. As usual, Anna had put her finger directly on the crux of the case.

Sable's alleged victims ranged from teenaged to elderly, six men, eight women. Among the murdered were four prostitutes, an emergency room intern, a policeman, a local crime reporter...others. All the victims were in some way connected with the seedier side. All had been abducted, strangled, and mutilated so horribly that they had to be identified with fingerprints and dental records. Their foreheads had been split open and pried apart — with a crowbar, the coroners' reports suggested. Much of the victims' cerebrums had been ripped out in order to get at the personal recorders implanted at the bases of their brains. Sable had paid attention to detail: not only were the wafer-thin central storage units removed, medical examiners also found no trace of the spidery control leads that connected the units to the frontal lobes. The victims' eyes had been gouged out to get at the optic nerve leads; the sides of their heads had been cracked open to retrieve the auditory sensors. Even the output jacks, located in the back of the neck, had been removed.

Some pundits in the media had speculated that the murders were the future of crime. After all, personal recorders — or black boxes, as they were called — were marketed as the last word in security: the ultimate, omnipresent eyewitness. Ripping out a person's black box, the pundits suggested, was only logical.

"Yes," Jeremy said. "It's a sticking point, I know. Destroying the black boxes demonstrates an understanding of how they could incriminate him. But I've visited the guy. I'm telling you, he has no idea what's happening to him."

"He's faking it."

"You sound so sure of yourself."

"Years of experience, Jeremy. Don't let this guy fool you."

"Thanks." He cradled his head in his hands, staring at his scattered case file.

"Oh, quit pouting," she said. "I'll take your leftovers."

He glanced at her, surprised. "Really?"

"Don't ask me twice."

He held his hands up in front of him. "All right. I won't tempt fate. Thanks, Anna."

"What do you have?"

He gave her a brief overview of his current client list, a typical assortment of losers:

An accused rapist who had inexplicably saved some playback from the "date" in question. As the monitor had displayed scenes of a woman struggling and screaming, he had pointed to the screen and said, "You see? She wanted it. She wanted it like that."

A drunk driver, third offense, who had resisted arrest. The state trooper who had made the bust had used force to subdue the man, who now saw himself as the next Rodney King. His playback had been laughably spliced — editing out footage to make it appear as though he had been unfairly attacked. The trooper's playback painted a different picture of the arrest.

A middle-aged housewife accused of stalking her neighbors. "But look," she had pleaded, as the screen displayed an image shot from outside a bedroom window — the neighbors', Jeremy presumed. The young couple on the bed groaned and perspired with the exertions of anal intercourse. "It's sinful, Mr. Aldrich!" she had exclaimed. "The Bible says so! They should be arrested, not me!"

And a dozen others just like her.

"I'll download the case files in the morning," Jeremy said. "But I feel bad about dumping all this on you. Are you sure it's all right?"

"Buy me a beer sometime, and we'll call it even."

"Deal." He scratched at the back of his neck.

"What's wrong? Is your jack still bothering you?"

"A little."

"Let me see." She stood and came around the table. Jeremy inclined his head obligingly. Hesitantly, she reached out and touched the knobby protuberance. "It's really red and irritated, Jeremy. You should have a doctor look at that."

"I have. He says it's psychosomatic."

Anna snorted, returning to her seat. "That's crap. I never have any kind of trouble with my jack."

"Yeah. Well." Jeremy was silent for a moment.

"Anna, why did you have your recorder implanted?"

She crossed her arms. "What...what does that have to do with any-thing?"

"The standard reason, right?" Jeremy said. "Personal security? Just like they tell you in the commercials?"

"Why else?" She turned her head slightly, watching him from the corners of her eyes. "You don't think I'm one of those weirdos who sells her playbacks to cable television, do you?"

"I suppose not."

"Why are you asking me this?"

Jeremy shook his head. "It doesn't matter. Listen, Anna, thanks again for helping me out."

Still wary, Anna uncrossed her arms and stood. "Just remember to buy me a beer sometime. It's late, Jeremy. Go home." She left him alone in the conference room once more. Jeremy watched her go, then turned back to the monitor and cued up the playback again.

THE MEDIA LOCATED JEREMY the next morning. In half an hour, he received twenty phone calls from tabloid reporters offering to buy whatever playback Franklin Lee Sable might have saved in his black box. The offers began in the mid five figures and quickly escalated. Jeremy eventually had to pull the phone cord out of the wall.

He returned to the corrections center to visit Sable. Once more, he sat on the cot and watched the man rock himself, cross-legged, on the floor. According to the guard outside, Sable had neither slept nor eaten all night.

"Let me tell you several things," Jeremy said. "I've formulated a preliminary strategy. First, I believe we'll ask for a competency hearing to determine your fitness to stand trial. I've ordered a psychiatric examination for you. With the right diagnosis, we may be able to avoid a trial altogether.

"But I have to be honest: the case against you is strong. The taser and the trash bags have your fingerprints on them. And if the DNA tests in the pathologist's report can link the brain tissue found on your premises to any of the victims, the case is going to get a lot stronger. Do you understand me so far?"

Sable rocked. He made a low crooning noise.

"Under these circumstances," Jeremy said, "I'd normally recommend an insanity plea. But your case has certain… peculiarities… that preclude such a defense." He paused, remembering his conversation with Anna the night before. "What I'm getting at, then, is this: if you're faking this psychosis — and your records show that you're intelligent enough to try it — then you're wasting your time."

He let the words sink in. Sable muttered something, repeated it. Jeremy leaned closer, cocking an ear.

"Little brother loves you. Do you love little brother? Little brother loves you."

None of Sable's ramblings made any sense. The man had no family, no younger siblings. Both parents were dead. Jeremy watched him rock himself, waiting for any break, any hint of recognition, any glimmer of understanding.

"Mr. Sable, you may not realize it, but I'm trying to help you. You're not giving me much to work with here. If we go into court with nothing but this… this act of yours, you may very well wind up in the electric chair. Is that what you want?"

"The eyes are the windows of the soul," Sable said. "The eyes are the windows of the soul."

Jeremy sat back and passed a hand over his face. He tried to see Sable as Anna saw him — a cynical, sociopathic posturer — but he just couldn't do it. Anna hadn't sat with Sable, hadn't looked into his blank stare.

"This is a waste of time," Jeremy said under his breath. He called for a guard. A beefy man in police uniform appeared at the cell door, unsealed it for him.

"Let me know if his condition changes," Jeremy told the guard. "Any change, you understand? I need to be able to talk to this man. You call me, any time, day or night. Got it?"

The guard cast a dubious glance over Jeremy's shoulder. "Whatever you say, counselor."

"And if he doesn't eat tonight, I want him fed intravenously. Will you see to that?"

"Sure."

Jeremy detected the faintest traces of an amused smirk forming on the guard's fat face. Something in the expression reminded him of what Anna had said the previous night: What's the point?

He stepped into the corridor, leaving Sable alone in his cell, still rocking.

THE PATHOLOGIST'S REPORT IDENTIFIED DNA from at least five of the Black Box Killer victims. Upon receipt of the lab results, the prosecution filed notice that it intended to ask for the death penalty. Mobs of reporters followed Jeremy wherever he went. Strangers began recognizing him on the street; he couldn't help wondering if they were recording his every move. Sable rocked and rocked.

The psychiatrist's report came back with the results he had hoped for: dissociative psychosis. Armed with the diagnosis, he filed for a competency hearing and waited.

Jeremy spent the time in the conference room, reviewing every frame of playback he could legally obtain on the Sable case. He concentrated on the search of the premises. His hopes of finding some damning deviation from police procedure that would disallow the physical evidence had long since been dashed. He studied the playbacks for any clues, possible keys that might unlock Franklin Lee Sable.

Much of the exterior was disturbingly, maddeningly normal: a small one-story house with a weed-choked yard, sagging gutters, and wood siding marred by scabrous patches of flaked and peeling paint.

Inside, though, was a study in schizophrenia. Sable had ravaged much of the living room, ripping apart the television and the stereo, but the book-case in the corner still stood, the volumes on its shelves aligned in tidy rows. His bed was neatly made; his clothes hung in orderly fashion in the closet. But the other bedroom in the house was completely empty, its hardwood floor uncarpeted, its walls bare. The kitchen was small and clean, the sink clear of dirty dishes. But in the garage—

Anna entered the darkened conference room without knocking. She took a seat next to Jeremy, eyes downcast. "More home movies?" she said, nodding toward the wall monitor.

"Yeah," Jeremy said. "What's up?"

"I got a call for you. I took a message." Still averting her eyes, she passed him the phone memo she held in one hand.

He scanned the message, reading by the light from the wall monitor. On the playback, one of the investigating officers was providing a grim narration as he held up clear trash bags filled with dark blood.

Jeremy read the note twice before comprehending it. "Turned down? They turned a request for a competency hearing?"

"I'm sorry, Jeremy."

"Christ." He slumped in his seat. "This has to be a joke, right?"

"Jeremy," Anna said, shaking her head slowly, "didn't you know this was going to happen?"

"What do you mean?"

"Oh, come on." She faced him squarely. "Quit acting like a first-year law student. The Black Box Murders have galvanized the whole community. Everyone has seen playback of the victims' corpses. You knew that. And this is an election year; no one in office wants to appear soft on crime. And Sable was caught red-handed, for Christ's sake. When will you face facts? He's going down."

"He's insane, Anna. He has absolutely no understanding of the charges against him. The state is planning to execute a mentally incompetent man."

"It's an act."

"No, it's not. I just can't prove it."

"How on Earth would you prove something like that?"

"By finding the black boxes."

"Finding the— " Anna regarded him with a puzzled frown. "I thought they were destroyed."

"That's what the prosecution thinks. That's what they'll try to sell to the jury." Jeremy gestured to the playback on the wall monitor. "But where's the evidence of that? No one's found a trace of the black boxes themselves — no bits of wiring, no circuitry, nothing. That's a bit odd, don't you think? Considering what else has been found?"

"If he didn't destroy them, why did he go to the trouble of ripping them out?"

"I don't know." Jeremy flipped halfheartedly through the sheaves of paper on the table. "Maybe he's paranoid, thinks people are watching him all the time. Or maybe he just doesn't like black boxes."

Anna nodded slowly. "Sound like anyone you know, Jeremy?"

He stiffened, meeting her gaze. She stared back at him calmly. The playback droned on in the background.

"Suppose you're right," Anna said. "Suppose you manage to find the black boxes. What good do you think it will do?"

A wave of exhaustion, long delayed, washed over him. Jeremy rested his head on the table. "Not sure," he said, his voice muffled. "I'm just not sure."

"Face it, Jeremy: there is no defending this guy. William Kuntsler couldn't get him off. Jeffrey Dahmer tried an insanity defense, too. So did David Berkowitz. It didn't help them, and it won't help Sable." She laid a hand on his shoulder. "Don't do this to yourself. Nobody has all the answers."

"Yeah," Jeremy said. "Yeah."

The door to the conference room opened. "Mr. Aldrich?" a voice said.

Jeremy looked up. A young woman stood at the door — a support staffer, one of the college students who interned in the public defender's office over the summer.

"What is it?" Jeremy said.

"There's a phone call for you from the corrections center. They want you down there right away. There's been some trouble."

JEREMY PEERED INTO THE CELL. Sable had been strapped to his cot with a wide leather belt across the chest, arms secured against his sides. The man strained against the belt, eyes wide, teeth gritted. A red knot stood out on his forehead.

"You said you wanted to be called if his condition changed," the beefy guard said.

"Yes, that's fine." Jeremy had already seen the playback. A nurse had been admitted into Sable's cell at 5:34 p.m. To administer an intravenous feeding. Sable, normally docile, had flown into a shrieking rage. The nurse managed to escape unharmed, and the guard on duty had sealed Sable in his cell. The prisoner started throwing himself against the walls. The guard had recorded several minutes of Sable banging against the cinder block, turning, and banging into the opposite wall.

"I was waiting for backup to arrive," the guard explained. The playback became chaotic and jumbled as Sable, still shrieking, was subdued and restrained. It had taken three men to force him onto the cot and strap him down.

"Where did he get that bump on his forehead?" Jeremy said. "Did he do that to himself?"

"I'm not sure. That may have happened when we subdued him. But you saw the playback, right? No undue force was used."

"Right. No undue force." Jeremy knew that the guard was undoubtedly recording this conversation, too — protecting his own interests.

"He's been sedated," the guard said. "You probably have fifteen minutes or so before he loses consciousness."

"Who authorized that?"

"Standard procedure, counselor."

Jeremy sighed. "All right. Let me in."

The guard unsealed the door. Jeremy advanced slowly, approaching the cot as he would a venomous snake. "Mr. Sable?"

The scrawny man twisted and strained against the leather strap. He was chanting: "The eyes are the windows of the soul. The eyes are the windows of the soul. The eyes—"

More gibberish. Jeremy's head sank. "I don't have time for this," he whispered.

"Windows of the soul. Windows of the soul. Windows. Windows."

"Goddamn it, I don't have time for this!"

Sable's head jerked. Their gazes met, and for the first time Jeremy saw a faint flicker of recognition. "Oh, now you want to listen, is that it? Then listen to this." Jeremy lunged at Sable, grabbing him by his bony shoulders, shaking him. "You're going on trial for murder! Nobody gives a damn about how crazy you are! They just want to see you fry in the electric chair! Do you get it? Do you get that, you sick fuck?"

He was screaming. Sable stared back, glasses askew on his face.

Jeremy released him and turned away, disgusted with himself. The guard outside may very well have heard and recorded his outburst. Sable might have, too, for that matter.

Behind him, Sable whispered, "Eyes are the windows of the soul…eyes…pale blue eye…vulture eye…evil eye…eyes…"

Jeremy half-turned back to the cot. "What did you say?"

"Like to watch…like to watch…windows of the soul…windows of the soul…" Sable was gone, his gaze once again empty. His whisper trailed off to inaudibility. He continued mouthing the words, over and over.

Something he had said…Jeremy recognized it from somewhere. He concentrated, trying to recall where he had heard it before, a long time ago.

Dark suspicions blossomed in his mind. Slow horror suffused him. "Oh, my God."

He rushed to the cell door and pounded on it, demanding release.

HE WAS ESCORTED TO SABLE'S HOUSE in an unmarked car to avoid attracting media attention. It was on a suburban street, homes lined up in neat rows, most of them quiet with the lateness of the hour. Jeremy's heart rate accelerated as the car pulled up to the curb and parked.

He got out and approached the house with his escort — a cop dressed in beat blues — in tow, stepping over the sawhorses that cordoned off the premises. The front door had been sealed with yellow tape: POLICE LINE — DO NOT CROSS. A sticker was pasted to the door, printed with a warning of legal penalties for violating a crime scene.

Jeremy produced a pocket knife and sliced through the tape. "Do you have the key?" he said to his escort.

Wordlessly, the policeman stepped forward and unlocked the door.

"Wait here," Jeremy said.

The cop nodded toward the darkened house. "What do you expect to find in there?"

"I'll let you know." Jeremy stepped inside.

As he entered, the rank odor of decay, still strong, swept over him. Jeremy gagged and covered his mouth with one hand. He felt along the wall for a switch, found one, flicked it.

He was in the living room — a couch and chair with ragged upholstery, entertainment center, bookcase in the corner. The smashed television and stereo had been confiscated as evidence; only a few bits of broken glass remained in their stead. The carpet near the center of the room bore a dark bloodstain.

The scars on the back of Sable's neck flashed through Jeremy's mind. As if in reflexive response, he sent the mental command that activated his black box, knowing it would be good to have a record of this.

He ignored the signs of violence. Instead, he took a closer look at the bookcase. The volumes on its shelves were dusty but handsomely bound. He noted the names on the spines: Dumas, Dickens, Orwell...Poe.

"Son of a bitch," he whispered. He pulled the Poe volume off the shelf and opened it to the table of contents. Sure enough, "The Tell-Tale Heart" was listed there, page three hundred sixty-three. Jeremy set the book back in its place.

From the playbacks, he knew the layout of the house by heart. A short hallway extended off to the right. He flicked on another overhead light, revealing three doors — two on the right, one on the left. The first door on the right opened on the bathroom, he knew. The door on the left was the master bedroom. The second door on the right...

It was the empty room, the one with the bare walls and the uncarpeted hardwood floor. No furnishings. An empty closet with a sliding door. Jeremy stepped into the room and turned in a slow circle, peering at corners.

Heart pounding, he knelt and began pressing on the narrow floor-boards. They creaked under his weight. He worked methodically, from one side of the room to the other, feeling for what he knew had to be there.

He found nothing as he crawled across the floor. Doubts surfaced in his mind. Ignoring them, he slid open the closet door and checked the floor there.

A squeak sounded. Some of the boards were loose.

Jeremy got out his pocketknife again, inserting it between the boards, prying them apart. He removed two short slats, disclosing a lightless space beneath — a hole in the subfloor. A faint foulness, like an echo of the stench permeating the rest of the house, wafted from the hidden hole. A small black spider crawled out and scuttled away.

Jeremy cursed himself for not remembering to bring a flashlight. With bated breath and shaking hands, he reached into the hole.

His fingers brushed something wiry and delicate. He closed his eyes and grasped it, his gorge rising. He pulled it out and opened his eyes.

He held a square of wafer-thin circuitry with long, spidery wires. It twirled, dangling. A black box. Jeremy held it by one of the optic leads. Bodily fluids had crusted on the wires.

He dropped it; the thing clattered on the floorboards. His gorge surged. Shuddering, he fought it, forcing it back down, forcing himself to remain calm.

When he felt in control of himself again, he reached back into the hole. He pulled out another black box. And another. And another. He laid them out in a row in front of him, fourteen in all.

He reached deeper, found coils of wire and small component parts — like those from the television and the stereo. He felt around the hole a final time, found one last item: stapled sheets of crumpled paper printed with thick knots of circuit diagrams. Each sheet was labeled: AURAL LEAD (LEFT), AURAL LEAD (RIGHT), OUTPUT JACK—

Like to watch.

The eyes are the windows of the soul.

The scars on the back of Sable's neck.

A degree in electronics engineering.

Like to watch.

Jeremy thought of the woman who had stalked her neighbors, of the guard who had taped Sable slamming himself into walls, of the Rodney King wanna-be who had taped the police officer who'd pulled him over, of the police officer who'd pulled him over taping him…and of poor, twisted Franklin Lee Sable.

Like the rest of them, Sable watched. But he hadn't been satisfied with the mundane details of his own life. So he took the next logical step. He had stalked victims who had seen what he wanted to see — the prostitutes, the policeman, the emergency room intern — and had removed their souls, and had tried somehow to rewire his own output so he could look through their eyes.

"Little Brother is watching you," Jeremy whispered.

He chuckled, staring at the row of souls lined up before him. He was going to get Sable acquitted, after all.

After the operation, Jeremy called the office to check in. Anna answered the phone.

"It's Jeremy, Anna."

"How did it go?" she asked.

Jeremy lay back on the hospital bed. "The prognosis is good, the doctor said. I should be out of here tomorrow."

"That's terrific. We got a call from the Harvard Law Review, you know. They want to interview you."

"Yeah. Well. I'm not interested."

"They said your defense was brilliant."

"No," Jeremy said. "The black boxes won it, not me. The fact that they hadn't been destroyed took away the prosecution's case. That's all there was to it, really."

"Even so, Jeremy — congratulations."

"Thanks." The scar that marked where his output jack had been itched under the bandages. Gingerly, he touched his scalp, shaved at the temples and around the ears, all heavily bandaged. He tried hard not to scratch. Doctor's orders.

"I still don't understand why you had it removed, Jeremy," she said. "It seems kind of...extreme."

"Let's just say I've decided I have better things to do than worry about playback."

Anna laughed softly. "I suppose. See you at the office?"

"In about a week or so."

They said their good-byes, and Anna disconnected. Jeremy hung up the phone and stared at the ceiling.

"Black box," he said. "I'm a black box." He closed his eyes and tried to get some sleep.

MATTHEW S. ROTUNDO'S FICTION HAS APPEARED in various magazines in the U.S., Canada, and the U.K. In 2002, he won a Phobos Award for "Hitting the Skids in Pixeltown," which became the title story of a Phobos Books anthology. His novella "Ascension" appeared in 2004's Absolutely Brilliant in Chrome, also from Phobos Books. He is a 1998 graduate of Odyssey, where he wrote "Black Boxes." Matthew also plays guitar, and is passionate about movies, heavy metal, and college football. Though he and his wife Tracy live in Nebraska, he insists they are not hicks.

TIDES

BY TOBIAS S. BUCKELL

IT WAS MOONLIGHT-TIME AND THE SECOND SUN, orange and stately, slipped into the inky depths of the Roranraka sea. The first sun had been quenched for well over a tide. Siana played in the silver pools the tide had left behind, looking for spiraled shells that she could decorate her new room with.

She didn't skip from pool to pool. On the crumbly, wet coral skipping could cause a slip and fall, and Siana had learned about falls the hard way. She had fallen face first into a patch of firecoral when she was very little. Her mom said she'd cried so loud half the tall-village came looking for her. And the wickedly fierce burning left small patches of Siana's left cheek discolored.

Siana had to time her excursions for shells well. Her tall-village sat in the middle of the ocean, on the tallest mid-ocean peak where reef had grown and sand had collected over time. Several times during the day the Roranraka receded, and Siana could look for shells. But during the rest of the day the ocean lapped at the pillars of her entire village.

So Siana carefully stepped her way between the pools.

In a funny looking kidney-shaped pool she paused and squatted to try and peer through the mirrored surface. The hem of her gray skirt touched the water and turned even darker. It stirred ripples into the surface as she shifted.

Although Siana couldn't see very well through her reflection she was the best at finding beautiful shells. It wasn't a case of looking, she knew, but reaching her hand out over the surface and feeling through the water for the perfect shell.

There! Just tucked into the corner of the pool was a mahogany-brown cowlie. Rippled stripes ran in wedges around the spiral, and clean bone-white patterns twisted in between them. How beautiful. Siana carefully reached down and picked it up. Ah, and she was lucky, nothing had moved into the empty shell.

It sat large in her hand, dripping salty water down her palm and tickling her wrist when she held it up into the moonlight. This will go above the doorway, Siana thought. Right next to Toffhey, her stuffed dolphin.

A large shadow passed in front of Mainmoon: a long, thin, airship. Siana stopped admiring the cowlie. She'd never seen an airship before, though Mum talked about them sometimes in a sad way. Teamdroves of enormous wrinkled birds squawked and complained as they pulled the large silvery craft against the wind.

It was going towards her tall-village! Siana tucked the cowlie into a wet, dirty, canvas bag along with all the other shells she'd collected. She walked back home, but slowly. No matter how excited Siana got, she refused to chance the firecoral.

WHEN SIANA FINALLY GOT HOME she stood and looked up at the four massive wooden posts that kept home above the high-tide level. All the lanterns were lit, flickering a warm yellow light. Her new room, hanging off of the side of the main hut and propped up on the south post, also had a lantern in the window.

Even stranger, Siana could smell cooking and the excited rumbling of Dad's voice. Strange because they'd just had supper, and Mum had let her out to go look for shells while the tide was well out.

Siana grabbed the first rung of the ladder and climbed up and up. She paused halfway to catch her breath. When she reached the hatch of the entryway she clambered in and closed it behind her. She carefully set the canvas bag of shells down.

"Siana? Is that you?" Mum called, peeking around the corner of the door.
"Yes."

"Come in," she said with a big smile. "There's someone we'd like you to meet." Mum smelled reassuringly of bread and saltfish stew. She wore her apron, and had her long brown hair carelessly pulled back in a ponytail. Her hair, Siana thought, was almost the color of the cowlie in her bag. And so was her skin. Tanned and weathered.

Siana walked into the room. Dad sat in his driftwood armchair. He was also grinning. And next to him stood a woman. The woman looked a lot like

Mum: the same brown eyes, and the sharp cheeks. She looked the same age as well. But even though she smiled when she saw Siana, the woman's eyes looked really tired, like Dad's when he'd been out after a whale for many weeks and come home without a catch.

"Hello Siana," the woman said. "I can't believe how big you've grown. Look at you!"

Siana smiled politely. Adults always said things like this in a high-pitched voice. It actually annoyed her, but Mum would get angry if Siana got smart with the guest.

"Thank you," Siana said.

"Do you know who she is?" Mum asked excitedly.

Before Siana could hazard a guess, though she was thinking that the visitor was a cousin to Mum of some sort, the woman spoke.

"I'm Miasia. I'm your sister."

Siana pursed her lips.

"No you're not. Mum says my sister died in the Coastal War."

Mum made a half strangled sobbing noise, and Dad looked angry for a second. Then he grinned ruefully.

"No, Siana." He reached out with his long arms and pulled her closer. "No, this is really your sister, Miasia."

Siana regarded Miasia for a moment.

"Sorry," Siana said. "You looked old. You look just like Mum. But even older."

Miasia looked at Mum and shrugged.

"I've been through a lot," she said. There was a large duffel bag by her feet. She picked it up and opened it. "But, I do have a little something for you that I bought back from over the ocean." Miasia pulled out a small wooden box and gave it to Siana. It was made of old, dark wood, with brass hinges that creaked as Siana opened it.

Inside sat a purple and pink conch shell. It was stunning.

"Thank you," Siana breathed. She moved away from Dad and gave Miasia a quick hug. "It'll go well with the other shells in my new room."

Dad tapped his fingers on his chair.

"Siana, Miasia's going to sleep in your new room tonight." He glanced at Mum. "Until we figure out how things are going to work. Okay?"

Siana stood stunned. She knew how 'temporary' things like this worked in a tall-village. Where could Miasia sleep except here? She'd just come back, and it would take her a long time to get settled on the island. And Dad couldn't afford the wood for another new room; it had taken him years to work for the extra wood to build the small addition to their tallhouse.

There were few islands scattered on the ocean, and even fewer building resources traded between them and the Mainland. And tall-villages all across the Roranraka were fighting the Coastal War for access to forests, so that they could build their homes that barely stuck out of the ocean. Siana's mum often told her it made everyone sad to lose so many children, and brothers and sisters, for the sake of wooden pilings.

Siana looked at a sister she had almost forgotten. Her return was a good thing, Siana thought, but losing a room! Children in tall-villages dreamed and prayed for a room of their own most of their lives. And now…

She started to get a pout ready, but Dad gave her a stern look, knitting his eyebrows together. Siana sighed.

"It's not fair," she declared. "I'm going back outside."

"No you're not. Easytide comes in a few hours," Mum said.

"It's only a few inches," Siana started.

"No."

Siana bit her lip.

"I'll go to bed then."

"That's a good idea," Dad said. Siana changed into her nightclothes and crawled back into her old bed, the one next to the kitchen. The bed she'd spent most of her life in. Her elbows hit the shelves one end, and her feet the other. Bulbs of onions, dangling parsley, garlic, all swung in planters above her. Siana listened to the distant murmur of everyone talking while she mulled over various ways of running away from home.

None of them would work. There weren't any big vessels she could stowaway on besides the whaler Dad worked on, and the tides prevented anyone from walking to any of the other islets near hers. The nearest other tall-village was a week away by boat. The only other land was Mainland, hundreds and hundreds of miles away, where the world came up out of the ocean, and green trees grew, and people lived without worrying about tides. It sounded like a fairy-tale.

But the Mainland was crowded with people. And they guarded their precious trees with their lives. Tall-villagers were not welcome. The only way Siana could get there was if she got involved in the Coastal War. Children were not meant for that kind of fighting.

The thought of the Coastal War made her think of Miasia again, and got Siana even angrier.

Just before Siana fell asleep she heard someone walk carefully up to her. Siana feigned sleep, but peeked. Miasia stood there as if wanting to say something, but then apparently thinking Siana was asleep, left. Her footsteps creaked on the floorboards.

At least someone was getting their own room tonight, Siana thought. She turned back the other way trying to get comfortable.

SIANA FOLLOWED HER FRIENDS to the edge of the tall-village the next midtidemorning, and everyone kept questioning her about Miasia.

"Where has she been?"

"What does she look like now?"

"Why does she look so old when she is only a little older than you, Siana?"

"Did she use up all her magic?"

Siana looked at the excited faces, their hair blowing in the wind. The sand sucked under her feet as she walked.

"And how is Siana today?" she asked, annoyed. But even her close playfriends didn't find it all that horrible that Siana had lost her room.

In fact, most of the children in the tall-village weren't very nice to her. Siana's family had only been in this tall-village since her grandfather had fallen on hard times and been forced to leave the Mainland to become a whaler. So still, when they played war, Siana had to be the Evil Coastie.

"Really, Siana, it must be so neat to have a sister back from the wars," they all said. Then they rolled their eyes when Siana slurped off down the sandtrails in a huff.

It had been her room. Why did Miasia have to return at all?

SIANA ASKED MUM THAT SAME QUESTION with a calculated foot stomp. Mum looked down at her, then leaned over. Her shell necklace tinkled and shifted.

"It's not always easy," Mum said softly. "Sometimes we have to adapt. I wish we could just live on the beach, not on the poles. It would be so much easier to build a home."

But that was silly. Mum was being strange. The tides would wipe out a house without stilts in an instant. Its owners would never be heard from again.

Mum's silliness didn't change Siana's rage.

She stomped towards her bed. She looked at the shells on her shelf above her bed, and the cowlie she had picked out for Mum but hadn't given her yet. She might regret this later, but…

Siana swept the shells onto the floor with a shriek.

"I hate it! It's not fair."

"Siana," her mother yelled. "Your shells!" The fragile pieces lay on the floor, most of them okay. Shells were tougher than they looked. Some had chipped their spiraled edges, or the little horns sticking off their sides.

But the beautiful cowlie, Siana's new pride, had shattered against the little table by her bed.

"Siana," her mother pointed. Miasia's gift, the conch shell, also lay broken. "Why?"

Siana swallowed.

"I don't care," she declared, lying. "I don't care." She ran out of the kitchen and down the ladder.

SIANA SAT AGAINST ONE OF THE PILLARS of the tide-caller's station. It was the highest building in the tall-village, and the furthest out. She let her last few tears dry on her cheeks and sat watching the second sun rise as the first sun dipped below the horizon to fire the sky and clouds with patterns of deep red and purple.

Miasia crossed the sand with a slight limp. Siana scuffled to face the other way as Miasia got close.

"Hey," Miasia said.

Siana didn't answer.

"Mum says the conch shell fell off the shelf and you're pretty upset about it."

Siana looked at Miasia.

"No she didn't. You're just saying that."

Miasia leaned back in mock horror.

"Caught in my own lie! Okay, I'm sorry. I couldn't think of anything else to say that would be more comfortable for the both of us. Can I sit?"

"I guess."

Miasia scooped out some sand and then wiggled into the side of the pillar. She turned a bit to look at Siana. Siana resolutely stared ahead. Miasia pulled out a wooden bead with tiny lines of blue painted around it in a wiggly pattern. She held it up to the sun. Siana watched out of the corner of her eye, still trying to pretend not to.

Then Miasia opened her palm and dropped her hand below the bead a few inches. And the bead stayed where it was: in the air, just above Miasia's palm.

Siana couldn't not look. She shifted around to face her sister.

"How'd you do that?"

Miasia grinned.

"It's not that hard. You could probably do it. According to my teachers, the talent runs in blood."

"Wow," Siana breathed. The bead spun in the air. "But what about the price?" She'd been taught in school about it. Using magic was dangerous. Miasia sighed and the bead dropped into her fingers.

"Each little bit of magic takes a proportionately sized piece of your life," she said. The corners of her mouth tugged down briefly, and she looked past Siana's shoulder, out at the sand that went on and on into the distance.

"Miasia," Siana asked. "Is that why you look old like Mum?"

"Yeah." Miasia stood up. She grunted as she did so. But Siana was still thinking.

"You shouldn't have floated that bead," she said. "That cost you."

Miasia smiled and ran a finger through Siana's hair.

"It only cost me a few seconds," she said. "It's the least I can do for taking your room away from you."

Maybe, Siana thought, maybe Miasia wasn't so bad.

They stood up and started to walk slowly back to tall-home, Siana delaying to look for shells, Miasia limping. Halfway there, Siana paused at a leftover pool of water and looked in. There was a small shell she couldn't quite reach, but Miasia quite deftly leaned over past Siana and plucked it out of the water, only slightly wetting the edge of her sleeve.

"What did you do in the wars?" Siana asked, a bit bold, as Miasia dried the shell off on her dress.

"I made shells. Invisible shells, like bubbles, to protect the officers." Miasia shut her eyes. "Before battle ten or twenty of us spellcasters would stand in the tent. The officers came in one side, their uniforms bare to the danger of gunfire, and they came out the other side protected by my magic. I had to make the bubbles big for them, to give them enough air to come back and have the bubbles unlocked so they could breathe. I had to repair damaged shells, not far from the fighting. All the time around us soldiers died of horrible things, Siana, and I grew old quickly."

"Oh."

"One day the Coasties attacked the tent." Miasia looked around to see if anyone was about, then pulled up the edges of her skirt and showed Siana the angry red scar that ran down the front of her leg.

"Why didn't you have your own bubble?" Siana asked.

"They don't teach us that version of the spell. The rulers decided to take all the books about magic that spellcasters owned a long time ago, and only the rulers can decide what spells they should teach each spellcaster. That way no spellcaster gets too powerful, like they used to be in the barbaric Old Ages. But then the rulers still get to use the powers to help them. So other than that one powerful spell they taught me for the war, all I know are some simple little tricks."

Siana digested this all.

"Why did you leave the tall-village?" Siana asked. "If the magic was going to do this to you."

Miasia looked off into the distance.

"You know Dad promised the rest of his life to the whalers to afford our tall-house? Just because those on the Mainland drive the price of wood so high. I wanted to help Dad."

Siana scratched at the sand. Dad always looked glum. Always sea-tough, tired, and yet so proud of her shells.

The thought of fighting Miasia for the room suddenly seemed extremely selfish and petty. Siana realized she had much growing up to do. Her sister was drained and old from war, her father chained to the whaling ships for life, and mum did her best to find part time work around the tall-village, cooking and cleaning for established families.

But Siana didn't want to think about sober things. It was still a pretty day out, with the salt heavy in the air. All those adult things seemed so far away.

"Would you teach me the bead trick?" She asked.

After all, what were a few seconds of her life in exchange for the ability to really impress her playfriends?

But Miasia turned away. All the joy dropped from her face. Siana realized how old Miasia looked: her face had wrinkles, and some of her hair had begun to silver and grow wispy.

"Let's go back," Miasia said.

IT TOOK SIANA SEVERAL DAYS to get Miasia to ease up and show her the bead trick again. And Siana tried to look through Miasia, just like she looked through the pools of water to find her shells.

Miasia handed Siana the bead with a smile.

"Okay, you try."

Siana let the bead sit in the crease of her folded hand. It felt slightly hot. She scrunched her forehead and stared at the bead willing as hard as she could for it to rise.

Nothing happened.

Miasia put her hands underneath Siana's and smiled. The bead began to rise into the air.

"Oh," Siana giggled. The bead hovered, and then it slowly began to spin, gyrating like a top on the floor, wiggling all over the place. The little lines of blue painted onto the bead created a smooth mesmerizing pattern in the air. "I wish I could do it," Siana said, frustrated.

"You are," Miasia said. "Now." She pulled her hands away and the bead continued spinning, for a second. Siana gasped in surprise and the bead spun out from her hands and landed in the sand.

Miasia laughed and tousled Siana's hair.

"Not bad you little egg, not bad at all."

Siana looked at the little bead in the sand.

"Can I try again?"

Miasia leaned over and picked the bead up.

"Sure," she said.

They spent the rest of the hour laughing and together making the bead dance over their hands.

SIANA'S GUILT AT THE SMASHED SHELLS was weighing on her mind, and she decided she should find a good shell for Miasia and Mum as a way of making up. She left after one of the littletides, just before the rushtide, to go out and look for the best shells. The best shells were to be found just beyond the edge of the tall-village, past the lookout towers who would no doubt call Mum to come and fetch Siana back into the tall-village because she was wandering too far out. Again.

She squelched out eastwards over the sand, and then after a while started picking her way over rock as the ground slipped downwards. Walking around great round pieces of brain coral that were orange-gray, wrinkled, and covered in mucus, Siana began to zero in on a few tide pools that felt promising.

Mainmoon sat gray in the sky, along with first sun. This was further than Siana usually went.

Siana found the perfect pool. She carefully squatted at the edge and waddled down in. Her careful movements sent ripples across the peaceful surface. Despite her caution Siana's foot slipped in between two rocks and she fell into the tide pool.

The cold water shocked her, and for a moment she floated there. Then her foot began to throb and Siana started to cry. She was scared, her foot hurt, and she knew she'd definitely walked too far away: she would get into trouble from Mum.

"Hey, hey," came Miasia's voice. "Don't cry. It's okay." Her sister's face appeared at the edge of the pool, and Siana stopped crying.

"Miasia?"

"Yep. The lookout sent someone to fetch Mum to bring you back. I decided to come instead. Figured you'd get into less trouble." Miasia reached over and grunted as she helped Siana out of the pool.

Cold water streamed from Siana's dress and she shivered, glad to be out in the first sun's warmth.

"I'm sorry," Siana said. "I was trying to find the best shells for you and Mum."

"Well, that's sweet of you," Miasia said. "But come on, let's go home, rushtide is coming soon."

"My ankle hurts."

"All the more reason to leave now. We'll go to the nearest lookout."

Siana grabbed Miasia's shoulder and they both slowly hobbled back towards the tall-village. They passed the brain coral step by step with Siana stopping to rest when her ankle hurt too much.

Miasia tried not to look worried, but Siana knew she had done something very bad. Miasia kept looking north when she thought Siana wasn't looking. They both knew rushtide was coming soon. Siana had been hoping to find her shell and walk back, with just enough time, to the nearest lookout. Any tall-villager knew the tide schedule instinctively; their lives revolved around it in every way.

Siana should have made it back to the tall-village already. And because they were on the slope no one from the lookouts could see them to come out and help.

She tried to hobble faster, but it only hurt more. She tripped and fell, and Miasia couldn't move quickly enough to catch her. Siana's chin hit a piece of rock.

"Oww…" she forced tears back. "Miasia, I'm scared."

"It's okay," Miasia said. Her feet began squelching in sand that had become slightly wetter. "I'm going to try and carry you."

Siana got on Miasia's back and grabbed her thin shoulders. Miasia grunted and began slowly walking.

"Mum's going to be really mad at me." Siana said.

"Maybe not," Miasia said, out of air and panting out the words. "If we don't," she shifted Siana's weight, "tell her."

They walked a little while longer, and then Miasia set Siana down, breathing heavily.

"I'm sorry," she said, her voice breaking, "I can't do it. I'm too spent. I'm too old."

Siana, scared, grabbed Miasia's hand.

"Come on, I can keep walking, we have to make it."

She hobbled on faster, leaning on Miasia, but after a minute the ankle began to give out, and Siana was hopping. And in the sand and rock, every hop was almost a disaster. She flopped to the ground twice more, once bringing Miasia down with her.

Siana tasted salt water. A thin trickle was beginning to flow up the slope with them.

Miasia sat down and ripped at the hem of her skirt. She took the strip of cloth and bound Siana's leg to her own.

"Now try," Miasia said.

They began to walk in tandem. It took a few tries, they started slow, splashing through the water, then got into a good peg-legged rhythm. But the water was beginning to trickle louder around them, and Siana heard a familiar distant roar.

"Faster," Miasia ordered, an edge in her voice.

They cleared the rocks and stepped onto wet sand. Siana lost her step and they both tumbled. Siana could see tall-village. The nearest lookout was frighteningly far away. If she'd been able to jog she could have made it in time.

Siana struggled to get back up, crying out from the stab of pain in her ankle, but she couldn't. Miasia was still sitting. She had a distant look on her face. She started unwrapping their legs.

"What are you doing?" Siana asked. The cold water swirled around her lap and tugged the strip of cloth away when Miasia let it go.

"Pay attention," Miasia said. "To what I'm going to teach you."

Siana's heart thudded in her chest and her mouth went dry.

"Now," Miasia said. "I'm going to create a bubble around that rock, and then teach you how to unlock the bubble on your own."

"No, that will take too long." Siana said. "Teach me how to make a bubble and we can make them on each other."

Miasia looked at Siana, the lines in her face crinkling as she smiled.

"It took me weeks and weeks of training, sister. This isn't just a bead trick you can learn in a day. The unlocking trick is hard enough, but I know you can do it."

"No," Siana said again. "If you put me in a bubble without teaching me how to unlock then you can run back to the lookout tower and come get me after rushtide."

"What if I don't make it? Who will come unlock it? You will run out of air and die as well."

"Don't say that," Siana begged, starting to cry again. "You will, you have to. You just got here. I'll lose you again."

"Stop it," Miasia said. "Pay attention." She grabbed Siana's hands. "Please. Pay attention."

And maybe it was just her ability to stay calm that she'd learned abroad, at war, but Siana responded to Miasia's calmness by falling quiet.

"Okay."

Miasia spread her hands and murmured some words. Siana didn't understand them, but she could feel them coming out of Miasia and caressing the rock. The rock shimmered, half in and half out of the rushing water. Then a clear bubble formed around it, trapping the air and protecting the rock. The water rushed around it.

The spell was powerfully subtle, and Siana could not grasp what Miasia had done no matter how much she strained to hear and see and understand.

She had to learn to save Miasia with a bubble. But the understanding never came to Siana. Miasia sighed and relaxed. She looked tired.

"Okay. Now feel with me as I unlock it."

Miasia took Siana's hands in her own and Siana followed as they both reached out and felt the bubble around the rock. There was a spot Siana could feel, a spot where she could put in her finger and twist. Miasia twisted the bubble and it collapsed. Water rushed around to fill the empty space. It burbled over Siana's belly now, threatening to sweep her away.

"Now I'm going to put one around you," Miasia said. "And make it large enough to last through the tide."

"No," Siana begged. "Please…" she trailed off and began to cry. Miasia hugged her.

"I love you, little sister," she said. She stood up and stepped back, and Siana closed her eyes and cried some more.

The water around her quit rushing.

She looked back up from inside the now massive bubble surrounding her and saw Miasia moving through the water back towards the tall-village. Through the ground she could feel the vibration of rushtide, and the wall of rapidly rising water took Miasia's shrunken figure.

Siana ran over and slapped the wall of the bubble with her small fists and cried until it hurt, then cried some more, and still the pain didn't go away.

Eventually she slipped into the now tepid water floating around in the bottom of the bubble. The water level all around her rose until she was totally underwater. The surface lay many feet overhead, and torpedo shaped scudderfish began to nose around the edge of the bubble. Every breath sounded loud inside the bubble, and the light that filtered down to her danced and rippled around her.

The tall-village now stood alone in the center of the Roranraka Sea, alone for hundreds of miles.

AT TIMES THE TIDE THREATENED to wash the bubble away, but Miasia had grounded it well, including a great amount of sand and water in the bottom. She had put it near a large rock, so it moved a little, but stayed still.

After the many hours of rushtide, the people of the tall-village emerged from the houses and came to look for Siana. When they found the bubble they gathered around and began hammering away at it with whatever they could find. Hammers, chisels, axes.

Mum and Dad pressed up against the side with frantic faces, but Siana ignored them. She pressed her cheek against the bubble, trying to touch that last piece of her sister that lay deep in the filmy nothingness between Siana and the outside.

No one outside understood what Siana could feel and understand; that when she unlocked the bubble Miasia's presence, contained in the bubble which she had given a piece of her life to create, would dissolve. Siana's tears ran freely and she pressed her fingers against the bubble.

"I'm so sorry," she sobbed as she found the lock with her mind. When she put her finger in and turned, the bubble fell apart. The water in it burst out and soaked everyone around it, and the pieces of bubble whisped out at them in little filmy fragments that passed harmlessly right through them and evaporated in a flash of rainbow colors.

And inside Siana, something else broke, and her tears stopped cold.

Siana flinched when Mum and Dad hugged her. She was looking far, far off into the unseen distance, to where there was real land, land that didn't have the tides. She felt hard inside, and friends, fun, and shells fell from her mind.

After she had been carefully tucked into the new bed in Miasia's room, Siana looked at the broken conch shell on the floor. It would be a long time before the next airship touched at her tall-village, but Siana knew she would leave with it. Out there, she could learn the magic that would have let her save Miasia. She would practice what little she knew, and try to learn what she couldn't. She would erase anything of herself to lose the pain of Miasia's memory.

And all the village who saw her in the days, and months after, whispered to each other. Though they didn't think she could hear them, Siana could. They whispered that she seemed different from the village folk. They said that she was no longer a wild, young child, favored by her parents. They thought she had a far-off look in her eyes, and that she seemed…older.

TOBIAS S. BUCKELL IS A CARIBBEAN BORN science-fiction and fantasy writer who now lives in Ohio. Over 30 of his short stories have appeared in various magazines and anthologies, and his first novel debuted from Tor in 2006. His second is due out in the summer of 2007. You can visit his website at www.tobiasbuckell.com.

URBAN RENEWAL

BY TOM PENDERGRASS

MEMORANDUM TO: Felix Shodclaws, Special Assistant to the Mayor
FROM: Reginald Armbruster, Deputy Assistant to the Special Assistant for Urban Renewal
SUBJECT: Task Force Report Recommendations to Resolve "Old Woman in Shoe" Issue

The Urban Renewal Task Force completed on 11 June the site survey of the riverfront property in the Mayor's "Strive to Revive" proposal. There is enormous potential of the site for the proposed luxury marina/condominium complex. It is accessible to major thoroughfares and the electrical and sewage infrastructure in existence will support development. Initial soil and hydrographic results indicate the site is ideal for a multi-story facility.

The existing neighborhood is largely unoccupied as most buildings were destroyed in the riots of '98. Absentee landlords were heavy contributors to the mayor's campaign, and almost all have agreed to accept fair-market value for the property. Initial estimates of site environmental cleanup are well below the city's current Superfund allotment.

Indeed, the program should be considered a go if it weren't for one minor impediment. The area zoned for the main reception area and martini bar is currently occupied by the family of Mrs. Euphonia Hubbard, a widow. Her residence, it seems, is a shoe that has been in her family for some generations. Actually it's really more a boot. But it is occupied and has been continuously for at least seventy years. Mrs. Hubbard refuses to let us access the dwelling to examine the structure, nor will she discuss the possibility of selling the site to the city.

The Task Force is confident that this is only a minor inconvenience. Given recent Supreme Court rulings, it is recommended we exercise the power of eminent domain and claim the property as essential for the public good. Alternatively, the mayor, given recent opinion polls, may wish to avoid publicity in this matter. Given the dilapidated condition of the residence, the task force recommends the city condemn it for human habitation, effectively driving down the fair market price and saving the taxpayers thousands of dollars.

Yours in service,

Reginald Armbruster

MEMORANDUM TO: Felix Shodclaws, Special Assistant to the Mayor
FROM: Gobborn Seer, Municipal Building Inspector
RE: Old Woman Who Lives in a Shoe

This morning, June 14th, given the complaint issued by your office of unsafe living conditions, I inspected the residence of Ms. Hubbard of 101 Wharf Street. Ms. Hubbard was hesitant to let me in at first, but I have a way with people. It's called "honesty" and you should try it sometime. Eventually she gave me free rein to inspect the entire house. I found her to be a charming woman.

It seems that the "shoe" she lives in was once a novelty cobbler shop owned by her husband who was killed in the riots. It was built in the early 1920s as a marketing promotion. The workmanship of the house actually was quite spectacular, but this was back before they used compressed particle beams that so-called architects throw into houses these days to save a few bucks. This house is made of real wood and bricks and nails, built by men who knew what they were doing.

The house was in an internal state of disrepair. But this can be easily understood since she has 13 children, all under the age of 10. It's not surprising that she can't clean the house, or that there are holes in the plaster. It's so crowded in there I'm sure they can't all get dressed at the same time. Despite these fairly minor cosmetic issues, the building is sound.

Given the results of my inspection, I cannot recommend this structure for condemnation nor do I find it unfit for human residence. In fact, I have encouraged Ms. Hubbard to place the home on the Historic Register.

MEMORANDUM TO: Felix Shodclaws, Special Assistant to the Mayor
FROM: Daisy O'Leary — Chief, Fire Department
RE: Old Woman Who Lives in a Shoe

My Dear Mr. Shodclaws,

Thank you for your kind words. I do appreciate the mayor's confidence in me despite the unfortunate incident at the fireworks plant last week. It warms my heart to know that the mayor understands all of the issues of the fire department and that we truly are committed to the safety of our fair city.

Regarding the mayor's request for a fire inspection of subject residence, I accompanied our chief inspector to 101 Wharf Street. The structure stands in the middle of a block that was burned to the ground in the '98 riots, shortly after the mayor was elected to office. I understand he is being attacked by his opponent on the poor emergency response, but as you will remember, the fires occurred during the tenure of my predecessor and we have put procedures in place to ensure such a tragedy does not happen on my watch.

The building in question — the "shoe" — was not damaged in that fire. On further inspection, there was minor scorching on the outside of the building, but the intense heat did not affect the structure's integrity. Our fire inspector determined that the building had been covered with heat resistant tiles, both inside and outside, making it virtually impregnable to fire.

So it is with a heavy heart that I must tell you, despite the wretched overcrowding of the building by her horrendous children, that I cannot condemn the building as a fire hazard. Unfortunately, it is as sound as a castle.

I know this is important to the mayor, especially with Ms. Hubbard's acquisition of legal representation. There may be another issue that you wish to pursue. Ms. Hubbard's children are in dreadful shape, malnourished, and look like scarecrows. I believe that you may wish to follow up with this. Please give my best wishes to the mayor.

Regards,

Daisy O'Leary

MEMORANDUM TO: Felix Shodclaws, Special Assistant to the Mayor
FROM: Stone Zoop — Deputy Director, City Relief Services
RE: Old Woman Who Lives in a Shoe

Mr. *Special* Assistant,

I am writing again to inform you that the food bank program is dreadfully underfunded and has been consistently ignored by this administration. Please see my earlier memos of February 2, March 14, April 27, and May 12. This city has a real problem with hunger and homelessness, as unemployment levels have skyrocketed while public assistance has declined. After defending the administration for the past two years, I have come to the conclusion that the root of these ills is the mayor's poor fiscal policies and rampant cronyism of which I suspect you are the biggest beneficiary.

I thought it only fair to notify you that I will be publicly announcing my resignation at 3 p.m. today at a press conference to be televised by all local channels. I am prepared to lay out the whole sordid history of the use of the food bank as a repository for overpriced luxury items, tins of beluga caviar and Norwegian smoked salmon, for the mayor and his "special" advisors. I warn you, do not cross me, as I have the goods on everyone in this stinking administration and I can take you all down if you make me angry.

PS: Of course the old lady's kids are starving given the state of the welfare program in this city, you moron. All she has is broth and bread. Have you ever tried to go to sleep hungry? Why don't you feed them instead of siccing some overmatched public servants on the working poor?

PPS: If you had a shred of decency left, you would see to it that Ms. Hubbard received parenting classes ASAP.

PPPS: By the way, Hubbard has gotten a press agent. You guys are toast.

PPPPS: You disgust me.

See you in court,

Stone Zoop

(soon to be ex) Deputy Director, City Relief Agency

MEMORANDUM TO: Felix Shodclaws, Special Assistant to the Mayor
FROM: Barbara Yaga — Director, Department of Child Welfare
RE: Old Woman Who Lives in a Shoe

Dearest Felix,

It has been too long since we have talked. I know you are busy with your important job and all, but we really should get together some evening like we did in the old days. Remember when you were running the mayor's campaign and I was the ward chairman for the second district? And that night after the first snap poll? You were so giddy and full of life, and we spent the evening stuffing the ballot box. Those were great days.

I still get emotional when I think of you, even though it's getting harder to picture your face since I see it so seldom.

Anyway, I followed up with your request, dearest, to visit that horrid old woman on Wharf Street. She lives in a knock off Buster Brown mid-rise suede shoe. I mean, if she had lived in a Prada pump, maybe a sling-back with squared-off toes, that would be one thing, but this is so common.

This woman has all of these brats, thirteen I believe, and they are thin as rails and they run around the shoe all day and won't shut up. It's amazing she hasn't killed every last one of them.

Believe me; I thought about it the thirty minutes I was there. They were whining about not having any meat at dinner so the woman, Hubbard I believe it was, spanked them all soundly and told them to go to bed.

The fact that she would do that in front of a child welfare worker impressed me. It showed spunk, and I like that. Believe you me, the lady was justified. Spare the rod spoil the child, as they say. Anyway, I don't think this constitutes child abuse. Besides, we're a bit hesitant now to remove children from homes, particularly since that unfortunate child labor incident. How was I supposed to know that when the guy said he would give the kids vocational training he meant having them tan leather eighteen hours a day in the basement of his house?

So anyway, I'm being just a bit cautious these days, especially since there were so many reporters there. I have closed the file on the Hubbards. The kids stay with their mother in the damned shoe. Serves them right for whining all the time anyway.

Call me soon,

Babs

MEMORANDUM TO: Felix Shodclaws, Special Assistant to the Mayor
FROM: Dick Whittington, Mayor
RE: Old Woman Who Lives in a Shoe

Shodclaws, what the living crack addict are you doing? This Hubbard woman has the city papers wrapped around her gnarly old fingers. It's like she's running some sort of guerilla public relations campaign and making us all look like fools.

And the statement you prepared for me at the press conference? When I read the part about doing some soul-searching, the entire press corps busted a gut. And when I had to say we were trying to do this project on a shoestring, well I've never been so embarrassed in my life. My polls have dropped a dozen points since last week. It looks like I have no empathy. Me, the man of the people. And after I've done so much for the little wretches.

You need to come up with a way, quick, to get us out of this mess. The election is only weeks away, and I do not intend to lose to that skinny little do-gooder Sprat. Remember, if I lose, you lose.

MEMORANDUM TO: Felix Shodclaws, Special Assistant to the Mayor
FROM: Tuesday Childe, Press Secretary to the Mayor
RE: Old Woman Who Lives in a Shoe

It is with deepest regards and affection that Mayor Sprat expresses his sincere thanks for the admirable work you have done to revive our fair city's troubled neighborhoods and improve the lives of our citizens. Your work has been nothing short of genius, and an inspiration to our community.

Mrs. Hubbard is enjoying her new house and the celebrity that accompanies appearing on national television on that extreme home makeover show. How did you ever convince Mr. Jordan to come to the dedication ceremony? Nike's sponsorship of Mrs. Hubbard's renovated home was truly divine inspiration. And the home is beautiful with the bright red swoosh and the manicured yard. I also hear the floors are a bit springier than the old ones. By the way, the marina facility is gorgeous. Mrs. Hubbard has gained quite the reputation for her hospitality, and there is a constant line around the heel of her house for her martinis.

On behalf of the Mayor and the citizens of our fair city, we present you with this key to the city. We all wish you much success in your new career in Hollywood.

Warmest regards,

Tuesday Childe

TOM PENDERGRASS FORMERLY WORKED AS A COUNTERTERRORISM OFFICER for the U.S. government, but now works for a technology company in Huntsville, Alabama in a distinctly non-technological role. In addition to writing, Tom grows bonsai trees and once was invited to tour the bonsai collection at the Emperor's palace in Tokyo.

As the Stars of the Sky

BY MIKE SHULTZ

INFINITE ROWS OF SHIPS.

That's what I remember most. At that moment, I knew nothing would be the same anymore. Yes, our ship had gotten sucked down an invalid transfer pathway; yes, we took severe damage and most of the crew was dead; yes, they exiled me from the crash site, and yes, I stumbled upon a strange ship and crawled in. But it wasn't until I woke up who knows how far from our crash site and saw the rows of ships that I knew I was unimaginably far from home.

I lifted my binoculars and gazed down the rows. A thousand meters, two thousand, three thousand… Still, the ranks of ships went on and on, crouching like a well-disciplined army of locusts.

I let my binoculars fall to my side. Now, what? Explore? Investigate the alien vessel I had arrived in? I recalled how it hummed to life when I first crawled in, just before I collapsed into a dazed slumber. Why did it bring me here? Did my crew see me lift off? What did its controller want with me?

I tried not to be afraid.

I decided to study the other ships. Probably best to leave the hatch open, I thought, before gingerly hopping two meters down from the top of the one I'd arrived in.

I approached the neighboring ship and stroked my hand over its gleaming grey hull, which seemed to be made of plastic. Miniscule channels pitted its shiny surface. It was all angles and no curves, a geodesic space dart. I noticed something else — it was symmetrical around a horizontal plane — the top and bottom were mirror images. If I could figure out how to open the bottom hatch, entry would be easier. I circled the ship, looking for other details I had missed before.

Hmmm. That beacon there could have been communications lasers. That one looked like exterior lighting. No visible field generators, no weapons. The engines at the rear were completely alien in design.

Alien, I thought, stopping. Where were the builders?

They could have been human, but I doubted it. The Europic Enclave and the Asiatics had surely explored transfer points that we'd never found, but these ships didn't seem earth-based. They bore no markings of any kind that resembled a written language — or any type of language. The field-web seat I had laid in inside the ship was not specific to any particular body shape. No interior instruments were visible. It did have wide, smooth panels arcing along the entire circumference inside, and I recalled some activity on them when the ship first awoke, but nothing I saw was even remotely familiar. The obvious conclusion: the ships were alien.

So I was the first.

Government conspiracy theories aside, humans hadn't found alien intelligence anywhere, despite having explored four galaxies. There were protists on Ganymede. Diatoms in the oceans of Cignus IV. Primitive grasses covering every square centimeter of the moons of Capella Prime. But nothing sentient. I had found the first convincing evidence of nonhuman intelligent life in the entire universe.

Now, that was a humbling thought.

And I needed to be humbled. My own arrogance had gotten me kicked out of my crew.

The troubles had started when something hit us on our way through the transfer point closest to Earth. It happens about one time in a million. As soon as we came through, we set to figuring out where we were, despite the flames roaring around us, the breaches in the hull, and the damaged sensors. Charles, lead pilot, told us what we didn't want to hear: we weren't in the Milky Way, and he couldn't detect our end of the transfer pathway. We weren't going home anytime soon.

That concern quickly faded. Our cruiser, the Eridanus, couldn't go much farther without repairs. We had to touch down somewhere. To our delight, Alfonso found a moon with an oxygen atmosphere around the eleventh planet in the system, a gas giant. Oxygen meant water and possibly cyanobacteria — at least it did in the Milky Way. Andromeda had taught us other rules, so we couldn't tell for sure. We weren't going to breath it; too much sulfur dioxide. We just wanted the oh-two to replenish our reserves and the atmospheric pressure so we could wear lighter exploration suits.

We landed.

Three quarters of our crew dead… Some of them coughed into space during hull breaches… The memory terrifies me even now as I record it sixteen years later.

Most of them were pretty much out of their minds. When we realized it would take weeks to fix the transfer point scanners and navigators, and that the food would run out first, a few people went wild. Four were shot before the rest settled down.

At the time, what I did made sense. They had ruined some food fighting over it; we needed order. I tried to take charge. Told them that they either listened to me or I'd shoot them. I still think it was a decent idea; it just shouldn't have been me. I lacked the proper personality. Most of the survivors didn't like me; I've always been a man of a very few close friends, and none of them had lived. The rest complained that I thought I was smarter than everyone else, and they might have been right.

So, they tackled me, beat me up, and told me to take a hike. Charles and Darla didn't like the idea, but Alfonso and Holmes had taken control, and they were serious. It was martial law, and I was the criminal.

Away I went, figuring that if I stumbled back the next day, they'd have pity on me. I was exhausted and delirious when I found the open alien craft and crawled inside.

Next thing I knew, I was in the biggest parking lot imaginable.

I returned my scrutiny to the ship that brought me here. It still hummed, low and quiet. What din would arise if these ships lifted off all at once? Surely this fleet was meant to fly together. Why else would anyone build millions of identical ships?

I crawled in. The field-web crackled to life. It was the only component that was even vaguely familiar. Avoiding the field-web, I took three paces to the rear. The back panels were the same smooth, grey plastic as the exterior. Upon closer inspection, I discovered that they, too, were etched with tiny channels, like the lines of a child's maze or the circuits of an old microchip.

A panel lit, centimeters from my face.

I stumbled backward. "What the—"

Half a second later, the glowing panel echoed, "What the—"

A recording device? No — it wasn't my voice. I waited, sweating. Nothing happened.

"Repeat after me," I said then.

"Repeat after me," it replied. Then it said "Re."

I froze. "Repeat," I replied.

"Repeat." A few seconds later, it added, "Aff."

"After," I told it.

"After." Pause. "Me."

"Me," I replied, touching my chest. My heart thudded louder than the detonations that ravaged the Eridanus.

More panels lit, spanning the entire rear of the ship, dozens of images of myself appearing on them. Each was shaped correctly but off in color; for example, one was grayscale and another looked like images I've seen through night vision goggles. One was almost correct in coloration. On a hunch, I touched it. The others vanished.

Another set appeared, all nearly correct in color. I touched the best one. After three more cycles, a perfect one appeared. By that time, I had figured it out, though it was hard to accept. It didn't know what wavelengths of the electromagnetic spectrum my eyes perceived. There had been some blank areas on the panel the first time — probably IR or UV images, or even microwave.

"Me," the panel said, emitting a beep. A white line extended from my image's chest. I realized that it was pointing right where I had touched myself when I had said "me."

"No," I said. I motioned to my whole body. "Me."

"Me," the panel said, lighting a white circle around my entire image.

"Yes," I replied. Maybe it thought "Me" was my name, but the depth of our communication was already beyond what I might have imagined possible with an alien intelligence. In Earth books and movies, the aliens always spoke English already.

"No me," the panel said. It created and pointed to an image of the ship.

"Ship," I told it.

AFTER TEACHING IT WORDS for about an hour, I concentrated on telling it my need for food and water. I named most parts of my body and the ship; it had me identify images of planets and stars as well. Then, we went on to simple actions, though 'simple' is a misnomer because it became extremely difficult. I had to tell it no frequently. The panel showed variation after variation of an action, even after I "yessed" something, seemingly wanting to understand the exact nuance of every word. When I decided to explain food and water, though, I had no idea where to start.

I solved the water dilemma when I went outside, peed on the floor, and brought back a drop that I had intentionally dribbled onto my boot. I illustrated the idea of a mixture and was able to communicate that my urine was a mixture and that I wanted only the main component of it. Again, the panel painstakingly sought clarification, leading us into chemistry. After much confusion, a barely recognizable model of a water molecule showed up on the screen. The model emphasized electron orbitals more than I was used to, but when it showed me the nucleus and demonstrated charge attractions and repulsions, I understood.

I was exuberant, of course.

"Water," I said. "Water to Dave's mouth." We had established earlier that I was Dave rather than "Me."

But the panel was still interested in our investigation of water.

"Dave no atoms." Or know atoms? Question or statement?

"Yes," I replied.

"Panel not know Dave know atoms," it replied.

"You didn't know that I knew about atoms," I replied. I had the feeling that it would gradually learn pronouns and prepositions if I used them in context.

"Water," the panel said abruptly. "Talk atoms after water."

"Yes," I replied. "We will talk about atoms after I drink water."

It instructed me via pictures to exit the ship. I complied immediately.

THIS WILL SOUND TERRIBLE, but I was glad that my companions weren't with me. They never would have gotten to the point of teaching it language. Charles probably would have started gunning it with his laser rifle, and Darla wouldn't have even gotten back inside the ship. Later, of course, I would have welcomed any of them.

I saw the other vessel approaching from my left as soon as I climbed out. It drifted, low and noiseless, in the gap between the double rows. Its glide was slick and rapid and it arrived before I reached the ground.

A glowing panel lit on the exterior of the new vessel as it settled to the floor. "Water," it said.

I took a deep breath. That was one question answered. The "panel," or whatever entity was behind it, could speak through other ships — maybe even all of them. It only made sense. Some intelligent being sat in a command center somewhere, operating all of them, watching me though whichever panel it liked. More likely, there was a group of beings working together, brainstorming. That would explain the multiple questions about each topic. Perhaps their society, or their own twist on the scientific method, required all of them to agree on a meaning before they were willing to move on. They were using sophisticated computers, too — they hadn't forgotten a word thus far.

I approached the ship and paced around, but didn't see anything resembling a spigot. Maybe it was inside. I climbed the craft and opened the hatch.

It was filled with water.

I sniffed first. No odor at all. In fact, the only thing I had smelled was myself, the whole time I was there. I braved a fingertip next. Rather warm. I withdrew my finger and spread it on the exterior of the ship. Organic liquids evaporate quickly and have low surface tension. Oil spreads thin, for example. This stuff beaded just like water.

I dipped again and licked.

Water. It was lukewarm, around body temperature — disgusting to drink — but I dropped my face and sucked like a horse.

OVER THE NEXT FEW HOURS, we discussed every atom and molecule that I could remember. I established that some were harmful to me, and the panel was meticulous in clarifying that. It brought another ship filled with physical samples of various materials that we had discussed. I didn't recognize a few at first. The sucrose, for example, was in the form of a flawless single crystal the size of a bowling ball. Not the form I was used to seeing sugar in.

Time came next. Solar system models established days and years. Simple math took us to hours, minutes, seconds.

As soon as it understood time, we discussed the intervals at which I would need water. It had taken away the water vessel, and when questioned, explained that the water was no longer pure. Soon, I learned what it meant — my own saliva and bacteria from my mouth had contaminated it. Food came next. I ate a few chunks of sucrose, but that would never be enough. I knew the formulas for most sugars, but proteins, fats, carbohydrates — they were a different story. I knew the general gist, but I was afraid to guess on their exact composition. What if I made a mistake of a few atoms here or there? It could kill me. I would have to let better food wait until our communication improved.

I wanted to ask Panel how it knew the water in the first ship was contaminated.

"How did Panel know water not pure?" I asked.

"Unknown: How. Unknown: did. Unknown: Dave drink five water. Water one. Yes/No."

Blurring-fast thought, as always. Panel didn't know the words "how" or "did," that was clear. But "Dave drink five water..." Ah! It brought me water five different times, and it didn't know which time I was referring to. Thus, water one, yes or no.

"Yes. Water one."

"Explain 'how'."

Darn good question. How do you explain the word how?

"Question word," I replied.

Panel maybe understand. It showed me images of tiny sensors all over the interior of the vessel.

Sensors! This was the answer to the food dilemma. We went through some sensor-related terminology first.

"Sensor me," I said, pinching my skin. It had detected trace amounts of saliva in the water, so it should be able to take a tiny sample of skin and blood and isolate fats, carbohydrates, proteins — everything. We dickered for a while until Panel understood.

"No sensor Dave," it said.

That was new. It hadn't refused to do anything before. Maybe I hadn't phrased it correctly.

"Question: no sensor Dave?" I asked.

"No sensor Dave." It showed an image of my blood dripping out of my body and said "No."

"Explain," I replied, brow creased. Maybe Panel thought it would hurt me, even though I had tried to convey that it wouldn't. In any case, I was touched by its concern.

And I couldn't help but to think of Panel as "it," an artificial intelligence, because of its lightning-fast responses and perfect recall. I wasn't so arrogant as to believe that an organic being couldn't be vastly more intelligent than me, but I had only my own experiences to draw upon. Even so, humanity's artificial intelligence was nowhere near this — all it could do was guide a vehicle and keep it from running people over, and stuff like that.

Time for more math. We worked on fractions first.

I WAS BEGINNING TO FEEL SICK from living on sugar and water. To my embarrassment, I had diarrhea on the floor right underneath the ship. It was weird knowing that an alien watched it happen. Why should I be ashamed in front of it? But I was — very. The second time exhausted me, and I fell asleep in the ship.

WHEN I AWOKE, I WENT OUT, peed on the floor and munched on a few sugar crystals. I was sipping from the water ship, my face submerged, when the alarm blared. I sat bolt upright and then nearly fell into the water. A nearby panel lit.

"Dave, see this," Panel said.

Images filled the screen — the moon my team had crash-landed on. We had named it Mars because it had red soil. The image zoomed in. Panel must have sent a scout ship to "Mars." I wondered how far away it was.

I saw the crash site and my crew members. White flashes punctured the gloom at regular intervals — weapons firing. Damn! What were they shooting at?

Panel zoomed me in and I saw. Each other. Probably fighting over the remaining food or the water recycler. I saw Darla duck behind a scrap of the torn hull, dodging blasts. Her cover didn't help — the bolts punched through the metal and sizzled into her flesh. She slumped to the ground.

It will have to be enough for me to say that three more went down in the next few minutes. I didn't like them — suddenly found myself liking them more — but I can't clinically describe them dying. The two survivors, Charles and Alfonso, were wounded. They didn't look happy with each other.

"What distance?" I asked, pointing to them. "How many hours?"

"One day," Panel replied. Very non-computer-like in its imprecision, I noted.

One day. If Charles and Alfonso kept their hands off of each others' throats for a day, we might be able to rescue them.

"Dave and Panel go to them!" I shouted, stabbing my finger at the screen.

"Yes," Panel replied.

Alfonso was dead when we arrived.

I watched it happen through Panel en route. I should have asked Panel to pick them up without me. It was difficult to discuss anything with such limited language. But it didn't seem likely that they would have trusted an alien craft — they'd probably have fired on it.

They had grabbed packs and stumbled off downriver, probably hoping to find... something. Anything. Maybe me. They came to a canyon and Alfonso slipped. Panel's scout ship didn't catch an image of his impact, but it moved in and found him bleeding to death.

The next images showed Charles returning to the Eridanus and lifting off.

I couldn't blame him. When he'd argued for taking off before, the others rejected it. Where could we go? But he was alone. So what if our cruiser was crippled and could barely limp along. So what if the chances of finding a transfer point before we died were one in a thousand. And so what if the chances of a successful rescue from earth were far less than that. What was Charles supposed to do, sit on Mars and starve?

After it was too late, I thought of an idea that I should have suggested to Panel. Panel could have faked having his scout crash-land. My companions probably would have rushed to the site and investigated — armed, surely, but it would get them close. Then, he could have displayed images of me and spoken to them.

Maybe the scout couldn't have done that. Maybe it wouldn't have worked. But I should have suggested it. I'd abandoned my companions, found safety, found a way to save them, and then bungled the chance. I felt miserable.

A darker thought intruded. Panel was intelligent and highly creative — it had demonstrated that numerous times. Why hadn't it thought of a way to approach my companions before they died? Panel seemed concerned for my life. Why not for theirs? I brainstormed as many reasons as I could, and only two stood out. Either Panel simply hadn't thought of anything, or it hadn't wanted to help them. Perhaps I had been foolish, trusting this alien intelligence. It rescued me and fed me and hadn't wanted me to sacrifice a drop of blood, for heaven's sake, but that didn't mean it had my best interest in mind. I resolved to remember that.

In the meantime, we had to find Charles. I asked where he was. Panel showed me shifting images of Mars and the gas giant, but not the Eridanus. No trace of Charles, apparently.

"Go back," I said.

Panel displayed the dorsal region of my body.

"No. Go to Darla."

Panel displayed Darla's dead body, lying amongst discarded scraps of metal on Mars.

"Yes."

I donned my suit before we landed. Once outside, I scavenged every-thing of potential use that Charles hadn't taken — a broken knife, a dam-aged minicomputer, and a chair — and threw them all aboard Panel's ship.

I dreaded my next task. I'd never touched a dead body before. I could smell the burnt flesh of her wounds as I dragged her — suit filters don't catch non-toxins. At one point, I had to stop and step aside. My heart fluttered and I dizzied; it took me a while to calm down. Eventually, I managed, and threw a stiff plastic sheet over her that I'd torn from an interior wall of our cruiser.

"Go home," I said to Panel.

"Charles?" Panel asked, showing an image of him while flashing green.

"Panel see Charles?" I asked.

Barren planet and moonscapes flickered before me.

"No Charles," I said.

"Find Charles," Panel said.

"Yes," I said, and we lifted off.

The gas giant had a huge moon nearby. Panel showed me measurements in kilometers — circumference, diameter, distance from the gas giant, distance from the sun. Larger than earth's moon and far more pocked with craters. It looked like a used pinata. He had finally detected the Eridanus, sitting in a crater doing who knows what — maybe scanning for raw materials.

I felt fairly safe with ship-to-ship contact. Granted, the cruiser had potent weapons. The lasers were damaged, but it still had missiles. In this situation, though, we could radio him before we got too close, erasing the threat that the alien vessel would be to him. The thought excited me. Charles and I weren't exactly chums, but I hadn't talked to another human being in days. And it would be fantastic to be able to tell him that I had found a way for us to survive, and hopefully a way for us to get back to earth.

Of course, these thoughts were before I told Panel that I wanted to find a way home.

"Talk to Charles," I said.

Panel flashed some images, and I realized that it was asking me what to say. We didn't have time for that, though. The longer we waited, the greater the chance that Charles could decide we were a threat and open fire. And he had detected us, I could tell. The Eridanus was powering up for lift-off.

"Quick," I shouted.

A thin red laser beam pierced the gap between Charles and us.

I knew what it was immediately, even though ours were invisible — a communications laser. But that's not how the Eridanus communicated. Charles would interpret the beam as an attack.

"Missiles," I said, staring in dread at the white arrows streaking out from the cruiser. "Lance Missiles. Danger! Hurt Panel! Hurt Dave!"

We were already angling away. My alertness skyrocketed. This ship better have incredible maneuvering technology, I thought. If not, we were dead. Lance missiles rarely miss a target. Just one of them would blow us away — it would be like killing a bird with a grenade. Unless this ship was made of superior materials, I reminded myself, or had a defense system that humans haven't even conceived of.

We sped away, but it was clear that we weren't going to outrun the Lances. Not encouraging. Lance missiles aren't that hard to defend against — you just have to shoot them down before they hit you. But Panel didn't seem to have that capability.

The screens showed a dozen Lances coming in four waves. The first wave was about to hit. Panel executed a full-stop that no earth vessel could have accomplished. I was tossed forward rather than backward — the inertial equilibrators had overcompensated. The first wave flew past. Impressive, but not good enough. They'd circle back in seconds.

The comm laser kept flicking out at the missiles. I thought Panel had a new plan, but then it said, "Panel talk to missiles."

Well, maybe it could. Maybe it could reprogram them—

Second wave coming in, first wave redirecting. So much for reprogramming.

Panel quickly took up a leading trajectory in front of a small asteroid orbiting the gas giant. An earth ship would've needed minutes of intense astrogation calculations to do that.

A couple of the Lances whisked past us and then slowed; a couple stayed behind. The other two crept up alongside the asteroid. Damn their variable programming!

My turn. I touched the asteroid on the screen. "Asteroid," I said, then touched our ship. "Us." I smacked my hands together.

Panel understood. It landed on the asteroid, bringing it within the effect of our electromagnetic guidance fields. Then it veered sharply toward the gas giant, punching the asteroid in the opposite direction.

It struck a Lance and detonated it, shattering the asteroid into a dozen fragments. Two more missiles exploded from the shrapnel. The rest swerved to intercept us.

"Third wave and fourth waves," I said, gripping the arms of my chair. No asteroid nearby. No ability to fire back or to dodge fast enough. We were running out of options.

"Go," I shouted, pointing at the gas giant. We dove in instantaneously. Panel and I were thinking alike. The Lances followed like teenage boys after the only girl on the planet.

Our ship shuddered as it slid into the atmosphere. The missiles couldn't track as well in air, but they were more aerodynamic. I had hoped they'd blow from the heat, but it wasn't happening. Not good. Our tactic had failed already — we had to get out.

"To Mars," I shouted. Panel agreed, yanking us out of the gas giant. We emerged so close to Mars that it must have been Panel's plan all along, to go there under atmospheric cover.

The remaining nine Lance missiles came out of nowhere, hot on our exhaust. Panel dropped into a very tight orbit around Mars. Yes! Slingshot out! It could buy us another minute or so…

But the missiles would gain the same effect. Forget that. What was Panel doing?

"Five seconds," Panel said.

Everything after that was blurry. I remember one last twirling maneuver. It was brilliant evasion, four missiles detonating off target, but it wasn't enough. One detonated close by and this time the inertial equilibrators couldn't compensate. The blast tossed me against the hull as if I'd been swatted by God.

I AWOKE TO THE AROMA OF ROASTING CHICKEN. Potatoes, too. It couldn't be. I sat up and sniffed, then rubbed my eyes and stood — ouch. My entire right side ached. Bruises covered my leg; my right shoulder burned. I found a lump on my head that felt like someone had surgically implanted a wad of razor blades. No dried blood, though. Panel had cleaned me.

Well, it had its blood sample.

But the food? I opened the hatch and lifted myself out, wincing.

The sight outside nearly knocked me back in.

Ships swarmed everywhere, like bees in a meadow; tiny devices scuttled across the floor, a few of which were cleaning up my diarrhea. I saw Darla and Charles, their bodies lying on bier-like floaters.

"Panel, what is going on? Explain!" I shouted.

A solitary horizontal panel hovered over. On it was a human-style cup full of red liquid. I picked it up and sniffed. Next thing I knew, I was gulping it down. Fruit juice. I recognized the exact brand — it was the kind we had on board the cruiser.

"Panel, explain," I said.

Another square floater approached and rotated so a flat surface faced me. The images unfolded the story.

Our ship couldn't escape the missiles, so Panel decided to crash into one of the rivers on Mars. The impact still disabled the ship, but the missiles exploded when they hit the surface of the water. Ships from the vast armada then came and picked me up.

Another swarm of ships went after Charles, who apparently had taken the Eridanus to the crash site. This swarm of ships was of a different design, I could see. They formed a ring; gigantic holographic images lit the space inside. Images of me. But Charles ignored them. The swarm approached and attached to the hull. Within moments, images from inside Eridanus appeared — Panel had boarded. I caught glimpses of spheroid floaters drifting through my old vessel. They found Charles's body quickly enough, clutching his laser rifle with its barrel toward himself, a gaping hole in his chest. He looked like a deflated balloon. I shuddered, wanting to turn away, but I had to watch.

They wrapped him in plastic and took him out. Then, they explored the Eridanus. When they found the food stores, they took samples of everything.

But the smell of roasting chicken? All of our food was precooked. I looked around, still unable to see its source.

I found out soon enough. The next images were of them returning, Eridanus in tow. I didn't understand their entry into the hanger; it looked nothing like going through a transfer point, yet at one moment they were in empty space and the next they were here. Then, I saw them working with the food samples and could hardly believe my eyes.

They cloned a chicken.

Sure, cloning is no big deal when you have a living organism to work from; all Panel had was a freeze-dried dinner. But Panel didn't just clone it. It built it up much faster than any chicken could ever grow. I understood little of what I was seeing. Organic microtubules protruded from the chicken and stuff pumped in and out. Cells grew like a crazy colony of E. coli.

I soon saw that it wasn't a whole chicken, after all. Panel had cultivated a hunk of chicken meat. But it was chicken on the molecular level, or so Panel was trying to convince me. Molecule after molecule appeared on the screen, each compared to a molecule from the sample it had collected. They all matched.

They rolled it out to me on a small floater and I devoured it. The potatoes were much more normal-looking, but I wasn't really paying attention. I hadn't eaten normal food for days.

And I hadn't really been aware of what I was dealing with.

"Panel, what are you?" I mumbled between bites.

FOR THE NEXT SEVERAL WEEKS, we worked exclusively on language. Written language blew Panel away — it had no context for it whatsoever. I also found out that it couldn't make sense of my minicomputer, or the ones on Eridanus. I figured they would be a treasure trove of information — what better way to learn our language? But Panel stored data on the molecular level, like biological memory. In fact, as far as I could tell from the images it showed me, its memory was biological — nothing remotely similar to a computer's digital storage. Panel electrically interfaced with Eridanus's computers, but it didn't help.

That had been the cause of Panel's failure to communicate with Charles, too. At first I thought Panel didn't use radio signals, but of course it did. Each band of the electromagnetic spectrum has certain uses, not because a given intelligent mind was biased toward that use, but because each frequency is absorbed and transmitted by certain materials. Panel's ship tried to communicate by laser and radio, but the Eridanus simply hadn't been able to decode the transmissions. They weren't sent in anything resembling digital format.

I didn't find out much about Panel during those several weeks, stifling my curiosity in favor of the greater goal of actually being able to talk. Finally, our conversation reached the point where we could say mostly what we wanted to. We decided to switch our focus from learning language to learning about each other.

That's when I remembered something: Panel didn't necessarily have my best interest in mind.

"WHAT ARE YOU?" I ASKED.

"An array of microscopic organic lasers that—"

"No, Panel. Not this screen. What is the nature of your intelligence?"

It showed me nerve cells.

"So there is a living creature, like me, somewhere I can't see?"

"No. This brain is inside this ship."

"So each ship is an independent organism."

"No. Can I show you with pictures?"

Panel always wanted to show me with pictures. I nodded.

It showed me the entire armada of ships in this place for the first time. The view zoomed in and out, focusing on hundreds of different types of ships, all the size of the vessel I was in or smaller. All of them were mobile. All of them were in sets of at least a hundred thousand identical vessels. There were vessels filled with scores of smaller devices, some mobile and some not, all of them capable of specific functions.

Ships and devices flowed from one place to another. Most of the action centered on me; Panel showed me what some of the others were doing. Studying my dead companions. Repairing the cruiser. Exploring the solar system. I wanted to ask why about the latter, but the images moved on. I still didn't understand what Panel was.

Until it superimposed the image of its swarming ships on a magnified image of a human blood vessel, red blobs whisking by.

"Cells," I said. "This ship is a cell."

"Yes," Panel said. "Made to familiar a cell."

"Made to resemble a cell," I corrected. "Why?"

Panel depicted a ship being dismantled and a new one being built.

"Biology is made smart," Panel said. "One piece bad or old doesn't make whole organism bad or old."

"True," I said. "So are you a biological organism or a computer? A collective of some kind?"

"I don't understand," Panel replied. "All ships here make one organism. Biological? Computer?"

"What controls you?" I asked it.

"Each cell is controlled by me."

"What controls the whole you? Who makes decisions?"

There was a long pause. "I do," it replied. "Panel."

"So you are a sentient being?"

"I don't understand."

"You make your own choices. You have your own goals that you have chosen. You are aware that you can think."

"Are you a sentient being?" it asked.

"Yes."

"I don't know. I make choices. I have goals. I know I think."

"Can you make another being like yourself, but not yourself?"

"No. Can you?"

It had me there. I guess that wasn't a requirement for sentience. "No. What made you?"

"All cells here was made by older cells."

"Were made. What made them?"

"I won't tell until my study finish."

A rare refusal. Not good. "Study of what?" I asked.

"Of Dave."

I grimaced. "What about me are you studying?"

"I have goals for you," it replied.

That sent chills down my spine. Time for my biggest question.

"Will you help me get back to earth?""

"Maybe."

I rose and stalked away.

WE DIDN'T TALK FOR THE NEXT FEW DAYS. Panel tried, but I wasn't biting. If it could withhold, so could I. In fact, I was tired of cooperating. Resisting or fighting would be stupid, yes. But doing nothing would be more stupid.

It had goals for me. I shuddered again. I meant to get back to earth. I had thought Panel would help me, but obviously I was wrong. I thought I had finally found a kindred being, one that I understood. But I was wrong. And though I had come up with a hundred theories in the last few hours, I had no idea what it wanted from me.

I wanted answers. It was testing me. Time to test back.

I asked to be transported to the Eridanus (why repair it if I wasn't to go home?) and was obliged. Panel tried to engage me in conversation again, but I gave terse answers. It was clearly confused.

When we arrived, I climbed inside. Hovering devices — Panel's organelles — zipped around, carrying parts to and fro. I went straight to the weapons closet, yanked out a laser rifle, turned it on the nearest organelle, and pulled the trigger.

The rifle whined sharply and the blast ripped a hole in the organelle. Shards flew everywhere.

The change around me was abrupt and immediate. Most of the organelles darted away; meanwhile, a hovering communications panel entered the room. "Dave, stop," it said.

I blasted it.

Or tried. the bolt reflected off its surface and scorched the wall next to me.

"Dave, do not harm you."

Grapefruit-sized spheres flew into the room and closed in on me from all directions. I blasted a few, but there were too many. Soon, they were pressing up against my body, lifting me gently off the ground. A few pressed themselves over my eyes. The rifle got jerked from my grasp, I'm not sure how. I struggled uselessly.

"Dave, my study finish soon."

"Tell me everything," I replied.

"Yes."

What? "You'll tell me, now?"

"Yes."

The orbs dropped me and moved away from my eyes. A panel hovered before me.

"I was built by fully organic beings," it began.

I NAMED THEM TRILLS because the earth creatures closest in appearance were trilobites, the common prehistoric fossils. The alien Trills were about the size of an armadillo; their shape resembled the dart-like form of Panel's ships. They had a mass of appendages that could protrude from the forward arc; images showed them to be superior to hands in their manipulative skills.

They didn't have sensory organs anything like a human's; the sensor-coated surfaces of Panel's ships were a much closer analogy. Trills could see and hear in all directions in many wavelengths. They could generate light on their skin. They could deliberately release chemicals for communication purposes. In fact, if a fish is specialized for swimming, a Trill was specialized for communicating. I wondered if Panel and I ever would have managed to talk otherwise.

"How could they be so intelligent with such small brains?" I asked.

Panel dissected their anatomy. "No brain," it said.

"I don't understand. Group intelligence, like your cells?"

"Yes and no." Panel showed me the Trill's cells.

Each cell had the capacity of a nerve cell. A brain-like associative network ran throughout the entire Trill: every appendage, every drop of blood, every internal organ. My mind swam with the problems and the possibilities.

"How could they function with such cellular uniformity?" I had to rephrase the question a couple times, but eventually Panel understood.

"Your cells are equal in uniformity but different."

"Explain."

"Example: your cells all reproduce."

"Not a Trill's?"

"No. Special cells do reproducing."

That was a novel alternative to mitosis. What alien biology! Every cell on earth could reproduce itself. Well — brain cells stopped dividing eventually. That almost made sense if all of a Trill's cells were brain cells.

"The Trill were like you," I said.

"Yes. In many ways."

"Was a Trill easy to hurt?" I asked. After all, if every cell was a brain cell…

"Yes and no. One hurt could kill a Trill. But Trill be good at not being hurt."

It showed me some images to the effect that Trill were hiders, not predators. Brilliant mice.

"That's why you are so cautious," I said.

"Yes. Trill were cautious."

"That's why you didn't take a blood sample from me!" I burst. "You thought it would be like taking brain cells!"

"Yes. Lost Trill cells maybe change Trill. Make it less smart. Make it act different."

"A change in personality from getting a cut," I marveled. They must have been very cautious indeed.

I thought of a new angle to pursue: "Did Trill love?"

"Not understand love," Panel said.

"Welcome to the club. Did they help each other for more reasons than survival?"

"Yes. Each Trill has help thoughts."

"How about feelings? Emotions?"

"Do you think I have feelings, emotions?"

It was a good question. "Did it hurt you when I shot that organelle? Other than the physical damage?"

"Yes. Scared. Frightened."

"Really? That scared you?"

"Yes. You maybe hurt me more. You maybe not same thoughts. You not agree my goal."

Goals, again. I decided to save that for later. "Anything else?"

"Yes." It paused. "I thought before you shot me that you would not."

"You didn't like being wrong about me?"

"I didn't mean that meaning. Correction: You showed me Dave. I thought Dave wouldn't hurt me. I cannot explain this."

"I hurt your feelings," I said.

"Maybe."

"You hurt my feelings," I told Panel.

"I didn't tell you my goals," it replied.

"Yes, that's right. But worse. You won't let me return to Earth."

"You cannot return to Earth. I have no knowledge of transfer points and you cannot explain."

I pounded my hand on the wall. "Have you tried?"

"I have information on every solar system in this galaxy," it replied. It irritated me that its voice inflection never changed. "The Trill and I didn't find transfers points."

"Transfer points," I mumbled, turning away.

It could be lying, but how would I ever know? For all I knew, it killed Charles and fabricated those images. Maybe if it let me take the cruiser.

"Why are you repairing the cruiser?" I shouted, turning back to face it.

"To understand. To have place you know."

I stuck my face centimeters from the screen. "What if I can use the cruiser to find a transfer point?"

"Do not go, Dave." It showed me an image of the galaxy we were in, and I backed away. "Your offspring will number as these stars," Panel said.

I laughed out loud. "What are you now, God?"

"Explain God."

I laughed again, shaking my head. "Impossible." There was a way, though, that would tell me if Panel had any concept of a creator. "God made everything. Every atom. Every particle. All energy."

"I am not God," Panel replied. "Some Trill thought all everything made itself."

"So do some humans."

"Do you?"

"No," I replied. But the conversation was straying from where I had so carefully guided it. "You hurt me by keeping me here," I told it. "Doing that is wrong."

"I don't understand your use of the word 'wrong,'" Panel said. "I was made to find life like you for our goal."

I glared at the screen filled with the image of the galaxy, my stomach twisting. "To make my offspring fill the galaxy." I felt sicker the more I thought about it.

"No. Different."

"What, then? Where did you get this 'fill the galaxy' idea from?"

"From me."

I stared at the panel. "Why?"

"I like you."

That pissed me off. "What, I'm your pet? You're trapping me here for your own amusement?"

"I don't understand."

"How are you going to do it? Clone me?" The room felt like it was a hundred degrees Fahrenheit.

"No." Panel showed me images of the rest of the crew, focusing on Darla. The image zoomed in on her lower abdomen and went inside. Egg cells appeared on the screen.

I closed my eyes. Of course it could do this. If it could make fresh chicken from a hunk of dehydrated meat, it could pop out some test-tube babies. And if I didn't cooperate, it could use any of the men's sperm — or their dandruff flakes, for that matter.

I shared none of my thoughts with Panel and blurted, "Why do you need me?"

"You live. You must teach them."

Of course. Play daddy for Panel's slaves.

"I want to leave in the Eridanus," I told it.

"Don't go," Panel said.

"I don't care if you don't understand what wrong is. It's wrong to keep me here. Just like it would be wrong for me to destroy all of your cells with a laser rifle. I don't want to be part of your plan. I want to go."

"I will make food," Panel replied.

IT ONLY TOOK ME A MONTH.

When I left Panel, I decided that I would search for a year. I got the transfer point equipment running as well as I could — enough to detect one at ten thousand kilometers. Panel even helped me find the Eridanus's entry point into this solar system, even though I confirmed it independently.

Nothing there, but that didn't stop me. I spent days running sweeping searches through the system. I couldn't cover more than a speck of it, of course, but I had to try.

How could I be a father? I couldn't even get along with my shipmates, let alone raise a bunch of people from artificially fertilized eggs. They'd turn out more monstrous than me.

Eventually, though, I couldn't bear the loneliness. Panel said it liked me. Well, I liked Panel. My anger with it faded daily. I woke some mornings and had to whip up my rage just to stop myself from going back.

But in the end, Panel had succumbed to my arguments. Had helped me. Once, in conversation, Panel had told me that it knew of no sentient life in this entire galaxy, that my crew was the first in thirty thousand years, but Panel was wrong. Something very alive, very human, lived here. Panel.

Years later, Panel got the jist of Eridanus's transfer point detectors and made thousands of them. We searched half of a spiral arm and found nothing. A theory among old earth scientists, long discounted, said that transfer points were artifacts left over from an extinct civilization. Maybe they had been right after all, and maybe that ancient race never visited this galaxy. But I'm getting ahead of myself.

"Why?" was the first word out of my mouth when I returned. "And don't tell me it's because you like me."

Panel understood; it was getting better. It was still cautious, though, even in conversation.

"Do you ask why the Trill made me to find one like you?"

I nodded. "Yup."

"Haven't you wondered why there is no other sentient beings in this galaxy?"

Good question. Maybe I just hadn't wanted to ask. "Tell me," I said.

Images flashed, and it explained. "A virus killed all Trill. It made them stupid first, and then they died. They quarantined solar systems, but it went everywhere. It took four hundred years. The Trill thought the virus was intelligent. Sentient."

I sank to the floor, feeling the blood drain out of my face.

"Don't fear, Dave. It can't kill you."

"How do you know?" I said softly.

"The virus is everywhere. It was in you. Your body destroys it."

I suddenly felt itchy all over. An alien virus throughout my body —it was like being told that your house was infested with millions of invisible fleas.

"What if it mutates? You said it was smart."

"Your proteins and DNA use different base pairs. Also, the virus doesn't mutate well. The Trill thought it couldn't mutate well because then it would lose its thinking."

"A virus can't think." I spoke my proclamation with no conviction. All the life force had fled from my body. Viruses had killed millions of humans, hundreds of millions. But even the worst account I'd ever heard was a mortality rate of about sixty percent. This was different. One hundred percent mortality. I wanted to crawl into a corner and shrivel up.

"The Trill gave me a goal," Panel went on. "They made me for this purpose: find an intelligent being the virus doesn't kill. Give it one planet to populate. Make it learn how to make the virus not hurt Trill."

"And then you revive the Trill from a few DNA samples you happen to have stored away," I said, smiling in spite of myself.

"Yes."

Talk about a will to survive! They must have foreseen their own destruction a century in advance. They constructed Panel, a machine organism that could withstand the virus and the ravages of time. The Trill's entire galaxy was devoid of any other intelligent life, but they crafted a living net that would catch any intelligence that happened to drop by — and they knew someone would. After all, they were explorers themselves.

I suddenly wanted to meet a Trill. What if we could succeed in my lifetime? I hadn't felt so excited in years.

"Tell me again," I said, smiling, "why you want my offspring to fill the stars, instead of just one planet."

"The Trill will like you," Panel said. "And I think it is good."

I wasn't so sure. But Panel had such high regard for me — he even thought I could be a father. I'd never met a crazier being in my entire life.

"We'd better get started," I replied.

"We?"

"Yes, we. I can't beat this virus or raise kids without you."

— **CHAPTER ONE OF DAVID'S BOOK**, *As the Stars of the Sky*, written in the sixteenth year after his arrival in our galaxy. As of Year 70, required reading for all humans and Trill.

MIKE LIVES NEAR PHILADELPHIA, PENNSYLVANIA. At his day job, his students frequently ask him to blow something up. At home, he plays ping-pong with his ravishingly beautiful and insanely intelligent wife. Then he works toward his writing goal of 2.5 words/day, but often peters out around 2.4. His novel is due out in December of 2114. Mike is a husband, teacher, writer, gardener, prophet, priest, and king. He has published three stories in The Magazine of Fantasy and Science Fiction. *His future goals include procreating, publishing more stories, and swallowing fifty dollars in pocket change.*

RAINMAKER

BY RUTH NESTVOLD

WHEN REKAYA STEPPED OFF THE SHUTTLE on Chepanek, the air had that balmy warmth she associated with vacation planets, and the blooming succulents were a riot of color. Even that was little comfort. She wished she could have turned this assignment down, but Evans, her boss in the Foreign Worlds Service, hadn't really given her a choice. Rekaya had successfully avoided intolerant worlds like Chepanek until now, but this time, the combination of promises and threats had been too much to resist.

Haden Corbett, the administrator of the Allied Interstellar Community colony at New Hope, was waiting at the head of the welcoming party. He squinted into the sun as she approached. "Ambassador Dhasir," he said with a nod, holding out his hand.

She shook it. "Commander Corbett." He was about her age, she guessed, no more than fifty — fairly young for such a powerful position — and he wore his dark hair tied back in a queue in accordance with Chepanek tradition. She wondered if he'd gone native and if that was going to be a problem too.

Wide-trunked, purplish-green irella trees with their immense, waxy leaves lined the walkway to the station, and the air smelled like summer, cloying and dusty. "The news reached you of the ultimatum?" he asked, leaning into her with a fake smile as they marched past soldiers and towards the camera crews.

She waved graciously at one of the cameras and nodded. "Yes, unfortunately."

They came up against the thick crowd of waiting reporters, and their procession came to a halt. Microphones were shoved in her face, and Rekaya continued to smile. "Ambassador, have you heard about the ultimatum of the Traditionalists?"

Rekaya spoke into the bevy of microphones. "I was informed about it on the way here."

"How do you propose to find a compromise between such mutually exclusive positions?" asked a journalist in the traditional robes of Chepanek.

"The essence of diplomacy is compromise." She danced around the question. "We must each reexamine our positions and make concessions."

Another woman in a suit resembling an AIC uniform pushed forward. "The ultimatum leaves no real room for compromise. I quote: 'They must remove the ungodly technology from our world before the usoqua herds begin to move south or it will be removed for them. It is destroying the native Chepanek way of life, replacing change with stability and undermining the moral values of our people.'"

Rekaya hated it when people quoted things at her that she had long ago memorized. She smiled. "Consider: the 'world' of the people of Chepanek consists of the habitable zone north and south of the equator. Perhaps within this framework some kind of compromise can be reached allowing Traditionalists and AIC to live together on this planet."

She was about to step away from the encroaching microphones when another question was called out that made her stop short. "Ambassador, is it true that you are in an unnatural relationship?"

Rekaya resisted the urge to glance back to find Xi among her assistants. "I don't know what you're talking about," she said decisively.

Corbett took her arm. "This way please, Ambassador Dhasir." He guided her to a ground vehicle the color of sand and slipped into the seat beside her. An AIC soldier closed the door and waved them off.

There was a brief silence in the back seat of the simple sedan. It was glassed off from the driver and had an intercom and fine leather upholstery, but otherwise it was bare of any diplomatic perks. "You will have to forgive the lack of luxury," Corbett said. Rekaya could hear a hint of unwillingness in his voice. "Given the attitude of many of the natives to AIC technology, we restrict ourselves to a minimum as much as possible."

"I can understand."

"Can you?" He crossed his arms in front of his chest. "Was what the reporter asked back there true?"

Rekaya gazed out the window, disdaining to answer.

The commander obviously took this for assent and slammed his fist on the seat between them. "Damn! How could you have taken an assignment on a world like this?"

She turned to him, keeping her temper under control. "I was not given much choice, Commander."

This at least turned his anger away from her. He shook his head. "Why would AIC send someone with your sexual proclivities here, where homosexuality is a crime?"

"My 'sexual proclivities' as you call them are not generally known."

"Apparently well enough known for someone here to find out. Is your partner here with you?"

She nodded.

"With all due respect, Ambassador, I think it best if we give her an assignment somewhere other than New Hope."

Rekaya leaned her head back against the leather headrest and thought of Xiheru's smile. Xi kept her grounded, kept her sane in the midst of the high-pressure craziness of interstellar politics. "Perhaps I should report back to the AIC Central Committee that my position has been compromised by rumors and ask that a new ambassador be sent."

"There's not enough time. As far as our geophysicists can determine, the rainmakers of the tribes will be giving the command to move south within the next month. We need to go forward with negotiations now."

Rekaya gazed out the window, wondering why AIC didn't just promise to move off the planet — from everything she'd read, there wasn't anything particularly valuable here. But that would be admitting that the decision to allow colonization had been a mistake, and political entities did not like to admit making mistakes.

They came over a rise marking the outskirts of New Hope. The small capital of the colony was nestled on the northwest shore of the Inner Sea, in the northern part of the habitable equatorial zone. Rekaya couldn't quite get her mind around the geology of this world, with its extreme axial tilt and extreme seasons, the glaciers at mid-latitudes and the deserts of heat and cold at the poles. Her own homeworld only had minimal axial tilt and very little seasonal variation, with the opposite result of the situation on Chepanek — the equator was uninhabitable, not the mid-latitudes.

But though it was referred to as the habitable zone, permanent settlements within the equatorial region were only possible with advanced technology. The natives who still lived by the old ways avoided the brutal heat of the summer months by crossing the equator twice a year — once north, once south. And soon it would be time for the southern migration.

"Should I speak to your partner for you?" Corbett volunteered when she remained silent.

She straightened her shoulders and repressed a sigh. She didn't always like what her job forced her to do, but sacrifices were part of being in the Foreign Worlds Service. "Yes, perhaps you should."

REKAYA TOOK A BITE OF THE HOT USOQUA DISH, vaguely reminiscent of the foods of her homeworld culture, also a warm world. On Chepanek, the need to preserve foodstuffs for the long treks across the equator had resulted in a cuisine salty and highly spiced.

"You must not think that Shuntaino and her followers are representative of our planet," Toray said, her right-hand neighbor at the formal dinner. He was the leader of a nearby tribe, enthusiastic and attentive, and he wore an AIC-style suit rather than the comfortable robes of his people.

On her other side, a member of the Allied Interstellar Research Association by the name of Nebel spoke up. "Life here on Chepanek is not easy. There are a number of people who appreciate what our technology can bring them."

Toray smiled. "Yes. My tribe no longer needs to have me make the weather to take with them. The smart houses of AIC create their own weather."

"You are a Rainmaker?" Rekaya asked. She missed the presence of Xi in the room, to exchange a smile or a secret.

The young chief nodded. "Most tribal chiefs are. If the tribe has no Rainmaker, they must find another tribe to travel with during migration. Dr. Nebel is studying the abilities of Rainmakers at Mukotsa Station."

Mukotsa Station — where Xi had been sent. Rekaya turned to her left-hand neighbor, looking at him more closely. He seemed to have had little age-correction done, given his graying hair and wrinkles; an eccentricity widespread among academics, she had long-since noticed. "And how is your research progressing?"

Nebel shrugged. "The project has only just started. We have no decisive results as yet."

She turned back to Toray. "What precisely does a Rainmaker do?"

"He or she is responsible for the weather of the tribe when they move."

The material Rekaya had received with her assignment had included that much information on the Rainmakers, but she still didn't quite understand what it meant. "But how do you 'take the weather with you'?"

He gazed at her, obviously baffled how to explain something so elementary. She examined a beaded wall hanging in the shape of a curving pentacle in shades of sand while she waited. "We speak to the earth," he said finally.

Rekaya nodded and let it pass. She asked Nebel about life at Mukotsa Station, but he had no conversational skills to speak of, and she learned little more than details of labs and studies.

She was relieved when the dinner was over and Haden Corbett drew her aside. "May I suggest a brief stroll in the gardens, Ambassador? The auroras can be quite spectacular this time of year."

"Certainly, Commander Corbett."

"Please, call me Haden. There are no last names on this planet, and I'm no longer used to mine."

His grin was infectious, and she smiled. "Then you might as well call me Rekaya."

Together they strolled through the colorful, cactus-like bushes known as yanui while the sky darkened. "Soon they will close up, a kind of summer hibernation," Haden said, indicating a flowering bush with wide, thick leaves.

"I've read about that. About the lights as well, how unusual it is that they appear so close to the equators."

He nodded. "When the seasons change on Chepanek, compasses go crazy and auroras appear all over the world. Our scientists are still working on the precise magnetic phenomena causing it."

Rekaya paused and cupped her hand around a flower, bright orange in the slanting light between sunset and dusk. The leaves were waxy to the touch. "But isn't it a relief to know there are some things the scientists can't figure out either? Now politics…"

Corbett laughed out loud, and Rekaya found herself smiling again in response. "Ah, but as long as you operate under the assumption that people are basically selfish?"

She shook her head. "Even if that were always true, you still don't know what action is in the best interest of anyone but yourself."

"True." He stopped and faced her, his stance that of a soldier, shoulders square, hands clasped behind his back. "The Traditionalist faction sent a courier to me tonight."

"A courier?"

"They refuse to use our technology for communication."

"I see."

"Shuntaino has agreed to enter negotiations with us, but she will not come north this time of year. She says it is against nature." Behind him, the sky was growing darker, and the night lights of Chepanek were rising, a faint hint of blue and green like a playful strobe.

"Then we will have to go to her. How much time do we have before the ultimatum runs out?"

Corbett turned to gaze at the lights as well. "I wish I knew."

Rekaya gazed at the shifting shades of blue in the sky and how the light played on the dark hair of her companion's queue, too distracted by the beauty of the night to continue thinking about business. The aurora seemed to fill her head, and she had a strange sensation of lightness and joy.

She drew in a deep breath, wishing Xi were here to share it with her. "Is it like this every night?"

The commander shook his head. "It hasn't been this brilliant for weeks."

"At least having seen this is worth something," she murmured.

"Yes." Love for a foreign world was in his voice.

REKAYA STOOD IN THE COOL MORNING AIR, shaking off the dregs of vivid dreams of the auroras which had left her strangely uneasy, as if there was something she had to do or say, but she didn't know what it was. She hoped Xi would be safe. To the East, she had an excellent view of the Inner Sea and the colorful native waterfowl the locals called chabwalish; to the north, the bluish-purple Mukotsa mountains rose up like a wall.

She had only spoken with Xi a few brief times since she had moved to Mukotsa Station, and then almost exclusively of business. While the Traditionalists disdained to use "ungodly" AIC technology, which would include using bugs or monitors, they couldn't assume that everyone was as squeamish.

After all, someone had leaked information about her "unnatural" relationship in the first place. Only who, and why?

It had taken Haden Corbett three days to prepare for their trip south to the camp of Shuntaino, but finally everything was ready. They could not arrive in the camp with motorized vehicles, so they would have to pull livestock trailers for shemath: nearly hairless, camel-like creatures that stored water in a large hump above the withers as well as in a wide, flat tail descending nearly to the ground. The shemath would act as their mounts once they made their own camp far enough away from that of Shuntaino so as not to offend.

"Rekaya!"

She turned, shaking off the fear and loneliness and unpleasant dreams that had been bothering her since she arrived on this planet.

"Good morning, Haden."

The commander put his hand on the small of her back, an intimate gesture, light and sure, a hint of courtship to dispel "rumors." "Toray has arrived. If you're ready, we can leave now."

Rekaya nodded, trying to repress the discomfort Haden's fictional courtship was causing her. She had agreed to the ruse, after all.

She greeted Toray, who was accompanying them as representative of the tribes who welcomed AIC presence on Chepanek, and they and their military escort got into their sand-colored desert vehicles. Rekaya had been surprised at all the soldiers (she counted fifteen), but Haden had only said shortly that the situation was unprecedented and it was better to be safe than sorry.

Shuntaino's camp was a drive of about two and a half standard hours south of New Hope. While half of the soldiers set up their own camp in the clearing between flowering yanui and giant jade plants, wide-trunked pines and colorful irella trees, Rekaya, Haden, Toray and the rest of the soldiers mounted their shemath and made their way southwest through the sparse forest. After riding the slow, heavy beasts for about fifteen standard minutes, they came out onto a broad plain. A herd of usoqua grazed in front of a village of round tents in purples and greens and beiges and browns to match the landscape of sand and earth and grass and irella.

Rekaya wiped the sweat from her forehead with the back of her hand and gazed at the scene before her. The beasts resembled any number of bovine breeds on the seeded worlds such as the kerskal of Sherba and the cattle of Earth. But while other seeded planets usually had several species related to those on other planets, Chepanek had only humans and the usoqua. Sometimes Rekaya wished she had become an archeologist or anthropologist; the mystery behind where the people of the seeded worlds came from, where their similarities were, how their differences developed, fascinated her.

And sometimes she couldn't help wishing she could deal with those differences on a more abstract level.

As they approached the settlement, a number of Chepanek soldiers with long robes and long swords stepped out from between the tents. Haden dismounted and spoke with them rapidly in their native language. Rekaya had studied up on the language for her assignment, but she understood only little of the governor's rapid speech without being able to consult her AI. She and Haden and Toray wore AIs disguised as pendants, but she couldn't access it without revealing that they were violating their promise not to bring any AIC technology to the meeting.

Haden motioned them forward, and she and Toray dismounted and followed the Chepanek soldiers. They pushed aside the flap of a large tent in sandy shades of brown, allowing Rekaya to step through first.

Inside, it was surprisingly cool. As Rekaya's eyes adjusted to the dark, she saw a tall woman flanked by soldiers. Black hair streaked with gray was tied back in a traditional Chepanek queue, and her intense brown eyes were fixed on Rekaya. For a moment, Rekaya was hardly aware of the rest of their party filing into the tent behind her. She felt her chest contract, and she took a deep breath, the shock of attraction making her feel foolish and at a loss.

Haden stepped forward, introducing her to Shuntaino and breaking the odd, unlikely spell. If the moment had occurred at a cocktail party among people with whom she shared the same cultural mores, Rekaya would have sworn the attraction was mutual. But this was Chepanek, and Shuntaino was the chieftain of a nomadic tribe which punished homosexuality with banishment, the next-best thing to a death penalty in this climate of extremes.

Shuntaino approached Rekaya and draped a pendant around her neck over the AI, a curving pentacle in shades of sand. "We are glad the woman from the stars could find time to speak with us."

"Thank you," Rekaya said in the language of Chepanek, and gave her a gift Haden had deemed appropriate, an armband of silver and gems the color of the auroras.

They settled into the soft pillows strewn around the tent, and a young man served them manchiluk wine from a ceramic jug.

"You see the way we live," Shuntaino said with a sweeping gesture indicating everything in the tent and beyond. "It is a good life. But the presence of your AIC is destroying it. Twice since the people from the stars arrived, we have followed the usoqua herds north, and once followed them south. Each time the Rainmakers take the weather with us to a new place, there are fewer who walk with us, fewer who ride the shemath at our sides. Technology," (this was an approximation of the Standard word) "this thing you bring with you, this magic to keep the weather in one place, must leave our world."

"Yours is a good life," Rekaya said in the native language, hoping her memory enhancements would be enough to get her through this without the help of her AI. She had long-since noticed that diplomacy was greatly assisted by being able to communicate in the local language without an interpreter. "But if it is change you believe in, is not what AIC brings to Chepanek a great new change? A number of your people see it so. We have brought Chief Toray with us to speak for them."

Toray touched her elbow and spoke low in Standard. "The change my people believe in is the change brought about by the goddess Sasne, and is called by her name, not 'peshun.'"

Rekaya was glad she did not have a light complexion which would show the heat she felt rising to her cheeks. "Peshun" was the only word she had known for "change" and was of course the one she had used.

"Because it is named for the goddess," Toray continued, "'unchanging' and 'ungodly' are the same thing."

"Thank you," Rekaya murmured.

Shuntaino cut them off with a gesture. "I have no interest in speaking with the Rainmaker who has sold himself to your AIC," she said. "He no longer follows Sasne."

With what Toray had just told her she understood: he no longer followed change, he no longer followed the goddess. Shuntaino glanced sternly at Toray before turning back to Rekaya. "Your people bring 'peshun,' yes, but they do not bring the 'sasne' of following the herd, the change of moving with the seasons, the change those of us with the power to speak to the earth know we must follow."

Rekaya felt Toray tense next to her — although spoken to her, the last had been aimed at him. "Our people may yet be able to live here together. Chepanek is vast."

"Not vast enough. Will you remove the ungodly technology before the usoqua herds move south?"

"I do not know when that would be."

"I have spoken to the earth. We must move south before the small moon outdistances the big moon."

Rekaya glanced over at Haden. "That's less than a week from now," he said to her in Standard.

She turned back to Shuntaino. "That is not enough time. We must send news of the results of our meeting back to the Central Committee on Agmir to discuss with them what is to be done."

"You can make no decisions yourself?"

"We must make our decisions together."

"Then I fear your technology must be removed by us."

Rekaya was silent for a moment, trying to comprehend such total unwillingness to negotiate. She took a deep breath. "Your people do not want to go north, mine do not want to go south — if the ultimatum were pushed back, zones could be established in which the presence of AIC could be tolerated."

Shuntaino leaned forward, staring Rekaya straight in the eyes. "Will your people stop stealing my people?" she asked, her voice low.

"Stealing your people?" Rekaya repeated, too surprised to retain her diplomatic cool.

"Yes, stealing. Taking them away. Showing them a life too easy to resist, sending them to foreign worlds."

"We cannot forbid your people to go where they will."

"You cannot make decisions, you cannot promise our people will no longer be stolen, how can you claim to speak for your 'A.I.C.'?"

"Among my people there are no Rainmakers who have the authority of the earth." She hoped she was using the right terminology this time. "We must discuss the possibilities before we decide."

"Then Chief Rekaya, take this possibility back to your people: the people of Chepanek will no longer be ruled by the Off-Worlders." At that, she rose abruptly, and Rekaya too got to her feet.

"From our camp, I will send a message to my people."

"Good. Then you will come again tomorrow?"

Rekaya nodded, and Shuntaino's soldiers led them out.

On the way back to their camp, she guided her shemath next to that of Haden. "Given the resistence to AIC among tribes like Shuntaino's, have you ever wondered how the planet could have been opened up for colonization?"

He gazed at her as steadily as the bouncing gait of his shemath would allow. "Often."

IF DAY WAS THE COLOR OF SHIFTING SAND and pale grass and filled with riddles, night was the color of gems and riddled by mystery. Rekaya once again slept uneasily, dreaming of nomads and curving pentacles and Rainmakers and a chieftain with eyes of earth in rain and hair of night laced with clouds. She awoke feeling less rested than when she had sought her tent the night before, once again uneasy.

It was time to go south, to follow the usoqua herds. What steps would the Traditionalists take? She was only glad that Xi was far away, hopefully safe at Mukotsa Station.

Rekaya draped the pentacle from Shuntaino around her neck, mounted her shemath, and found herself relieved to be traveling in a southerly direction again. She smiled, wondering at how indoctrinated she had become in such a short time.

But when they arrived at the plain again that morning, her relief fled. The camp of Shuntaino was gone.

Haden shook his head, staring at the empty clearing, at the flattened grass where the tents had stood, at the pastures cut clean by the grazing usoqua. "I don't understand. The tribes of Chepanek set great store by keeping their word."

"She did not break her word," Toray said. "She asked us if we would come again, but she did not promise that she would be here."

Rekaya nodded. "True. I wonder..."

From the direction in which they had come, an explosion shook the earth.

For a frozen moment, they all looked at each other, then Haden pulled out the comm hidden in the woven belt he wore, while Rekaya checked the monitor on her pendant.

"The signal must be garbled. My AI isn't getting anything."

"No response from the camp either," Haden said. "I'll try New Hope." He punched in an I.D. and waited for a moment. "Lasky? Can you hear me? I think our camp was attacked. What? The base stations? Lasky? Lasky?"

"Damn!" He looked like he was tempted to throw his comm in the trampled earth at his feet. "It seems the receiving stations in our area have been destroyed."

He remounted his shemath and turned back in the direction of their camp, Rekaya, Toray and their small troop of soldiers following. They heard another explosion in the distance as they tried to force their mounts to a gait faster than an amble.

"Stupid beast!" Haden dismounted again and began to run. Rekaya followed suit, drawing the weapon concealed beneath her robes.

Their own camp was about two kilometers from Shuntaino's. Rekaya was not as fast as the commander, but with effort she kept up with him, and they arrived in the camp together.

She saw the body of a young guard near one of their blackened ground vehicles, her legs twisted at an unnatural angle, her arms flung above her head. The scent of smoke and death hung in the air.

"It seems they no longer disdain using AIC technology," Rekaya said between pants. She leaned her hands on her knees and tried to catch her breath while she watched him.

He examined the destruction, not answering.

She straightened. "What do you think they did with the rest of the soldiers?"

Haden shook his head. "Let's find out how many dead we have first, shall we?"

In addition to the female guard, they found another casualty on the other side of the camp near where their tents had stood.

"That makes five soldiers missing," Haden said. His renewed attempts to contact New Hope had been unsuccessful; they were on their own.

"What are we going to do?" Toray asked. Still mounted, the rest had arrived shortly after Haden and Rekaya, Toray at their head; he was obviously better at urging shemath to a run.

"New Hope had our last coordinates," Rekaya said. "Perhaps we should wait." Without smart suits, without vehicles, without supplies, she didn't bother to add. That was obvious enough to all of them.

"We have to bury our dead first," Haden said. "We don't know how long it will be before a rescue team gets here, and it will be too hot today to leave the bodies out."

They fashioned shoveling utensils out of scrap metal from the sabotaged vehicles and rods from the tents. The sun was halfway towards the horizon by the time they had laid the two soldiers to rest.

Rekaya leaned her arm on the handle of her makeshift shovel and bent her head while Haden spoke a few words over the graves. Her job had never involved dealing with death before.

When Haden's deep, melancholy voice came to a halt, she shouldered her shovel and headed to where they had tethered the shemath and collected their meager belongings. She found the portable AI unit, and after checking the location monitor again (still dysfunctional), she settled herself cross-legged in the shade of an irella tree and called up the communications leading to her assignment on Chepanek.

Haden found her playing back a statement by Commander Evans.

"Still no sign of rescue," he said, settling down next to her.

She nodded. "And my locator is still on the blink. Yours?"

He shook his head. "None of them are working. All the nearest base stations must have been destroyed."

"No news from New Hope or Mukotsa Station?" Xi, where are you? Are you all right?

"None." The image of the twisted limbs of the dead soldier flashed in her mind, and her gut twisted.

She turned off her AI. "What do you know about the background of the Chepanek colonization?"

"A lot. Why?"

"I'm starting to get the impression that my mission was supposed to fail. Do you have any idea why that would be?"

Haden shook his head. "No one could have intended that New Hope be attacked."

Rekaya stood and brushed the dust and grass off her pants. "But what if they hadn't realized it would be? The ultimatum wasn't sent until I was already in transit. And no one expected them to fight us with our own weapons."

Haden wrapped his arms around his knees and gazed up at her. "True. But why would they want it to fail?"

"To have an excuse to take over the planet?"

"What for? Chepanek has no valuable natural resources to be mined, and with the extreme seasons, little value as a vacation planet."

Rekaya examined the heavy-leafed trees surrounding them. Now that the rainy reason was almost over, they would soon begin to fold up in preparation for the long, dry summer, and the semi-sandy jungle would become a semi-arid desert. "I don't know. But why send someone with my 'proclivities' as you so delicately phrased it — insist even that I take this assignment?"

From the direction of what was left of their camp, a series of short, sharp screams rent the air, followed by shots.

Haden and Rekaya turned and ran back to where Lea was crouched in the grass next to Jesimir, who was jerking uncontrollably. Beside them stood Toray, weapon in hand, a scaly, green and gray lizard almost a meter long dead at his feet.

"It won't help," Toray said to Lea, who had already begun first aid, tying a salvaged piece of cloth from one of the tents around Jesimir's knee above where the beast had bitten him. "There is no antidote for the poison."

"What's the name of the creature?" Rekaya asked, switching on her AI.

"Deewuk."

Haden laid a hand on her arm. "Rekaya, there really is no antidote that we know yet."

She ignored them and spoke into her pendant. "What can be done against the bite of a deewuk?"

"The medical researchers on the planet of Chepanek have not yet found an antidote," the professional female voice answered her.

The other six soldiers had joined them, and they all looked on as Jesimir's spasms became less and less and finally stilled. Lea held his hand tightly, silent tears running down her cheeks.

"The deewuk have already begun to hunt," Toray said quietly. "It is time to go south."

It seemed Toray's command of Standard was slipping now that he was back living under the stars and the auroras of his people.

"Is there anything we can do to make an attack less likely?" Rekaya asked.

"If we camp with the pack animals on the outside as my people do, when a deewuk springs, it is more likely it will get a shemath than one of us."

"Then that's what we'll do." At the words, she realized she was taking over command from Haden, but he made no move to stop her.

"First we have to bury Jesimir," Haden said.

Good. He would be responsible for their dead, and she would be responsible for their living.

DEATH AND BURIAL HAD HELD THEM UP, and by evening, they had hardly begun to salvage what they could from the ruins of the camp.

"Do you know where the next base station is?" Rekaya asked Haden as she pulled away the torn tarp of a tent in search of whatever treasures she could find: a scorched but intact canteen, a lighter, pencils, rope, a spool of thread, a needle.

Haden looked up from the metal cups he was stacking together. "I checked on the map earlier — it's about halfway between here and New Hope."

"Then if it's not destroyed too, we may be able to reach someone by lunch tomorrow."

Toray put aside a pack he was fashioning from some of the material they had salvaged. "You want to go north tomorrow? Without the magic of your people?"

Rekaya stared at him for a moment, and Lea glanced up from the pile of lightweight metal bars she had pulled out from the tangle of what used to be a tent.

"To go north when the deewuk spring is to go against nature," he continued, his voice earnest.

"What do you suggest?" Rekaya asked shortly. She too felt a strange reluctance — that damn indoctrination — but they had to get north, had to contact New Hope, had to reach Mukotsa Station. Xi.

"Isn't there a base station to the south?" Toray asked.

"Yes, but it's farther away," Haden replied.

Toray took a deep breath and looked at the rest of them. Behind him, the sun dropped below the horizon. "I would like to speak to the earth tomorrow morning before we leave. Perhaps I can call the weather to take with us, although it is against nature."

Haden and Rekaya looked at each other, and Rekaya shrugged. "Good," Haden said, "After we've made a breakfast for ourselves with whatever we've been able to find, you will speak to the earth, and then we will head north."

Toray didn't look happy, but he nodded.

They had managed to find some functioning flashlights, and as the sky grew dark, they distributed their finds in even piles beneath the light of the shifting aurora. After a silent meal of salvaged camp rations, they wrapped themselves in their Chepanek robes and settled down around the fire burning to scare away the night creatures. Tethered in a ring around them were their shemath. Soon Rekaya was dreaming deeply, despite death and burial and fears for Xiheru. Physical exhaustion took its toll.

Then a dream came which was much more vivid than a dream should be, a dream of Shuntaino, next to her on the hard earth of Chepanek, the gray streaks in her midnight black hair reflecting the flickering lights of the aurora.

"Do you understand now?" Shuntaino murmured.

"Understand what?"

"Our way of life."

Rekaya shook her head. "I understand it is hard." She lifted herself up on her elbow and glanced over at the sleeping figure of Haden not far away. "Are you really here?"

"As real as the lights in the night sky."

"That's not much of an answer." Rekaya leaned back again, gazing up at the beautiful, hard woman above her. "Isn't it against nature for you to come north this time of year?"

Shuntaino smiled and touched the swirling pentacle dangling between Rekaya's breasts. "I always go against nature. You saw this."

"Yes."

"This is why you must go against your nature and represent us for your people. Your kind must leave our planet before worse happens."

"But I don't understand your people. You kill in order to live a life of hardship."

At the word "kill," Shuntaino winced. "No. In order to live a life of change, as the earth dictates."

She rose. "You will understand us yet, Rekaya."

TORAY STOOD ON THE PLAIN FACING SOUTH, the direction nature wanted him to go, naked to the waist, a pendant like the one Shuntaino had given Rekaya gracing the dark skin of his nearly hairless chest. He had a long stick in his hand taken from an irella tree, stripped of its leaves, one end whittled to a sharp point. He stood completely still for a moment, obviously gathering himself, as the rest of them watched. The spot he had chosen for speaking to the earth was bare of grass, the dirt slightly sandy, more beige than brown.

After meditating for a few moments, he began to draw in the dirt with the irella branch, a swirling pentacle like the ones both of them wore. When the design was complete, he stepped to the center and lifted the branch to the sky. The pentacle on his chest seemed to glow.

And the pentacle on Rekaya's chest began to grow hot.

She grabbed the pendant in her fist, staring at the archaic ritual Toray was performing. How could the pendant have a physical reaction?

She hardly noticed as clouds began to gather on the horizon, hardly noticed as she stepped forward, like a sleepwalker, to join Toray in the middle of the pentacle. She had no irella branch, but she lifted her arms parallel with his, calling the weather to them, speaking to the earth. She could feel the energy flowing through her, a pulse, a wave of heat.

She didn't know how long the whole procedure lasted as the sky grew dark; she only knew she was channeling something. When Toray finally lowered his arms, she collapsed in the middle of the circle behind him.

Toray knelt next to her, lifting her head into his lap. "You did not tell me you were a Rainmaker."

She took a deep breath and opened her eyes again. "I didn't know."

Haden knelt down on her other side. "What was that all about?" His voice sounded angry.

Rekaya still felt light-headed. "I'm a Rainmaker, didn't you hear?"

"That's a Chepanek title. You can't be."

Toray looked at Haden. "Yes, she can; she has the ability to speak to the earth. I felt it."

Rekaya could see the way the commander was fighting with himself not to say something derogatory about Toray's beliefs in front of the young chief. Because despite his Chepanek robes and his queue, Haden didn't believe in the power of the Rainmakers.

And despite her AIC suits and her short hair, Rekaya did.

She pushed herself up to a sitting position, shaking her head, still dizzy from whatever had just happened to her. "Have you ever witnessed a Rainmaker at work before?" she asked the commander.

"Yes, but only once." He gazed up at what looked like rain clouds on the horizon. "And not with quite such dramatic effects."

"The ambassador is very powerful," Toray said.

"And someone wants to harness this kind of power," Rekaya murmured, gazing at Haden.

"You think ...?"

"... we've found the reason why this planet is so valuable, why AIC wants my mission to fail, why they want an excuse to be able to operate here unhindered. Until now, psychotronic energy has been little more than a theory." She turned back to Toray. "Have you ever worked with Dr. Nebel on his research project?"

The Rainmaker nodded. "He said I was a very good subject. He would like to send me to Agmir."

She and Haden stared at each other. "Stealing their people," he murmured.

"Help me up please," Rekaya said. "I still feel a bit dizzy." With Haden holding one elbow and Toray holding the other, she stood, and put a hand to her forehead as the ground seemed to shift beneath her.

"It will get better with time," Toray said. "When I first began to speak to the earth, I too could not stand up again after."

Rekaya nodded, staring to the south — the direction Shuntaino had gone. And Xi was somewhere to the north, somewhere Rekaya could not reach her, perhaps a victim of a Traditionalist attack, but if not, worrying that there was no word.

But if the Traditionalist attacks continued, AIC would send in its troops and take over the planet completely, to mine the human potential.

She gripped Haden's hand and took a deep breath. "We must go south, try to find Shuntaino before more damage is done."

For a moment, Haden didn't answer. "There is a distinct possibility that they may want to assassinate us."

"They could have done that yesterday, but instead they attacked our camp." She suppressed the image of the twisted body of the first soldier they had found. Could she really negotiate with people who would not even stop at murder? With a social system so intolerant she herself would have been a victim of it? Would it be so bad if AIC took over the planet?

Yes, it would. There was such a thing as playing fair, after all, and AIC had not done so, had pretended to be interested in negotiations, but had assumed from the very beginning that negotiations would not be successful.

With such a one as herself leading them.

Only one thing the Foreign Worlds Service had not reckoned with — that Rekaya would prove to be a Rainmaker.

"I HAD NOT EXPECTED TO SEE YOU AGAIN," Shuntaino said. The chieftain with eyes of earth in rain gazed at Rekaya. There was caution there, but no murder.

"Did you know I was a Rainmaker?" Rekaya asked.

"I felt something, but I was unsure. It could have been the one who has turned away from the earth."

"Will you listen to me now?"

Shuntaino raised her chin and pushed a strand of graying, night-black hair away from her temple. "Why is now different than before? You are still one of those who speak for your 'A.I.C.'"

Rekaya inclined her head respectfully. "But now I understand your ways better, and I beg you to allow me to help you save them."

"We can save our ways ourselves."

She looked past the chief's shoulder at the swirling pentacle on the wall of the tent. "I mean no disrespect, but I am afraid you cannot. I understand now why your people are being stolen, and there are those who will listen to me. But only if no more blood is spilled."

Shuntaino shook her head. "You listen to me only because blood has been spilled."

Rekaya was silent for a moment. How could she persuade this proud woman? Would it be too daring to refer to what she was sure they had both felt? There was little too lose.

She gazed straight into Shuntaino's dark eyes, calling that awareness from her. "That is not true," she said quietly. "I know you understand the truth of my soul, and I tell you now, I listen to you because I have spoken to the earth and I understand what it means."

Shuntaino gazed at her for a long moment, and wisps of dreams spirited through Rekaya's mind.

The rebel leader leaned forward. "Then tell me how I can save Chepanek."

RUTH NESTVOLD LIVES IN A HOUSE *with a turret and spends much of her free time among her roses in a garden on the outskirts of Stuttgart, Germany. Sometime-English-professor, sometime-IT-professional, she has sold stories to numerous markets, including* Asimov's, Strange Horizons, Scifiction, *Gardner Dozois's* Year's Best Science Fiction, *and several anthologies. Her novella "Looking Through Lace" made the short list for the Tiptree award and was nominated for the Sturgeon award. She maintains a web site at www.ruthnestvold.com*

RADICAL ACCEPTANCE

BY DAVID W. GOLDMAN

"YOUR PROBLEM, MR. KAROLEV," said the otter, "is angels."

I wasn't sure that I had heard him correctly over the hot tub's burbling. "Angels?"

He nodded his smooth brown head. "I don't specifically mean, of course, your *personal* problem."

"Ah." As I watched him duck his head underwater for a long moment, I wondered what specifically he *did* mean.

He came up for air, shaking the water from his head with a quick up-and-down jerk. The spray missed me by inches. His sleek body rolled twice, just below the water's surface, before he settled back onto the fiberglass bench opposite me.

If two years ago you'd told me that I would be sitting in a backyard tub high above Malibu, chatting with a six-legged, tenor-voiced river otter from outer space, you would have been pitching me a bad screenplay. Tonight, though, it was just a Tuesday evening business meeting.

"It's angels, Mr. Karolev, that stand between humanity and the rest of galactic civilization. Of all your people's memes, angels are the most destructive you've invented."

"Call me Jack." I had assumed that I'd been invited over to discuss a business proposition. But if one of Earth's dozen visiting otters — their species had its own name, of course, but it was very long and involved a lot of gasps and whistles; they were the ones who had suggested we just call them "otters" — wanted to talk philosophy, who was I to complain?

I asked, "Your people don't go in for religion, then?"

His brief high-pitched chittering was an otter's version of a chuckle. "Oh, you wouldn't *believe* some of the religions out there! Why, among the species of the Yowsh domain alone there are over four thousand highly-subscribed belief systems — everything from absolute solipsism to a pantheon of a million omnipotent, if largely apathetic, deities." He reached for a walnut from the large glass bowl perched on the edge of the tub; he balanced the nut upon his chest. "No, no shortage of gods and believers anywhere in this galaxy." With another forepaw he grabbed the nutcracker from beside the bowl and cracked open the walnut. I figured he was just being polite, since he then scooped the whole nut into his mouth, shell and all.

I looked past the munching otter to the sunset, its pinks and oranges spreading wide over the Pacific far below us. I'd heard that he had purchased this house outright, with cash from the sale of some sort of otter power technology to a South American government. Though that might just have been a rumor started by Isolationists.

"How about you?" I asked. "What do you believe?"

He'd been reaching for another nut; now his arm froze and his deep brown, pupil-less eyes zeroed in on my own. "Some," he said without a trace of his former amusement, "would consider that an insultingly personal question."

Uh-oh. I held up a dripping hand. "Hey, no offense intended. If I—"

But then he chittered, and slapped the nutcracker down onto the water — sending a chlorinated splash across my face, right into my mouth. "Sorry," he said, still chittering. "But I wish you could have seen your expression!"

I coughed several times. Real jokers, these space otters; there were plenty of stories about their very *alien* sense of humor. Last year, though, I'd made some discreet inquiries of a few of the otters' human staff (strictly business — I'm a producer, after all, and the otters are your quintessential Small But Influential Market); it turns out that the otters' number one viewing preference is slapstick — Keaton, early Chaplin, the Three Stooges. Go spend an hour watching Earth otters in your local zoo, then tell me you're surprised.

He cracked another walnut and popped it into his mouth. "My own people," he said, his voice somehow unaffected by his vigorous chewing, "never invented a god meme. Just didn't occur to anyone, apparently."

I frowned. Yet another area where the otters doubtless looked down at us as superstitious primitives.

He seemed able to read my expression. "Don't get me wrong," he said. "We've got creation myths, tricksters, an afterlife — the whole ball of wax. Just didn't come up with gods."

"Or angels?"

He grinned. Otters don't have individual teeth; just thick upper and lower plates with convoluted surfaces. It looked like his mouth was filled by a pair of dingy yellow hooves.

My curiosity had been piqued. "No gods," I asked, "but there's an afterlife? So who decides whether you go to heaven or hell?"

He shook his head. "Hell didn't occur to us, either. After dying, everybody just gets reborn, more or less. In a better world."

"Clouds and harps? Warriors and mead?"

"More like a really big water park. Also lots of food and copulation."

I lifted my bottle of Perrier from the plastic holder that was suction-cupped to the tub's inside wall, took a sip. The sunset had progressed into a streaky lilac phase. On either side of us a stand of pines shielded the otter's property from his neighbors; silhouetted branches waved up and down in a soft breeze.

He slipped his head under again, then swam two fast, tight circles around the tub, avoiding me by inches. As he surfaced and settled back onto his bench, he twisted his head over his shoulder — *way* over his shoulder — toward the sunset. And said, "You haven't asked what you want to ask."

What he meant by that, I didn't have a clue. But negotiating from a position of ignorance was nothing new for me. I took another sip of Perrier and waited.

"I've seen all your shows," he continued. "And the new pilot, too."

"What! How did—" Only one network had a copy of the pilot, and they certainly wouldn't be leaking it just as we started negotiations.

He ignored my outburst. "You're no Utopian, Jack. In fact, I doubt there's anything we've told your people that you assume is necessarily true. Since we arrived, what have you produced? Let's see… " He ticked them off on his stubby webbed fingers. "A movie where a fledgling human space empire gets into a shooting war with a devious alien federation. A remake of a mini-series in which extraterrestrials bearing gifts to Earth turn out to have a nefarious secret agenda. And a sitcom whose well-meaning but bumbling immigrants keep accidentally blowing up their suburban neighbors with inappropriate technology." His head remained turned toward the sunset. "All in all, a body of work that any Isolationist would be proud of."

I slid my Perrier back into the holder, and waited.

"But now," he went on, "there's this new series of yours. Plucky human explorers and entrepreneurs finding their way in a galaxy full of diverse species with diverse motivations. Carving out trading niches, forming tentative alliances; sometimes coming out ahead, sometimes not." He finally turned back to peer at me over his whiskered snout. "What do you think, Jack? Are you the only Optimistic Skeptic in Hollywood? Is anybody going to pick up your new show?"

I snorted. "Hollywood doesn't care what I believe. It's viewers that matter."

He grinned again.

I finally caught on. "This is why you invited me here tonight? You want to back my series?"

The otter just kept staring at me, his eyes blank as two brown marbles. "You still haven't asked. This is the first time you've ever been alone with one of us. Don't you want to ask why we've come to Earth?"

The conversation was spinning past me like a merry-go-round. I grabbed the latest passing horse and tried to hold on.

"And if I ask, I suppose you'll tell me the truth?"

He shrugged, the shoulders of his three forelegs breaking the surface of the water. Which, it occurred to me, was about as credible a response as he could give to that sort of question.

When the otters first showed up in Earth orbit, they came with a plausible story. The nearest members of galactic civilization had picked up our early radio and television broadcasts, deciphered them. After a couple of decades the otters, chosen for their relative similarities to humans, were dispatched to contact us — to study our world and report back on our suitability for admission to polite interstellar society.

Like I said, plausible. But then, what else would you expect from creatures who'd been listening in on a century of our radio and television broadcasts?

"Come on," said the otter. "Just ask me."

"Fine." I shifted my position so that a pair of the tub's jets massaged my shoulder blades. Then I stared back into those eerie eyes. "Why did you come to Earth?"

He leaned against the tub's side. He regarded me for a moment. Finally, in a very serious voice, he said, "*Babylon 5*."

For at least five seconds his expression remained impassive. Then he broke into a hoof-mouthed grin.

Disgusted, I reached for my Perrier.

"No, no," he protested, waving two of his paws at me. "I'm serious! Four years of loose ends and unresolved character arcs, and then what do they do? Take the final season to *cable*! Can you imagine how *frustrating* that was for me?" He spread his paws wide in supplication. "Visiting Earth was my only option."

I didn't really want to waste more time on this, but he had annoyed me. "You couldn't have watched it on the BBC?"

"Channel 4," he corrected. He shook his head. "The last season was delayed."

"Australia, then."

"Wrong hemisphere. Our ship was approaching from the other direction."

"Fine." I toasted him with my bottle. "You crossed countless parsecs of cold vacuum to rent a DVD. Whatever."

He chittered. "Don't be like that. Look — on the trip here we each took responsibility for monitoring and summarizing different genres from the incoming broadcast stream. One of us handled news, for example. Somebody else covered drama."

"Let me guess. You did science fiction."

"Exactly. You can learn a lot about a species from its dreams and night-mares."

Despite myself, I was starting to suspect that he really was being honest now — no matter how uselessly. "What else did you monitor, besides sci-fi?"

"Horror films. Fantasy series. Political campaign ads."

Assuming he was still telling the truth, I wondered how much further he would go. "Okay," I said, "now that we've established your *personal* motivation for landing on my planet, how about your people's collective purpose? And I hope you won't claim that you all came To Serve Man."

His snout dipped beneath the bubbly water's surface, then tilted upward to geyser an elongated mouthful of water vertically into the air, in what I took to be delight. "No, Jack — you won't find any cookbooks on *our* ship."

"You've read that story!"

"Story?" He shook his head. "*Twilight Zone.*" He paused then, and helped himself to another walnut. He chewed noisily as his eyelids slid halfway shut; he seemed to be studying me. He gave a little nod, finally, and said, "We've been telling the truth. Our team is here to study your world and report back, and to prepare humanity for joining the galactic community."

Disappointed with his pat response, I let my head fall back against the tub's edge. Above me most of the sky had gone deep blue; the horizon still glowed indigo and purple.

But there was something about what he had just said. "Prepare us?" I asked. "You mean by explaining how your society works? By giving us new technology?"

He nodded. "Adding to humanity's knowledge is the first phase of preparation, yes."

A shiver passed up my spine that had nothing to do with hot tub jets. Maybe the Isolationists had it right, after all.

"There's a second phase?"

He tossed a walnut into the air, caught it in his mouth. "Let's talk about angels," he said.

After all the deals I'd negotiated in my career, I knew non-nonchalance when I heard it. We had finally arrived at the actual starting point of tonight's discussion.

I thought back to his earlier comment. "Destructive," I quoted. "Isn't that what you called them?"

He shook his head. "It's the *concept* of angels that's destructive. I mean your current pop-culture version of angels — creatures lesser than God, but greater than man. Beings who are *almost* perfectly moral and good. It's a very old meme, one that's infected most human religions. In some it emerges in the form of supernatural beings; in others you can see it in the original humans themselves, before a fall from grace."

He ducked his snout for a swallow of water, then continued. "As a mere human, obviously you could never measure up to God, whether in knowledge, wisdom, power, or patience. But angels, they're not God. People compare themselves to angels all the time — and always come up short. *I should have been more forgiving!* you berate yourself: I should have been more like an angel. *I knew it was wrong, but I couldn't help myself!* Unlike an angel."

He was reminding me of a religious show I'd surfed past a few nights earlier. "An angel? Or do you mean a saint?"

His snout lifted, as if he were sniffing my words. "Saints! Even better! What's a saint, after all? A rare human who achieves angelic stature. In many of your religions, when a saint dies he even ascends to heaven, to serve God directly — he literally *becomes* an angel."

"So what's wrong with that? The saint provides an example for the rest of us, a model."

"Ah, but how many can ever match that model? And what do you tell yourself when you fail, as you're virtually guaranteed to do every time you're tested? *I should have behaved better — well, I guess I'm no saint!* It doesn't take many times to prove to yourself that saints, like angels, are simply a different breed from you. And then, unless you are truly unusual, you quite logically *give up*. You settle for being *fairly* moral. For trying *reasonably* hard. You feel guilt over past mistakes, but it doesn't occur to you to try and rectify them. After all, it's not like you're some sort of *saint*."

I frowned. "So you're saying — what? That our moral development is stunted because we can imagine something better to strive toward? That doesn't make any sense at all."

He let himself slide off the bench into the water, where he just floated near the bottom for several seconds. Why had he invited me here, really? Did he want me to air his bizarre argument in my show?

Shaking off the water as he retook his position, he asked, "Have you ever seen the movie *Lord of the Flies*? The story of how, in the absence of external forces, humans will inevitably revert to their innate savagery and evil?"

I nodded, wondering where he was headed now.

He slapped the water with his paw, hard, splashing us both. "That's exactly backwards!" He sounded genuinely angry, his voice squeaking up an octave by the end of his sentence. "It's the precise opposite of your actual phylogeny!"

"Our what?"

He lowered his snout to look directly at me. "Your development as a species. The history of each of your cultures. And the process that you, as individuals, repeat in your personal development." He dropped his mouth to the water's surface and blew bubbles for a few seconds, apparently collecting his thoughts. Then he looked up again. "The message of movies like that is that humans will always be failed angels. But you're *not!* You're actually incredibly *successful.* But not angels — you're incredibly successful *apes!* Apes who all by yourselves — without any guidance from either benevolent gods or sponsoring aliens — figured out language and agriculture and metalworking and love and morality and vaudeville. If *Lord of the Flies* told the *real* story of your species, it would show a shipwreck of illiterate savages struggling together to survive, then going on to invent epic poetry and Art Deco."

"Also beating their children. And occasionally massacring each other."

"Yes, yes, of course! You're *evolving monkeys!* What do you expect? Not everyone progresses at the same rate. For every forward step there are other steps backwards, or sideways — at the individual level, random influences will always dominate. But, *as a species*, look how far you've come!"

I didn't know what to say. I lifted my water bottle to my lips, but at some point I'd apparently finished its contents, or accidentally spilled them into the tub.

I studied him, this hyper-advanced space alien come to prepare my world for entrance into the greater galactic community. He lolled before me in the deepening darkness, half floating, two of his short arms pressed against the side of the tub. His snout pointed directly at me, nose twitching and head still pushed forward by the vehemence of his argument. Beads of water speckled his slick fur.

I said, "So humanity is, what, the galactic poster child for self-actualization?"

His head tipped back and he chittered loud and long. "Hardly," he said, his voice as unaffected by his still-chirping laughter as it had been by his earlier walnut-crunching. "How do you suppose *any* sentient species develops?" He shook his head, and then settled back into stillness. Once more he gazed at me over his long snout. "Unfortunately," he said, "the development of your particular species seems to have gotten stuck. Its moral development, I mean."

It took me a few seconds to work that out. Then I said, "You're talking about angels again."

He nodded. "In your present condition, we can't recommend allowing your species out of this solar system."

"What?!" Now *I* was angry. "As long as humanity is *stuck* on angels, we're not morally mature enough to join your society? We're not *good enough* for you?" I pushed myself upright on the slippery bench, so that I was looking downward toward his sprawled form. "That's what you're saying?"

He held up a paw. "To the contrary," he said, slowly shaking his head. "It's *we* who aren't ready for *you*."

I stared.

"Look at your Utopians," he said. "They've already cast my people as the messengers of the gods, bringing light and hope to the world. Can you imagine what will happen to them once your species starts interacting with the rest of the galaxy? They'll be the worst kind of suckers, patsies to the first fast-talking amoeba that gets its pseudopods on them. Before you know it they'll group themselves into feuding cults, each crazily loyal to its own alien race of perfect beings. Next step: interstellar Crusades — with all the rest of us caught in the crossfire.

"Or," he continued, "how about the Isolationists? To them we're *false* angels. They reject our offered technology, our culture. *No thanks*, they tell us. *We'll stick to the human way.* So where does that lead? Either to a dead-end existence stuck on your birth planet, or else to an independent human space empire. The first would be unfortunate for humanity — not really a problem, though, for the rest of us. But a growing, antagonistic human dominion? Eventually you'll collide with the rest of the galaxy. At first the conflicts will be economic, which is disruptive enough. But sooner or later, guaranteed, we're talking out-and-out war."

The sky had grown quite dark by now. It pressed down on me, as if someone were trying to smother the Earth with an immense pillow.

"You're not just guessing, are you?" I asked. "We're not the first race you've encountered that believed in something like angels."

He sighed. "If your people don't get past this meme soon, there's going to be a fleet of big, ugly warships embargoing your planet."

I stared at him. "Embargoing…?"

"Oh, you'll still be able to launch Earth-orbiting satellites. But manned flight beyond your atmosphere — that will be discouraged. Quite, ah, *rigorously* discouraged."

I pictured spacecraft exploding and falling ablaze back to Earth; the images left me chilled despite the heat of the water in which I sat. This would be humanity's fate? To remain forever imprisoned on our one small world, while throughout the rest of the galaxy other civilizations flourished and grew?

His face held no expression that I could read. *If your people don't get past this meme soon,* he'd said.

I asked, "What's *soon?*"

He shrugged. "Not up to me. Twenty-five years, maybe? Fifty, tops."

I couldn't speak. *Fifty years* to change our race's basic understanding of human nature. Or else.

Once again he seemed to appreciate the thought behind my expression. "Actually, that's plenty of time. Once every human truly understands how much humanity has already accomplished all on its own, how all of your ethics are the product of massive, ongoing self-improvement rather than a fall from unattainable grace, the rest will come quickly. Utopianism and Isolationism will both lose their meaning; humanity will recognize itself as simply the new kid among a galaxy of peers."

For a second he had me. But then I shook my head. "Great. So you put out a press release. You get people like me to spread the word. Then poof — the entire world changes its fundamental beliefs. Uh-huh."

He splashed some water onto his upper chest and started combing through the fur with his paw. "Some of your psychotherapists have a term, *radical acceptance*. Patients have to accept themselves as they truly are, not as they wish they were. Really, deeply, completely accept their actual nature. Once they've done that, it's remarkable how quickly they can finally alter longstanding dysfunctional behaviors."

"So that's your Phase Two? We bombard the world with anti-angel, pro-monkey propaganda until everyone achieves this 'radical acceptance'?"

He paused in his grooming. "Propaganda?" He cocked his head, as if he were surprised by my question. "No, Jack. Our techniques of memetic engineering have progressed a little farther than that. I'm not talking about some media campaign."

"Then *what*? And then why the hell have you been telling *me* all of this, if you're not asking me to help broadcast your message?"

"Ah." His snout bobbed up and down. "My apologies for any confusion." He dipped his head to take a mouthful of water, which he proceeded to gargle for a few seconds before swallowing. "I invited you here tonight because your new pilot indicated to me that you are someone who has already, if incompletely, come to accept humanity's true nature. Which qualifies you as a subject for the initial field testing of our memetic treatment. Safety and dosage trials, you understand?"

By now the only thing that could astound me was my earlier belief that I somehow had the slightest control over tonight's conversation.

"A *subject*," I repeated.

He nodded. "Once we've established the proper dose and ensured there are no side effects, we'll be ready to fully deploy the treatment. We figure two years for complete coverage. Not specifically for the deployment itself, you understand. But my people have ethical constraints — we must take as much time as needed to ensure that all subjects are fully informed. As I've done with you this evening."

I thought about it. "And the alternative to your treatment is a planetary embargo?"

He nodded again.

Maybe he was just toying with me, making up this entire story of warships and self-esteem treatments merely to be entertained by my reactions. Maybe in another minute an otter camera crew would jump out from under the hot tub and welcome me to Pan-Galactic Candid Camera.

But my gut said that he was telling the truth. And you don't last as many years in this business as I have without a perceptive gut.

Even if it were all true, though, why should *I* be the otters' guinea pig? What did the ultimate future of humanity matter to *me*? But that question answered itself; I hadn't produced a historical, or even a Western, for years — deep down, it had never been humanity's *past* that fired my imagination.

I took a deep breath, let it out. "Okay," I told the otter. "I'll do it. Do you want me to sign something?"

His head tilted to one side. "Excuse me?"

"You know, like in the hospital. Informed consent before a procedure, right?"

He stared at me for a few seconds. "Consent?" He shook his head, bemused. "*Before* a procedure?"

My eyes went wide. Wildly I scanned my surroundings. "You mean you've *already*—!" It was too dark to see more than a foot beyond the tub in any direction. "This *treatment*, how…?"

Calmly, he pointed to the bubbling surface of the tub's water. "Actually," he said, "you're soaking in it."

Horrified, I lifted a handful of the water into the air, let it pour from my palm. And then — like the terrified ape I was — I leapt out of the tub, landing half-crouched on the cool grass. I scrabbled for my towel, began frantically rubbing at my torso.

I was shivering something fierce, and not just because of the cold breeze that blew in from the ocean.

"Oh, come now, Jack," said the otter. "Calm yourself. You've been in here over an hour — you've already absorbed a maximal dose."

My rubbing slowed, ceased. Still holding the towel, my hand dropped to my side. The breeze blew over me; I felt goose bumps lift along my arms and chest.

"The treatment," he said, "will need another half-hour or so to complete its finer adjustments. But you won't mind, I hope, if I ask you a few questions now. Just a quick safety and efficacy screen, yes?"

I wrapped myself in the towel. I was ready to turn my back on him, march back to the house for my clothes, and drive away.

But then I recalled those exploding, falling spacecraft.

Besides, I *had* given him my permission. Even if it hadn't occurred to him to wait for it.

The otter must have taken my silence for assent. "Good," he said. "So, how do you feel? Any queasiness? Respiratory difficulty? Alterations in fundamental belief systems?"

My adrenaline surged all over again. Taking a quick inventory, I inhaled deeply, exhaled. Wiggled my fingers and toes. Tried my best, despite my resurgent panic, to observe my emotional responses as I pictured the faces of recent Presidential candidates. As best I could determine, everything still seemed to behave just as I remembered. Admittedly, at the moment Isolationism did strike me as a bit less obviously idiotic than usual — but under the present circumstances I figured that didn't count. So I told him, "No problems."

"Good." In the darkness, walnuts rattled. "Now, please try to imagine a species superior to yours. Not smarter, or stronger, or more experienced. But *morally* superior. Can you do that?"

"Sure."

"*What?*" A quick scratching sound — very much like that of nutcracker teeth slipping across a rough husk — was followed by a soft, walnut-sized splash. "*Innately* your moral superiors?" he squeaked.

"Oh." I wondered whether otter night vision could detect my shrug. "No, not innately. Actually, I was trying to imagine humanity a hundred years from now."

His breath whistled as he released it. "Ah. Well, yes, fine. But how about a non-human species? My people, for example?"

I snorted. "Hardly."

"Good. Very good."

I waited. The hot tub bubbled; pine branches rustled.

Had I offended him with my last answer? I said, "Please, go on with your questions."

"Oh, I'm done. Do be sure to phone, though, if any problems arise over the next few days."

I didn't like the sound of this. "Problems?"

"Physical symptoms, emotional issues, whatever. But don't worry — there won't be any. I just have to say that."

I couldn't believe his smugness. "So that's it? No brain scans? No electrodes measuring my subconscious responses to suggestive images? No DNA sequence analysis? You're not going to *check your work?*"

"Really, Jack, you watch too much television." I imagined him waving a forepaw to dismiss my concerns. "We *have* been doing this sort of thing for a rather long time, you know." Water splashed in the dark; a few drops sprayed against my cheek. "You're welcome," said the otter, "to tub a while longer if you like. It really can be very relaxing."

"Thanks," I said. "But I think I've been soaked enough for one night."

There was further splashing, and then his voice came from the near side of the tub. "Actually, I was hoping you could stay just a bit longer. You're now someone who can answer a question for me."

"Right. As if I—" Then I caught up with what he'd just said. "What do you mean, *now*? As in, now that you've reprogrammed my *mind*?"

"Merely the slightest rebalancing of your pre-existing belief system. Really." He spoke with a dentist's tone of calm reassurance. "Please. It's an important question. And you do look rather chilly." As I hesitated, he added, "Relax — the water won't do anything else to you."

Warships, I reminded myself. *Humanity embargoed.* I sighed, then dropped my towel and climbed back into the tub.

The water sloshed noisily from my entry; I couldn't hear or see where he was. "Does this thing have a light?" I asked.

A button clicked, and the tub filled with an eerie, pale green illumination. The otter was floating on his back toward the bench across from me, his head hidden within his torso's shadow.

While he made himself comfortable, I asked, "So how many people have you tested your treatment on, so far?"

"Actually," he said, "you're the first."

I wished he had mentioned that detail a bit earlier. "Ah," I replied, hoping that his smug confidence in the treatment's lack of side effects was well justified. "And how many do you plan on using, altogether, for these safety tests?"

"Including you?"

"Yeah."

"Hmm." He paused, as if calculating. "One," he said.

He chittered briefly as I stared, open-mouthed. He spread his three arms — apologetically? — and said, "Standard procedure for these situations. Locate an appropriate native, let him experience the treatment, then have him decide."

"Decide?"

He reached for a walnut. "I did *say* that I had a question for you."

"What—" But I cut myself off, suddenly realizing how he was once again jerking me around. The whole evening had been like this — before I had a chance to process whatever we'd just discussed, he'd distract me with yet another new idea. It was actually a negotiating tactic that I recognized; I just wasn't used to seeing it from the receiving end.

I held up my hand. "Don't say another word. I want a few minutes to think, all right?"

For a couple of seconds he just stared over his snout at me. Then he gave a little nod, and turned his attention to the nut resting on his chest.

I took a deep breath, released it slowly. Okay, then — for the first time, tonight's conversation would follow *my* timetable.

I let my head fall back against the tub, and stared upward at the few dozen stars that had managed to overcome the ubiquitous city-glow. Wisps of steam rose beside me like pale green wraiths.

I tried to sift my brain for evidence of the otter's tampering. I had never believed in literal angels — at least, I didn't *think* I ever had. But did I really view people as *failed* angels? Well, every morning I certainly shook my head at the human stupidity and viciousness evident in half the headlines in the *Times*. Not to mention ninety percent of the articles in *Variety*.

Now, though, I found myself thinking about the *other* news stories. The ones about people risking their lives to help strangers. About researchers achieving amazing breakthroughs. About novelists, sculptors, or athletes inspiring their audiences to look beyond what they'd always accepted as human limits. Not bad, I thought, for a bunch of monkeys. Maybe the otter's words had brought me to this point, or maybe it really was just some chemicals in a hot tub, but suddenly I felt a rush of unaccustomed *pride* in my species.

But how about aliens? Since my childhood reading of comics and science fiction, I'd always assumed that aliens from outer space would be vastly superior to us in their understanding of the universe — and, yes, in their wisdom and morality. When the otters actually did arrive, their descriptions of a longstanding, peaceful, multicultural civilization spoke to a level of sanity that I had never really believed within humanity's grasp.

Now the otter intended for me to get over this admiration. And as I tried to recall my previous feelings, I realized the degree of his success.

Sure, the aliens had been around longer than us, so of course their *technology* was more advanced. But that didn't make them *wiser* than us, or even smarter. And while they had reportedly solved profound social problems that still plagued humanity — poverty, war, tyranny — it now struck me that as increasing numbers of otter-treated humans started paying attention to those *other* news stories, we'd soon prove no less competent at getting along amongst ourselves.

I glanced over at the otter, who was idly juggling a walnut back and forth between his paws and snout. And realized that I could guess what he was going to ask me to *decide*.

I said, "You haven't been completely honest with me, have you? About your plans."

He snatched the nut from the air with his mouth, but didn't chew. Silent, he faced me. The tub's light glinted off his eyes.

"Why me?" I asked.

Still saying nothing, he crunched a few times, then swallowed. With a slow nod he acknowledged the assumption behind my questions. "Like I said, you were already close to accepting humanity's place in the universe. But also you're someone who's comfortable thinking about interstellar civilizations — albeit fictional ones. And your career requires that you understand the motivations and desires of many kinds of people."

"A unique combination, am I?"

"Not really." He plucked a bit of walnut shell from his fur. "But you were located conveniently near me, and within our delegation I do have a certain influence." He paused for a second, then broke into a big grin. "Also, I'm a big fan of your sitcom. That episode with the neutron bomb? Priceless!"

I had to smile. But the night was getting late. "Go ahead," I said. "Ask me your question."

He raised a webbed finger. "First," he said, "you should know that we'll be leaving Earth in a month."

"*Leaving?* All of you?"

Nodding, he said, "We've learned what we need to learn about your world, and we've laid the necessary groundwork for future interactions."

"But — what about those two years of fully informing the populace about your treatment?"

He gave a three-shouldered shrug. "Nothing we can't handle remotely."

"You'll be staying in touch, then?"

"No," he said. "Not after those first couple of years. Next it will be *your* people's turn to come contact *us*."

"Unless we're embargoed, of course."

For a few seconds he didn't say anything. The breeze rustled my hair; the otter's slick fur glistened in the tub's flickering light.

Finally he said, "Well, so what do you think? Should we deploy our treatment or not?"

There it was, then. The question I'd guessed was coming. The question I'd been dreading.

"It's really up to me? You'll follow my recommendation, however I decide?"

A nod. "That's the procedure. Unless you'd rather we asked someone else?"

I was certainly tempted to pass on this responsibility. But only in the same way I'd be tempted to pass on an exciting but daring new script, knowing that someone else would produce it — and knowing that I'd regret that decision for the rest of my career.

But his words did raise a new concern for me.

"My role in this — will anybody ever find out?"

"Only if you decide to go public. In which case we'll back you up, if you want us to."

I shook my head, relieved. At least there'd be no lynch mobs in my near future.

My decision, I knew, should be easy. Humanity had gotten itself stuck; the otters' elixir would give us the nudge we needed to get past our species-wide inferiority complex, and allow us to finally live up to our potential. Life on Earth would improve immeasurably; humanity would be accepted into interstellar civilization. A no-lose proposition if ever there had been one.

Of course, humanity would never know whether we could have done it all on our own. Maybe I could convince the otters to keep quiet for now about their treatment, but someday the truth would emerge. How would *that* revelation affect humanity's self-esteem?

I turned to the otter. "Other worlds have been through this, right? How has it worked out for them, learning that they needed alien assistance to get past their limitations?"

He shrugged. "Even here on your planet, there are cultures that wouldn't have a problem with that. Not everyone is John Wayne, you know."

I supposed that was true. But with the newfound pride I'd just begun feeling for my species, it rankled me that we wouldn't get the chance to manage this last step by ourselves. Not that the image of humanity being forcibly prevented from leaving our solar system sat terribly well with me, either.

I wasn't getting any closer to a decision. Then it occurred to me that I was approaching my choice as if it were a *plot* problem. What if I instead thought about it as, say, a *marketing* challenge? I had a great property on my hands, after all; what I needed to do now was help the audience learn to properly desire and appreciate what I had to offer. And — I realized with growing excitement — there was a tried-and-true method for accomplishing *that*:

I needed to attract a Small But Influential Market.

I pushed away from the tub's wall until I sat upright on the edge of the bench. The breeze was cold across my dripping chest as I asked, "This business of informing everybody about your treatment — how strict are you guys about that?"

His snout lifted as he tried to sniff out where I was headed. "Well," he said slowly, "I suppose we might have some *latitude*—" he waggled a paw from side to side — "in that regard."

I leaned toward him. "What if I asked you to deploy your treatment — but only on, say, one percent of humanity? Scattered all over the world?"

He cocked his head. "Randomly?"

"Not entirely."

"Ah." He nodded. "The political capitals."

I waved away that idea. "No. Toronto, Sydney, Bombay, Tokyo, Rome, L.A.... the *entertainment* capitals. But, yes, the remainder chosen randomly, all over the globe. Could you do that?"

"And not inform anyone about what we'd done?"

I waited.

He let go of the wall. Floating on his back, suddenly he applauded loudly with all six paws.

But his voice dripped with sarcasm. "Oh, bravo, Mr. Karolev! So we're supposed to give you tens of millions of unknowing teachers and prophets—"

"Trendsetters," I suggested.

"—and from that starting point, humanity is going to raise *itself* to maturity?"

"If we're capable of accomplishing that, yes. If your evolving-monkey meme can out-compete our angels."

"And you're not worried," he asked, his skepticism obvious, "about those rugged individualists among you? They won't be upset when they someday learn of our role in humanity's development?"

I shrugged. "Over the long haul, you can't sell people something they don't actually want. If we end up bettering ourselves, who cares whether the initial impetus came from Mahatma Gandhi, Gene Roddenberry, or you guys?"

He floated there, most of his legs slowly treading water. Then he shook his head, and in a tone of deep disappointment said, "Well, congratulations, Mr. Karolev. You've come up with one I've never heard before." He shook his head again. "Really, that's quite some pitch."

His reaction had leached away my former excitement. But I wasn't ready to drop this. "You *did* say you would follow my recommendations, right?"

He dismissed my question with a wave of a stubby arm. "Somehow," he said, "I don't seem to recall telling you to make up your own rules."

"But my idea—"

He stopped me with a peremptory paw — and then broke into a huge grin. "You really can be a sucker sometimes, can't you?" The hooves of his mouth glowed brightly in the tub's green light. "I *love* your idea! And I'm sure that my colleagues will, too." He paddled over and stuck out a paw. "Jack," he said, "you're brilliant! You've got yourself a deal."

I stared at his offered paw. Then — with more self-control than I'd realized I possessed — I restrained myself from hauling him up by his multiple armpits and shaking that nut-chomping grin off his pointy snout.

We shook hands. And then I let myself fall back against the side of the tub, spent.

He swam awhile, splashing quietly. After a minute or two he settled back onto the opposite bench. The nutcracker crunched, and the familiar chewing began. A few more seconds passed. Then he said, "You know, since you're here anyway…well, I had this idea for an episode of your show…"

From time to time I nodded, half-listening as his high voice rose and fell against the night's steady breeze.

Mostly, though, I was looking up at the stars.

It struck me that we were beaming an awful lot of programming out to all those worlds. Somewhere there had to be sponsors who'd like a piece of that.

DAVID W. GOLDMAN FINISHED PAYING OFF HIS LOANS from a well-known Boston trade school by moving to the Pacific Northwest, abandoning his trade, and becoming a software company. Eventually he wised up and found himself a day job. Now living in Portland, Oregon with his multi-talented wife (plus a pair of cat-shaped vacancies to be filled soon), he finally has time to pursue his childhood dream of writing the Great American SF Novelette.

Printed in the United States
77565LV00003B/139-198

9 780979 534904